# THE ICKABOG

LITTLE, BROWN BOOKS FOR YOUNG READERS

First published in Great Britain in 2020 by Hodder & Stoughton

1 3 5 7 9 10 8 6 4 2

A CIP catalogue record for this book is available from the British Library.

ISBN 978 1 510 20225 2

Printed and bound in Italy

The paper and board used in this book are made from wood from responsible sources.

Little, Brown Books for Young Readers
An imprint of Hachette Children's Group
Part of Hodder & Stoughton
Carmelite House, 50 Victoria Embankment, London, EC4Y 0DZ

An Hachette UK Company
www.hachette.co.uk

www.hachettechildrens.co.uk

J.K. ROWLING

With illustrations by the winners of
*The Ickabog* Illustration Competition

LITTLE, BROWN BOOKS FOR YOUNG READERS

*The Ickabog* is dedicated to:

Mackenzie Jean,
whose favourite story it always was
and who urged me for a decade to write it up properly;

Megan Barnes
and
Patrick Barnes,
in everlasting memory of
Lisa Cheesecake and the Llama;

and, of course, to two wonderful Daisies,
Daisy Goodwin
and
Daisy Murray,
proud daughters of the QSC

# Foreword

The idea for *The Ickabog* came to me a long time ago. The word 'Ickabog' derives from 'Ichabod', meaning 'no glory' or 'the glory has departed'. I think you'll understand why I chose the name once you've read the story, which deals with themes that have always interested me. What do the monsters we conjure tell us about ourselves? What must happen for evil to get a grip on a person, or on a country, and what does it take to defeat it? Why do people choose to believe lies even on scant or non-existent evidence?

*The Ickabog* was written in fits and starts between *Harry Potter* books. The story never underwent any serious modifications. It always started with poor Mrs Dovetail's death and it always ended… well, I won't say how, in case you're coming to it for the first time!

I read the story aloud to my two youngest children when they were very small, but I never finished it, much to the frustration of Mackenzie, whose favourite story it was. After I finished the *Harry Potter* books, I took a five-year break and when I decided not to publish a children's book next, *The Ickabog* went up into the attic, still unfinished. There it stayed for over a decade, and there it would probably be still if the COVID-19 pandemic hadn't happened and millions of children hadn't been stuck at home, unable to attend school or meet their friends. That's when I had the idea of putting the story online for free and asking children to illustrate it.

Down from the attic came the very dusty box of typed and handwritten papers, and I set to work. My now teenagers, who'd been *The Ickabog*'s very first audience, sat and listened to a nightly chapter once I'd nearly finished. Every now and then they'd ask why I'd cut something they used to like, and naturally, I reinstated everything they missed, astounded by how much they remembered.

In addition to my very supportive family, I want to thank those who helped me bring *The Ickabog* online in such a short space of time: my editors Arthur Levine and Ruth Alltimes, James McKnight of the Blair Partnership, my management team, Rebecca Salt, Nicky Stonehill and Mark Hutchinson and my agent, Neil Blair. It really was a herculean effort by all concerned, and I couldn't be more grateful. I'd also like to thank every single child (and the occasional adult!) who submitted pictures for the illustration competition. Looking through the artwork has been a joy and I know I'm far from alone in marvelling at the talent on display. I'd love to think *The Ickabog* gave some future artists and illustrators their first public exposure.

Returning to the land of Cornucopia and finishing what I started so long ago has been one of the most rewarding experiences of my writing life. All that remains to say is that I hope you enjoy reading the story as much as I enjoyed writing it!

J.K. Rowling
July 2020

# Contents

# CHAPTER 1

# King Fred the Fearless

Once upon a time, there was a tiny country called Cornucopia, which had been ruled for centuries by a long line of fair-haired kings. The king at the time of which I write was called King Fred the Fearless. He'd announced the 'Fearless' bit himself, on the morning of his coronation, partly because it sounded nice with 'Fred', but also because he'd once managed to catch and kill a wasp all by himself, if you didn't count five footmen and the boot boy.

King Fred the Fearless came to the throne on a huge wave of popularity. He had lovely yellow curls, fine sweeping moustaches, and looked magnificent in the tight breeches, velvet doublets, and ruffled shirts that rich men wore at the time. Fred was said to be generous, smiled and waved whenever anyone caught sight of him, and looked awfully handsome in the portraits that were distributed throughout the kingdom, to be hung in town halls. The people of Cornucopia were most happy with their new king, and many thought he'd end up being even better at the job than his father, Richard the Righteous, whose teeth (though nobody had liked to mention it at the time) were rather crooked.

King Fred was secretly relieved to find out how easy it was to rule Cornucopia. In fact, the country seemed to run itself. Nearly everybody had lots of food, the merchants made pots of gold, and Fred's advisors took care of any little problem that arose. All that was left for Fred to do was beam at his subjects whenever he went out in his carriage and go hunting five times a week with his two best friends, Lord Spittleworth and Lord Flapoon.

Spittleworth and Flapoon had large estates of their own in the country, but they found it much cheaper and more amusing to live at the palace with the king, eating his food, hunting his stags, and making sure that the king didn't get too fond of any of the beautiful ladies at court. They had no wish to see Fred married, because a queen might spoil all their fun. For a time, Fred had seemed to rather like Lady Eslanda, who was as dark and beautiful as Fred was fair and handsome, but Spittleworth had persuaded Fred that she was far too serious and bookish for the country to love her as queen. Fred didn't know that Lord Spittleworth had a grudge against Lady Eslanda. He'd once asked her to marry *him*, but she'd turned him down.

Lord Spittleworth was very thin, cunning, and clever. His friend Flapoon was ruddy-faced, and so enormous that it required six men to heave him onto his massive chestnut horse. Though not as clever as Spittleworth, Flapoon was still far sharper than the king.

Both lords were expert at flattery, and pretending to be astonished by how good Fred was at everything from riding to tiddlywinks. If Spittleworth had a particular talent, it was persuading the king to do things that suited Spittleworth, and if Flapoon had a gift, it was for convincing the king that nobody on earth was as loyal to the king as his two best friends.

Fred thought Spittleworth and Flapoon were jolly good chaps. They urged him to hold fancy parties, elaborate picnics, and sumptuous banquets, because Cornucopia was famous, far beyond its borders, for its food. Each of its cities was known for a different kind, and each was the very best in the world.

The capital of Cornucopia, Chouxville, lay in the south of the country, and was surrounded by acres of orchards, fields of shimmering golden wheat, and emerald-green grass, on which pure white dairy cows grazed. The cream, flour, and fruit produced by the farmers here was then given to the exceptional bakers of Chouxville, who made pastries.

Think, if you please, of the most delicious cake or biscuit you have ever tasted. Well, let me tell you they'd have been downright ashamed to serve that in Chouxville. Unless a grown man's eyes filled with tears of pleasure as he bit into a Chouxville pastry, it was deemed a failure and never made again. The bakery windows of Chouxville were piled high with delicacies such as Maidens' Dreams, Fairies' Cradles, and, most famous of all, Hopes-of-Heaven, which were so exquisitely, painfully delicious that they were saved for special occasions and everybody cried for joy as they ate them. King Porfirio, of neighbouring Pluritania, had already sent King Fred a letter, offering him the choice of any of his daughters' hands in marriage in exchange for a lifetime's supply of Hopes-of-Heaven, but Spittleworth had advised Fred to laugh in the Pluritanian ambassador's face.

'His daughters are nowhere *near* pretty enough to exchange for Hopes-of-Heaven, sire!' said Spittleworth.

To the north of Chouxville lay more green fields and clear, sparkling rivers, where jet-black cows and happy pink pigs were raised. These in turn served the twin cities of Kurdsburg and Baronstown, which were separated from each other by an arching stone bridge over the main river of Cornucopia, the Fluma, where brightly coloured barges bore goods from one end of the kingdom to another.

Kurdsburg was famous for its cheeses: huge white wheels, dense orange cannonballs, big crumbly blue-veined barrels, and little baby cream cheeses smoother than velvet.

Baronstown was celebrated for its smoked and honey-roasted hams, its sides of bacon, its spicy sausages, its melting beefsteaks, and its venison pies.

The savoury fumes rising from the chimneys of the red-brick Baronstown stoves mingled with the odorous tang wafting from the doorways of the Kurdsburg cheesemongers, and for forty miles all around, it was impossible not to salivate breathing in the delicious air.

A few hours north of Kurdsburg and Baronstown, you came upon acres of vineyards bearing grapes as large as eggs, each of them ripe and sweet and juicy. Journey onwards for the rest of the day and you reached the granite city of Jeroboam, famous for its wines. They said of the Jeroboam air that you could get tipsy simply walking its streets. The best vintages changed hands for thousands upon thousands of gold coins, and the Jeroboam wine merchants were some of the richest men in the kingdom.

But a little north of Jeroboam, a strange thing happened. It was as though the magically rich land of Cornucopia had exhausted itself by producing the best grass, the best fruit, and the best wheat in the world. Right at the northern tip came the place known as the Marshlands, and the only things that grew there were some tasteless, rubbery mushrooms and thin dry grass, only good enough to feed a few mangy sheep.

The Marshlanders who tended the sheep didn't have the sleek, well-rounded, well-dressed appearance of the citizens of Jeroboam, Baronstown, Kurdsburg, or Chouxville. They were gaunt and ragged. Their poorly nourished sheep never fetched very good prices, either in Cornucopia or abroad, so very few Marshlanders ever got to taste the delights of Cornucopian wine, cheese, beef, or pastries. The most common dish in the Marshlands was a greasy mutton broth, made of those sheep who were too old to sell.

The rest of Cornucopia found the Marshlanders an odd bunch – surly, dirty, and ill-tempered. They had rough voices, which the other Cornucopians imitated, making them sound like hoarse old sheep. Jokes were made about their manners and their simplicity. As far as the rest of Cornucopia was concerned, the only memorable thing that had ever come out of the Marshlands was the legend of the Ickabog.

*His friend Flapoon was ruddy-faced, and so enormous that it required six men to heave him onto his massive chestnut horse.*

*By Sophie, age 11 years, New Zealand*

# CHAPTER 2

# The Ickabog

The legend of the Ickabog had been passed down by generations of Marshlanders, and spread by word of mouth all the way to Chouxville. Nowadays, everybody knew the story. Naturally, as with all legends, it changed a little depending on who was telling it. However, every story agreed that a monster lived at the very northernmost tip of the country, in a wide patch of dark and often misty marsh too dangerous for humans to enter. The monster was said to eat children and sheep. Sometimes it even carried off grown men and women who strayed too close to the marsh at night.

The habits and appearance of the Ickabog changed depending on who was describing it. Some made it snake-like, others dragonish or wolf-like. Some said it roared, others that it hissed, and still others said that it drifted as silently as the mists that descended on the marsh without warning.

The Ickabog, they said, had extraordinary powers. It could imitate the human voice to lure travellers into its clutches. If you tried to kill it, it would mend magically, or else split into two Ickabogs; it could fly, spurt fire, shoot poison – the Ickabog's powers were as great as the imagination of the teller.

'Mind you don't leave the garden while I'm working,' parents all over the kingdom would tell their children, 'or the Ickabog will catch you and eat you all up!' And throughout the land, boys and girls played at fighting the Ickabog, tried to frighten each other with the tale of the Ickabog, and even, if the story became too convincing, had nightmares about the Ickabog.

Bert Beamish was one such little boy. When a family called the Dovetails came over for dinner one night, Mr Dovetail entertained everybody with what he claimed was the latest news of the Ickabog. That night, five-year-old Bert woke, sobbing and terrified, from a dream in which the monster's huge white eyes were gleaming at him across a foggy marsh into which he was slowly sinking.

'There, there,' whispered his mother, who'd tiptoed into his room with a candle and now rocked him backwards and forwards in her lap. 'There is no Ickabog, Bertie. It's just a silly story.'

'B-but Mr Dovetail said sheep have g-gone missing!' hiccoughed Bert.

'So they have,' said Mrs Beamish, 'but not because a monster took them. Sheep are foolish creatures. They wander off and get lost in the marsh.'

'B-but Mr Dovetail said p-people disappear too!'

'Only people who're silly enough to stray onto the marsh at night,' said Mrs Beamish. 'Hush now, Bertie, there is no monster.'

'But Mr D-Dovetail said p-people heard voices outside their windows and in the m-morning their chickens were gone!'

Mrs Beamish couldn't help but laugh.

'The voices they heard are ordinary thieves, Bertie. Up in the Marshlands they pilfer from each other all the time. It's easier to blame the Ickabog than to admit their neighbours are stealing from them!'

'Stealing?' gasped Bert, sitting up in his mother's lap and gazing at her with solemn eyes. 'Stealing's very naughty, isn't it, Mummy?'

'It's very naughty indeed,' said Mrs Beamish, lifting up Bert, placing him tenderly back into his warm bed and tucking him in. 'But luckily, we don't live near those lawless Marshlanders.'

She picked up her candle and tiptoed back towards the bedroom door.

'Night, night,' she whispered from the doorway. She'd normally have added, 'Don't let the Ickabog bite,' which was what parents across Cornucopia said to their children at bedtime, but instead she said, 'Sleep tight.'

Bert fell asleep again, and saw no more monsters in his dreams.

It so happened that Mr Dovetail and Mrs Beamish were great friends. They'd been in the same class at school, and had known each other all their lives. When Mr Dovetail heard that he'd given Bert nightmares, he felt guilty. As he was the best carpenter in all of Chouxville, he decided to carve the little boy an Ickabog. It had a wide, smiling mouth full of teeth and big, clawed feet, and at once it became Bert's favourite toy.

If Bert, or his parents, or the Dovetails next door, or anybody else in the whole kingdom of Cornucopia had been told that terrible troubles were about to engulf Cornucopia, all because of the myth of the Ickabog, they'd have laughed. They lived in the happiest kingdom in the world. What harm could the Ickabog do?

# CHAPTER 3

# Death of a Seamstress

The Beamish and Dovetail families both lived in a place called the City-Within-The-City. This was the part of Chouxville where all the people who worked for King Fred had houses. Gardeners, cooks, tailors, pageboys, seamstresses, stonemasons, grooms, carpenters, footmen, and maids: all of them occupied neat little cottages just outside the palace grounds.

The City-Within-The-City was separated from the rest of Chouxville by a high white wall, and the gates in the wall stood open during the day, so that the residents could visit friends and family in the rest of Chouxville, and go to the markets. By night, the sturdy gates were closed, and everyone in the City-Within-The-City slept, like the king, under the protection of the Royal Guard.

Major Beamish, Bert's father, was head of the Royal Guard. A handsome, cheerful man who rode a steel-grey horse, he accompanied King Fred, Lord Spittleworth, and Lord Flapoon on their hunting trips, which usually happened five times a week. The king liked Major Beamish, and he also liked Bert's mother, because Bertha Beamish was the king's own private pastry chef, a high honour in that city of world-class bakers. Due to Bertha's habit of bringing home fancy cakes that hadn't turned out absolutely perfectly, Bert was a plump little boy, and sometimes, I regret to say, the other children called him 'Butterball' and made him cry.

Bert's best friend was Daisy Dovetail. The two children had been born days apart, and acted more like brother and sister than playmates. Daisy was Bert's defender against bullies. She was skinny but fast, and more than ready to fight anyone who called Bert 'Butterball'.

Daisy's father, Dan Dovetail, was the king's carpenter, repairing and replacing the wheels and shafts on his carriages. As Mr Dovetail was so clever at carving, he also made bits of furniture for the palace.

Daisy's mother, Dora Dovetail, was the Head Seamstress of the palace – another honoured job, because King Fred liked clothes, and kept a whole team of tailors busy making him new costumes every month.

It was the king's great fondness for finery that led to a nasty incident which the history books of Cornucopia would later record as the beginning of all the troubles that were to engulf that happy little kingdom. At the time it happened, only a few people within the City-Within-The-City knew anything about it, though for some, it was an awful tragedy.

What happened was this.

The King of Pluritania came to pay a formal visit to Fred (still hoping, perhaps, to exchange one of his daughters for a lifetime's supply of Hopes-of-Heaven) and Fred decided that he must have a brand-new set of clothes made for the occasion: dull purple, overlaid with silver lace, with amethyst buttons, and grey fur at the cuffs.

Now, King Fred had heard something about the Head Seamstress not being quite well, but he hadn't paid much attention. He didn't trust anyone but Daisy's mother to stitch on the silver lace properly, so gave the order that nobody else should be given the job. In consequence, Daisy's mother sat up three nights in a row, racing to finish the purple suit in time for the King of Pluritania's visit, and at dawn on the fourth day, her assistant found her lying on the floor, dead, with the very last amethyst button in her hand.

The king's Chief Advisor came to break the news, while Fred was still having his breakfast. The Chief Advisor was a wise old man called Herringbone, with a silver beard that hung almost to his knees. After explaining that the Head Seamstress had died, he said:

'But I'm sure one of the other ladies will be able to fix on the last button for Your Majesty.'

There was a look in Herringbone's eye that King Fred didn't like. It gave him a squirming feeling in the pit of his stomach.

While his dressers were helping him into the new purple suit later that morning, Fred tried to make himself feel less guilty by talking the matter over with Lords Spittleworth and Flapoon.

'I mean to say, if I'd known she was seriously ill,' panted Fred, as the servants heaved him into his skin-tight satin pantaloons, 'naturally I'd have let someone else sew the suit.'

'Your Majesty is so kind,' said Spittleworth, as he examined his sallow complexion in the mirror over the fireplace. 'A more tender-hearted monarch was never born.'

'The woman should have spoken up if she felt unwell,' grunted Flapoon from a cushioned seat by the window. 'If she's not fit to work, she should've said so. Properly looked at, that's disloyalty to the king. Or to your suit, anyway.'

'Flapoon's right,' said Spittleworth, turning away from the mirror. 'Nobody could treat his servants better than you do, sire.'

'I *do* treat them well, don't I?' said King Fred anxiously, sucking in his stomach as the dressers did up his amethyst buttons. 'And after all, chaps, I've got to look my blasted best today, haven't I? You know how dressy the King of Pluritania always is!'

'It would be a matter of national shame if you were any less well-dressed than the King of Pluritania,' said Spittleworth.

'Put this unhappy occurrence out of your mind, sire,' said Flapoon.

'A disloyal seamstress is no reason to spoil a sunny day.'

And yet, in spite of the two lords' advice, King Fred couldn't be quite easy in his mind. Perhaps he was imagining it, but he thought Lady Eslanda looked particularly serious that day. The servants' smiles seemed colder, and the maids' curtsies a little less deep. As his court feasted that evening with the King of Pluritania, Fred's thoughts kept drifting back to the seamstress, dead on the floor, with the last amethyst button clutched in her hand.

Before Fred went to bed that night, Herringbone knocked on his bedroom door. After bowing deeply, the Chief Advisor asked whether the king was intending to send flowers to Mrs Dovetail's funeral.

'Oh – oh, yes!' said Fred, startled. 'Yes, send a big wreath, you know, saying how sorry I am and so forth. You can arrange that, can't you, Herringbone?'

'Certainly, sire,' said the Chief Advisor. 'And – if I may ask – are you planning to visit the seamstress's family, at all? They live, you know, just a short walk from the palace gates.'

'Visit them?' said the king pensively. 'Oh, no, Herringbone, I don't think I'd like – I mean to say, I'm sure they aren't expecting that.'

Herringbone and the king looked at each other for a few seconds, then the Chief Advisor bowed and left the room.

Now, as King Fred was used to everyone telling him what a marvellous chap he was, he really didn't like the frown with which the Chief Advisor had left. He now began to feel cross rather than ashamed.

'It's a bally pity,' he told his reflection, turning back to the mirror in which he'd been combing his moustaches before bed, 'but after all, I'm the king and she was a seamstress. If *I* died, I wouldn't have expected *her* to—'

But then it occurred to him that if he died, he'd expect the whole of Cornucopia to stop whatever they were doing, dress all in black and weep for a week, just as they'd done for his father, Richard the Righteous.

'Well, anyway,' he said impatiently to his reflection, 'life goes on.'

He put on his silk nightcap, climbed into his four-poster bed, blew out the candle and fell asleep.

*Fred decided that he must have a brand-new set of clothes made for the occasion... with silver lace, amethyst buttons, and grey fur at the cuffs.*

*By Kit, age 7 years, United Kingdom*

# CHAPTER 4

# The Quiet House

Mrs Dovetail was buried in the graveyard in the City-Within-The-City, where generations of royal servants lay. Daisy and her father stood hand-in-hand, looking down at the grave, for a long time. Bert kept looking back at Daisy as his tearful mother and grim-faced father led him slowly away. Bert wanted to say something to his best friend, but what had happened was too enormous and dreadful for words. Bert could hardly bear to imagine how he'd feel if his mother had disappeared forever into the cold, hard earth.

When all their friends had gone, Mr Dovetail moved the purple wreath sent by the king away from Mrs Dovetail's headstone, and put in its place the small bunch of snowdrops that Daisy had collected that morning. Then the two Dovetails walked slowly home to a house they knew would never be the same again.

A week after the funeral, the king rode out of the palace with the Royal Guard to go hunting. As usual, everyone along his route came rushing out into their gardens to bow, curtsy, and cheer. As the king bowed and waved back, he noticed that the front garden of one cottage remained empty. It had black drapes at the windows and the front door.

'Who lives there?' he asked Major Beamish.

'That – that's the Dovetail house, Your Majesty,' said Beamish.

'Dovetail, Dovetail,' said the king, frowning. 'I've heard that name, haven't I?'

'Er… yes, sire,' said Major Beamish. 'Mr Dovetail is Your Majesty's carpenter and Mrs Dovetail is – was – Your Majesty's Head Seamstress.'

'Ah, yes,' said King Fred hurriedly, 'I – I remember.'

And spurring his milk-white charger into a canter, he rode swiftly past the black-draped windows of the Dovetail cottage, trying to think of nothing but the day's hunting that lay ahead.

But every time the king rode out after that, he couldn't help but fix his eyes on the empty garden and the black-draped door of the Dovetail residence, and every time he saw the cottage, the image of the dead seamstress clutching that amethyst button came back to him. Finally, he could bear it no longer, and summoned the Chief Advisor to him.

'Herringbone,' he said, not looking the old man in the eye, 'there's a house on the corner, on the way to the park. Rather a nice cottage. Large-ish garden.'

'The Dovetail house, Your Majesty?'

'Oh, that's who lives there, is it?' said King Fred airily. 'Well, it occurs to me that it's rather a big place for a small family. I think I've heard there are only two of them, is that correct?'

'Perfectly correct, Your Majesty. Just two, since the mother—'

'It doesn't really seem fair, Herringbone,' King Fred said loudly, 'for that nice, spacious cottage to be given to only two people, when there are families of five or six, I believe, who'd be happy with a little more room.'

'You'd like me to move the Dovetails, Your Majesty?'

'Yes, I think so,' said King Fred, pretending to be very interested in the tip of his satin shoe.

'Very well, Your Majesty,' said the Chief Advisor, with a deep bow. 'I shall ask them to swap with Roach's family, who I'm sure would be glad of more space, and I shall put the Dovetails in the Roaches' house.'

'And where is that, exactly?' asked the king nervously, for the last thing he wanted was to see those black drapes even nearer the palace gates.

'Right on the edge of the City-Within-The-City,' said the Chief Advisor. 'Very close to the graveyard, in f—'

'That sounds suitable,' interrupted King Fred, leaping to his feet. 'I have no need of details. Just make it happen, Herringbone, there's a good chap.'

And so, Daisy and her father were instructed to swap houses with the family of Captain Roach, who, like Bert's father, was a member of the king's Royal Guard. The next time King Fred rode out, the black drapes had vanished from the door and the Roach children – four strapping brothers, the ones who'd first christened Bert Beamish 'Butterball' – came running into the front garden and jumped up and down, cheering and waving Cornucopian flags. King Fred beamed and waved back at the boys. Weeks passed, and King Fred forgot all about the Dovetails, and was happy again.

# CHAPTER 5

# Daisy Dovetail

For some months after Mrs Dovetail's shocking death, the king's servants were divided into two groups. The first group whispered that King Fred had been to blame for the way she'd died. The second preferred to believe there'd been some kind of mistake, and that the king couldn't have known how ill Mrs Dovetail was before giving the order that she must finish his suit.

Mrs Beamish, the pastry chef, belonged to the second group. The king had always been very nice to Mrs Beamish, sometimes even inviting her into the dining room to congratulate her on particularly fine batches of Dukes' Delights or Folderol Fancies, so she was sure he was a kind, generous, and considerate man.

'You mark my words, somebody forgot to give the king a message,' she told her husband, Major Beamish. 'He'd *never* make an ill servant work. I know he must feel simply awful about what happened.'

'Yes,' said Major Beamish, 'I'm sure he does.'

Like his wife, Major Beamish wanted to think the best of the king, because he, his father, and his grandfather before him had all served loyally in the Royal Guard. So even though Major Beamish observed that King Fred seemed quite cheerful after Mrs Dovetail's death, hunting as regularly as ever, and though Major Beamish knew that the Dovetails had been moved out of their old house to live down by the graveyard, he tried to believe that the king was sorry for what had happened to his seamstress, and that he'd had no hand in moving her husband and daughter.

The Dovetails' new cottage was a gloomy place. Sunlight was blocked out by the high yew trees that bordered the graveyard, although Daisy's bedroom window gave her a clear view of her mother's grave, through a gap between dark branches. As she no longer lived next door to Bert, Daisy saw less of him in her free time, although Bert went to visit Daisy as often as possible. There was much less room to play in her new garden, but they adjusted their games to fit.

What Mr Dovetail thought about his new house, or the king, nobody knew. He never discussed these matters with his fellow servants, but went quietly about his work, earning the money he needed to support his daughter and raising Daisy as best he could without her mother.

Daisy, who liked helping her father in his carpenter's workshop, had always been happiest in overalls. She was the kind of person who didn't mind getting dirty and she wasn't very interested in clothes. Yet in the days following the funeral, she wore a different dress every day to take a fresh posy to her mother's grave. While alive, Mrs Dovetail had always tried to make her daughter look, as she put it, 'like a little lady', and had made her many beautiful little gowns, sometimes from the offcuts of material that King Fred graciously let her keep after she'd made his superb costumes.

And so a week passed, then a month, and then a year, until the dresses her mother had sewn her were all too small for Daisy, but she still kept them carefully in her wardrobe. Other people seemed to have forgotten what had happened to Daisy, or had got used to the idea of her mother being gone. Daisy pretended that she was used to it too. On the surface, her life returned to something like normal. She helped her father in the workshop, did her schoolwork and played with her best friend, Bert, but they never spoke about her mother, and they never talked about the king. Every night, Daisy lay with her eyes fixed on the distant white headstone shining in the moonlight, until she fell asleep.

## CHAPTER 6

# The Fight in the Courtyard

There was a courtyard behind the palace where peacocks walked, fountains played, and statues of former kings and queens kept watch. As long as they didn't pull the peacocks' tails, jump in the fountains, or climb the statues, the children of the palace servants were allowed to play in the courtyard after school. Sometimes Lady Eslanda, who liked children, would come and make daisy chains with them, but the most exciting thing of all was when King Fred came out onto the balcony and waved, which made all the children cheer, bow, and curtsy as their parents had taught them.

The only time the children fell silent, ceased their games of hopscotch, and stopped pretending to fight the Ickabog, was when the lords Spittleworth and Flapoon passed through the courtyard. These two lords weren't fond of children at all. They thought the little brats made far too much noise in the late afternoon, which was precisely the time when Spittleworth and Flapoon liked to take a nap between hunting and dinner.

One day, shortly after Bert and Daisy's seventh birthdays, when everyone was playing as usual between the fountains and the peacocks, the daughter of the new Head Seamstress, who was wearing a beautiful dress of rose-pink brocade, said:

'Oh, I *do* hope the king waves at us today!'

'Well, I don't,' said Daisy, who couldn't help herself, and didn't realise how loudly she'd spoken.

The children all gasped and turned to look at her. Daisy felt hot and cold at once, seeing them all glaring.

'You shouldn't have said that,' whispered Bert. As he was standing right next to Daisy, the other children were staring at him too.

'I don't care,' said Daisy, colour rising in her face. She'd started now, so she might as well finish. 'If he hadn't worked my mother so hard, she'd still be alive.'

Daisy felt as though she'd been wanting to say that out loud for a very long time.

There was another gasp from all the surrounding children, and a maid's daughter actually squealed in terror.

'He's the best king of Cornucopia we've ever had,' said Bert, who'd heard his mother say so many times.

'No, he isn't,' said Daisy loudly. 'He's selfish, vain, and cruel!'

'Daisy!' whispered Bert, horrified. 'Don't be – don't be *silly*!'

It was the word 'silly' that did it. 'Silly', when the new Head Seamstress's daughter smirked and whispered behind her hand to her friends, while pointing at Daisy's overalls? 'Silly', when her father wiped away his tears in the evenings, thinking Daisy wasn't looking? 'Silly', when to talk to her mother she had to visit a cold white headstone?

Daisy drew back her hand, and smacked Bert right around the face.

Then the oldest Roach brother, whose name was Roderick and who now lived in Daisy's old bedroom, shouted, 'Don't let her get away with it, Butterball!' and led all the boys in shouts of 'Fight! Fight! Fight!'

Terrified, Bert gave Daisy's shoulder a half-hearted shove, and it seemed to Daisy that the only thing to do was to launch herself at Bert, and everything became dust and elbows until suddenly the two children were pulled apart by Bert's father, Major Beamish, who'd come running out of the palace on hearing the commotion, to find out what was going on.

'Dreadful behaviour,' muttered Lord Spittleworth, walking past the major and the two sobbing, struggling children.

But as he turned away, a broad smirk spread over Lord Spittleworth's face. He was a man who knew how to turn a situation to good use, and he thought he might have found a way to banish children – or some of them, anyway – from the palace courtyard.

*There was a courtyard behind the palace where peacocks walked, fountains played, and statues of former kings and queens kept watch.*

*By Charlotte, age 8 years, Republic of Ireland*

# CHAPTER 7

# Lord Spittleworth Tells Tales

That night, the two lords dined, as usual, with King Fred. After a sumptuous meal of Baronstown venison, accompanied by the finest Jeroboam wine, followed by a selection of Kurdsburg cheeses and some of Mrs Beamish's featherlight Fairies' Cradles, Lord Spittleworth decided the moment had come. He cleared his throat, then said:

'I do hope, Your Majesty, that you weren't disturbed by that disgusting fight among the children in the courtyard this afternoon?'

'Fight?' repeated King Fred, who'd been talking to his tailor about the design for a new cloak, so had heard nothing. 'What fight?'

'Oh dear… I thought Your Majesty knew,' said Lord Spittleworth, pretending to be startled. 'Perhaps Major Beamish could tell you all about it.'

But King Fred was amused rather than disturbed.

'Oh, I believe scuffles among children are quite usual, Spittleworth.'

Spittleworth and Flapoon exchanged looks behind the king's back, and Spittleworth tried again.

'Your Majesty is, as ever, the very soul of kindness,' said Spittleworth.

'Of course, some kings,' Flapoon muttered, brushing crumbs off the front of his waistcoat, 'if they'd heard that a child spoke of the crown so disrespectfully…'

'What's that?' exclaimed Fred, the smile fading from his face. 'A child spoke of me… disrespectfully?' Fred couldn't believe it. He was used to the children shrieking with excitement when he bowed to them from the balcony.

'I believe so, Your Majesty,' said Spittleworth, examining his fingernails, 'but, as I mentioned… it was Major Beamish who separated the children… he has all the details.'

The candles sputtered a little in their silver sticks.

'Children… say all manner of things, in fun,' said King Fred. 'Doubtless the child meant no harm.'

'Sounded like bally treason to me,' grunted Flapoon.

'But,' said Spittleworth swiftly, 'it is Major Beamish who knows the details. Flapoon and I may, perhaps, have misheard.'

Fred sipped his wine. At that moment, a footman entered the room to remove the pudding plates.

'Cankerby,' said King Fred, for such was the footman's name, 'fetch Major Beamish here.'

Unlike the king and the two lords, Major Beamish didn't eat seven courses for dinner every night. He'd finished his supper hours ago, and was getting ready for bed when the summons from the king arrived. The major hastily swapped his pyjamas for his uniform, and dashed back to the palace, by which time King Fred, Lord Spittleworth, and Lord Flapoon had retired to the Yellow Parlour, where they were sitting on satin armchairs, drinking more Jeroboam wine and, in Flapoon's case, eating a second plate of Fairies' Cradles.

'Ah, Beamish,' said King Fred, as the major made a deep bow. 'I hear there was a little commotion in the courtyard this afternoon.'

The major's heart sank. He'd hoped that news of Bert and Daisy's fight wouldn't reach the king's ears.

'Oh, it was really nothing, Your Majesty,' said Beamish.

'Come, come, Beamish,' said Flapoon. 'You should be proud that you've taught your son not to tolerate traitors.'

'I... there was no question of treachery,' said Major Beamish. 'They're only children, my lord.'

'Do I understand that your son defended me, Beamish?' said King Fred.

Major Beamish was in a most unfortunate position. He didn't want to tell the king what Daisy had said. Whatever his own loyalty to the king, he quite understood why the motherless little girl felt the way she did about Fred, and the last thing he wanted to do was to get her into trouble. At the same time, he was well aware that there were twenty witnesses who could tell the king exactly what Daisy had said, and was sure that, if he lied, Lord Spittleworth and Lord Flapoon would tell the king that he, Major Beamish, was also disloyal and treacherous.

'I... yes, Your Majesty, it's true that my son Bert defended you,' said Major Beamish. 'However, allowance must surely be made for the little girl who said the... the unfortunate thing about Your Majesty. She's passed through a great deal of trouble, Your Majesty, and even unhappy grown-ups may talk wildly at times.'

'What kind of trouble has the girl passed through?' asked King Fred, who couldn't imagine any good reason for a subject to speak rudely of him.

'She... her name is Daisy Dovetail, Your Majesty,' said Major Beamish, staring over King Fred's head at a picture of his father, King Richard the Righteous. 'Her mother was the seamstress who—'

'Yes, yes, I remember,' said King Fred loudly, cutting Major Beamish off. 'Very well, that's all, Beamish. Off you go.'

Somewhat relieved, Major Beamish bowed deeply again and had almost reached the door when he heard the king's voice.

'What *exactly* did the girl say, Beamish?'

Major Beamish paused with his hand on the doorknob. There was nothing else for it but to tell the truth.

'She said that Your Majesty is selfish, vain, and cruel,' said Major Beamish.

Not daring to look at the king, he left the room.

# CHAPTER 8

# The Day of Petition

*Selfish, vain, and cruel. Selfish, vain, and cruel.*

The words echoed in the king's head as he pulled on his silk nightcap. It couldn't be true, could it? It took Fred a long time to fall asleep, and when he woke in the morning he felt, if anything, worse.

He decided he wanted to do something kind, and the first thing that occurred to him was to reward Beamish's son, who'd defended him against that nasty little girl. So he took a small medallion that usually hung around the neck of his favourite hunting dog, asked a maid to thread ribbon through it, and summoned the Beamishes to the palace. Bert, whom his mother had pulled out of class and hurriedly dressed in a blue velvet suit, was struck speechless in the presence of the king, which Fred enjoyed, and he spent several minutes speaking kindly to the boy, while Major and Mrs Beamish nearly burst with pride in their son. Finally, Bert returned to school, with his little gold medal around his neck, and was made much of in the playground that afternoon by Roderick Roach, who was usually his biggest bully. Daisy said nothing at all and when Bert caught her eye, he felt hot and uncomfortable, and shoved the medal out of sight beneath his shirt.

The king, meanwhile, still wasn't entirely happy. An uneasy feeling stayed with him, like indigestion, and again, he found it hard to sleep that night.

When he woke the next day, he remembered that it was the Day of Petition.

The Day of Petition was a special day held once a year, when the subjects of Cornucopia were permitted an audience with the king. Naturally, these people were carefully screened by Fred's advisors before they were allowed to see him. Fred never dealt with big problems. He saw people whose troubles could be solved with a few gold coins and a few kind words: a farmer with a broken plough, for instance, or an old lady whose cat had died. Fred had been looking forward to the Day of Petition. It was a chance to dress up in his fanciest clothes, and he found it so touching to see how much he meant to the ordinary people of Cornucopia.

Fred's dressers were waiting for him after breakfast, with a new outfit he'd requested just the previous month: white satin pantaloons and matching doublet, with gold and pearl buttons; a cloak edged with ermine and lined in scarlet; and white satin shoes with gold and pearl buckles. His valet was waiting with the golden tongs, ready to curl his moustaches, and a pageboy stood ready with a number of jewelled rings on a velvet cushion, waiting for Fred to make his selection.

'Take all that away, I don't want it,' said King Fred crossly, waving at the outfit the dressers were holding up for his approval. The dressers froze. They weren't sure they'd heard correctly. King Fred had taken an immense interest in the progress of the costume, and had requested the addition of the scarlet lining and fancy buckles himself. 'I said, take it away!' he snapped, when nobody moved. 'Fetch me something plain! Fetch me that suit I wore to my father's funeral!'

'Is... is Your Majesty quite well?' enquired his valet, as the astonished dressers bowed and hurried away with the white suit, and returned in double-quick time with a black one.

'Of course I'm well,' snapped Fred. 'But I'm a man, not a frivolling popinjay.'

He shrugged on the black suit, which was the plainest he owned, though still rather splendid, having silver edging to the cuffs and collar, and onyx and diamond buttons. Then, to the astonishment of the valet, he permitted the man to curl only the very ends of his moustaches, before dismissing both him and the pageboy bearing the cushion full of rings.

*There*, thought Fred, examining himself in the mirror. *How can I be called vain? Black* definitely *isn't one of my best colours.*

So unusually speedy had Fred been in getting dressed, that Lord Spittleworth, who was making one of Fred's servants dig earwax out of his ears, and Lord Flapoon, who was guzzling a plate of Dukes' Delights which he'd ordered from the kitchens, were caught by surprise, and came running out of their bedrooms, pulling on their waistcoats and hopping as they put on their boots.

'Hurry up, you lazy chaps!' called King Fred, as the two lords chased him down the corridor. 'There are people waiting for my help!'

*And would a selfish king hurry to meet simple people who wanted favours from him?* thought Fred. *No, he wouldn't!*

Fred's advisors were shocked to see him on time, and plainly dressed, for Fred. Indeed, Herringbone, the Chief Advisor, wore an approving smile as he bowed.

'Your Majesty is early,' he said. 'The people will be delighted. They've been queuing since dawn.'

'Show them in, Herringbone,' said the king, settling himself on his throne, and gesturing to Spittleworth and Flapoon to take the seats on either side of him.

The doors were opened, and one by one, the petitioners entered.

Fred's subjects often became tongue-tied when they found themselves face-to-face with the real, live king, whose picture hung in their town halls. Some began to giggle, or forgot what they'd come for, and once or twice people fainted. Fred was particularly gracious today, and each petition ended with the king handing out a couple of gold coins, or blessing a baby, or allowing an old woman to kiss his hand.

Today, though, while he smiled and handed out gold coins and promises, the words of Daisy Dovetail kept echoing in his head. *Selfish, vain, and cruel.* He wanted to do something special to prove what a wonderful man he was – to show that he was ready to sacrifice himself for others. Every king of Cornucopia had handed out gold coins and trifling favours on the Day of Petition: Fred wanted to do something so splendid that it would ring down the ages, and you didn't get into the history books by replacing a fruit farmer's favourite hat.

The two lords on either side of Fred were becoming bored. They'd much rather have been left to loll in their bedrooms until lunchtime than sit here listening to peasants talking about their petty troubles. After several hours, the last petitioner passed gratefully out of the Throne Room, and Flapoon, whose stomach had been rumbling for nearly an hour, heaved himself out of his chair with a sigh of relief.

'Lunchtime!' boomed Flapoon, but just as the guards were attempting to close the doors, a kerfuffle was heard, and the doors flew open once more.

# CHAPTER 9

# The Shepherd's Story

'Your Majesty,' said Herringbone, hurrying towards King Fred, who'd just risen from the throne. 'There is a shepherd from the Marshlands here to petition you, sire. He's a little late – I could send him away, if Your Majesty wants his lunch?'

'A Marshlander!' said Spittleworth, waving his scented handkerchief beneath his nose. 'Imagine, sire!'

'Dashed impertinence, being late for the king,' said Flapoon.

'No,' said Fred, after a brief hesitation. 'No – if the poor fellow has travelled this far, we shall see him. Send him in, Herringbone.'

The Chief Advisor was delighted at this further evidence of a new, kind, and considerate king, and hurried off to the double doors to tell the guards to let the shepherd inside. The king settled himself back on his throne and Spittleworth and Flapoon sat back down on their chairs, their expressions sour.

The old man who now tottered up the long red carpet towards the throne was very weather-beaten and rather dirty, with a straggly beard, and ragged, patched clothes. He snatched off his cap as he approached the king, looking thoroughly frightened, and when he reached the place where people usually bowed or curtsied, he fell to his knees instead.

'Your Majesty!' he wheezed.

'Your Maaaaaa-jesty,' Spittleworth imitated him softly, making the old shepherd sound like a sheep.

Flapoon's chins trembled with silent laughter.

'Your Majesty,' continued the shepherd, 'I have travelled for five long days for to see ye. It has been a hard journey. I has ridden in hayricks when I could, and walked when I couldn't, and my boots is all holes—'

'Oh, get on with it, do,' muttered Spittleworth, his long nose still buried in his handkerchief.

'—but all the time I was travelling, I thought of old Patch, sire, and how ye'd help me if I could but reach the palace—'

'What is "old Patch", good fellow?' asked the king, his eyes upon the shepherd's much-darned trousers.

''Tis my old dog, sire – or was, I should perhaps say,' replied the shepherd, his eyes filling with tears.

'Ah,' said King Fred, fumbling with the money purse at his belt. 'Then, good shepherd, take these few gold coins and buy yourself a new—'

'Nay, sire, thank ye, but it bain't a question of the gold,' said the shepherd. 'I can find meself a puppy easy enough, though it'll never match old Patch.' The shepherd wiped his nose on his sleeve. Spittleworth shuddered.

'Well, then, why have you come to me?' asked King Fred, as kindly as he knew how.

'To tell ye, sire, how Patch met his end.'

'Ah,' said King Fred, his eyes wandering to the golden clock on the mantelpiece. 'Well, we'd love to hear the story, but we are rather wanting our lunch—'

''Twas the Ickabog that ate him, sire,' said the shepherd.

There was an astonished silence, and then Spittleworth and Flapoon burst out laughing.

The shepherd's eyes overflowed with tears which fell sparkling onto the red carpet.

'Ar, they've laughed at me from Jeroboam to Chouxville, sire, when I've told 'em why I was coming to see ye. Laughed themselves silly, they have, and told me I was daft in the head. But I seen the monster with me own two eyes, and so did poor Patch, afore he was ate.'

King Fred felt a strong urge to laugh along with the two lords. He wanted his lunch and he wanted to get rid of the old shepherd, but at the same time, that horrid little voice was whispering *selfish, vain, and cruel* inside his head.

'Why don't you tell me what happened?' King Fred said to the shepherd, and Spittleworth and Flapoon stopped laughing at once.

'Well, sire,' said the shepherd, wiping his nose on his sleeve again, ''twas twilight and right foggy and Patch and me was walking home round the edge of the marsh. Patch sees a marshteazle—'

'Sees a what?' asked King Fred.

'A marshteazle, sire. Them's bald rat-like things what lives in the marsh. Not bad in pies if ye don't mind the tails.'

Flapoon looked queasy.

'So Patch sees the marshteazle,' the shepherd continued, 'and he gives chase. I shouts for Patch and shouts, sire, but he was too busy to come back. And then, sire, I hears a yelp. "Patch!" I cries. "Patch! What's got ye, lad?" But Patch don't come back, sire. And then I sees it, through the fog,' said the shepherd in a low voice. 'Huge, it is, with eyes like lanterns and a mouth as wide as that there throne, and its wicked teeth shining at me. And I forgets old Patch, sire, and I runs and runs and runs all the way home. And next day I sets off, sire, to come and see ye. The Ickabog ate me dog, sire, and I wants it punished!'

The king looked down at the shepherd for a few seconds. Then, very slowly, he got to his feet.

'Shepherd,' said the king, 'we shall travel north this very day to investigate the matter of the Ickabog once and for all. If any trace of the creature can be found, you may rest assured that it shall be tracked to its lair and punished for its impudence in taking your dog. Now, take these few gold coins and hire yourself a ride back home in a haycart!

'My lords,' said the king, turning to the stunned Spittleworth and Flapoon, 'pray change into your riding gear and follow me to the stables. There is a new hunt afoot!'

# CHAPTER 10

# King Fred's Quest

King Fred strode from the Throne Room feeling quite delighted with himself. Nobody would ever again say that he was selfish, vain, and cruel! For the sake of a smelly, simple old shepherd and his worthless old mongrel, he, King Fred the Fearless, was going to hunt the Ickabog! True, there was no such thing, but it was still dashed fine and noble of him to ride to the other end of the country, in person, to prove it!

Quite forgetting lunch, the king rushed upstairs to his bedroom, shouting for his valet to come and help him out of the dreary black suit and help him into his battledress, which he'd never had the chance to wear before. The tunic was scarlet, with buttons of gold, a purple sash, and lots of medals that Fred was allowed to wear because he was king, and when Fred looked in the mirror and saw how well battledress became him, he wondered why he didn't wear it all the time. As his valet lowered the king's plumed helmet onto his golden curls, Fred imagined himself painted wearing it, seated on his favourite milk-white charger and spearing a serpent-like monster with his lance. King Fred the Fearless indeed! Why, he half hoped there really was an Ickabog, now.

Meanwhile, the Chief Advisor was sending word throughout the City-Within-The-City that the king was setting off on a tour of the country, and that everyone should be ready to cheer him as he left. Herringbone made no mention of the Ickabog, because he wanted to prevent the king from looking foolish, if he could.

Unfortunately, the footman called Cankerby had overheard two advisors muttering together about the king's strange scheme. Cankerby immediately told the between maid, who spread the word all over the kitchens, where a sausage seller from Baronstown was gossiping with the cook. In short, by the time the king's party was ready to leave, word had spread all through the City-Within-The-City that the king was riding north to hunt the Ickabog, and news was also beginning to leak out into wider Chouxville.

'Is it a joke?' the capital's inhabitants asked each other, as they thronged out onto the pavements, ready to cheer the king. 'What does it mean?'

Some shrugged and laughed and said that the king was merely having fun. Others shook their heads and muttered that there must be more to it than that. No king would ride out, armed, to the north of the country without good reason. What, the worried folk asked each other, does the king know, that we do not?

Lady Eslanda joined the other ladies of the court on a balcony, to watch the soldiers assembling.

I shall now tell you a secret, which nobody else knew. Lady Eslanda would never have married the king, even if he'd asked her. You see, she was secretly in love with a man called Captain Goodfellow, who was now chatting and laughing with his good friend Major Beamish in the courtyard below. Lady Eslanda, who was very shy, had never been able to bring herself to talk to Captain Goodfellow, who had no idea that the most beautiful woman at court was in love with him. Both Goodfellow's parents, who were dead, had been cheesemakers from Kurdsburg. Though Goodfellow was both clever and brave, these were the days when no cheesemaker's son would expect to marry a highborn lady.

Meanwhile, all the servants' children were being let out of school early to watch the battle party set off. Mrs Beamish the pastry chef naturally rushed to collect Bert, so that he'd have a good spot to watch his father passing by.

When the palace gates opened at last, and the cavalcade rode out, Bert and Mrs Beamish cheered at the top of their lungs. Nobody had seen battledress for a very long time. How exciting it was, and how fine! The sunlight played upon the golden buttons, silver swords, and the gleaming trumpets of the buglers, and up on the palace balcony, the handkerchiefs of the ladies of the court fluttered in farewell, like doves.

At the front of the procession rode King Fred, on his milk-white charger, holding scarlet reins and waving at the crowds. Right behind him, riding a thin yellow horse and wearing a bored expression, was Spittleworth, and next came Flapoon, furiously lunch-less and sitting on his elephantine chestnut.

Behind the king and the two lords trotted the Royal Guard, all of them on dapple-grey horses, except for Major Beamish, who rode his steel-grey stallion. It made Mrs Beamish's heart flutter to see her husband looking so handsome.

'Good luck, Daddy!' shouted Bert, and Major Beamish (though he really shouldn't have done) waved at his son.

The procession trotted down the hill, smiling at the cheering crowds of the City-Within-The-City, until it reached the gates in the wall onto wider Chouxville. There, hidden by the crowds, was the Dovetails' cottage. Mr Dovetail and Daisy had come out into their garden, and they were just able to see the plumes in the helmets of the Royal Guard riding past.

Daisy didn't feel much interest in the soldiers. She and Bert still weren't talking to each other. In fact, he'd spent morning break with Roderick Roach, who often jeered at Daisy for wearing overalls instead of a dress, so the cheering and the sound of the horses didn't raise her spirits at all.

'There isn't really an Ickabog, Daddy, is there?' she asked.

'No, Daisy,' sighed Mr Dovetail, turning back to his workshop, 'there's no Ickabog, but if the king wants to believe in it, let him. He can't do much harm up in the Marshlands.'

Which just goes to show that even sensible men may fail to see a terrible, looming danger.

*Lady Eslanda joined the other ladies of the court on a balcony, to watch the soldiers assembling.*

*By Radhya, age 9 years, India*

# CHAPTER 11

# The Journey North

King Fred's spirits rose higher and higher as he rode out of Chouxville and into the countryside. Word of the king's sudden expedition to find the Ickabog had now spread to the farmers who worked the rolling green fields, and they ran with their families to cheer the king, the two lords, and the Royal Guard as they passed.

Not having had any lunch, the king decided to stop in Kurdsburg to eat a late dinner.

'We'll rough it here, chaps, like the soldiers we are!' he cried to his party as they entered the city famed for its cheese. 'And we'll set out again at first light!'

But, of course, there was no question of the king roughing it. Visitors at Kurdsburg's finest inn were thrown out onto the street to make way for him, so Fred slept that night in a brass bed with a duck-down mattress, after a hearty meal of toasted cheese and chocolate fondue. The lords Spittleworth and Flapoon, on the other hand, were forced to spend the night in a little room over the stables. Both were rather sore after a long day on horseback. You may wonder why that was, if they went hunting five times a week, but the truth was that they generally sneaked off to sit behind a tree after half an hour's hunting, where they ate sandwiches and drank wine until it was time to go back to the palace. Neither was used to spending hours in the saddle, and Spittleworth's bony bottom was already starting to blister.

Early the following morning, the king was brought word by Major Beamish that the citizens of Baronstown were very upset the king had chosen to sleep in Kurdsburg rather than their splendid city. Eager not to dent his popularity, King Fred instructed his party to ride in an enormous circle through the surrounding fields, being cheered by farmers all the way, so that they ended up in Baronstown by nightfall. The delicious smell of sizzling sausages greeted the royal party, and a delighted crowd carrying torches escorted Fred to the best room in the city. There he was served roasted ox and honey ham, and slept in a carved oak bed with a goose-down mattress, while Spittleworth and Flapoon had to share a tiny attic room usually occupied by two maids. By now, Spittleworth's bottom was extremely painful, and he was furious that he'd been forced to ride forty miles in a circle, purely to keep the sausagemakers happy. Flapoon, who'd eaten far too much cheese in Kurdsburg and had consumed three beefsteaks in Baronstown, was awake all night, groaning with indigestion.

Next day, the king and his men set off again, and this time they headed north, soon passing through vineyards from which eager grape pickers emerged to wave Cornucopian flags and receive waves from the jubilant king. Spittleworth was almost crying from pain, in spite of the cushion he'd strapped to his bottom, and Flapoon's belches and moans could be heard even over the clatter of hooves and jingle of bridles.

Upon arrival at Jeroboam that evening, they were greeted by trumpets and the entire city singing the national anthem. Fred feasted on sparkling wine and truffles that night, before retiring to a silken four-poster bed with a swansdown mattress. But Spittleworth and Flapoon were forced to share a room over the inn's kitchen with a pair of soldiers. Drunken Jeroboam dwellers were reeling about in the street, celebrating the presence of the king in their city. Spittleworth spent much of the night sitting in a bucket of ice, and Flapoon, who'd drunk far too much red wine, spent the same period being sick in a second bucket in the corner.

At dawn next morning, the king and his party set out for the Marshlands, after a famous farewell from the citizens of Jeroboam, who saw him on his way with a thunderous popping of corks that made Spittleworth's horse rear and ditch him on the road. Once they'd dusted Spittleworth off and put the cushion back on his bottom, and Fred had stopped laughing, the party proceeded.

Soon they'd left Jeroboam behind, and could hear only birdsong. For the first time in their entire journey, the sides of the road were empty. Gradually, the lush green land gave way to thin, dry grass, crooked trees, and boulders.

'Extraordinary place, isn't it?' the cheerful king shouted back to Spittleworth and Flapoon. 'I'm jolly glad to see these Marshlands at last, aren't you?'

The two lords agreed, but once Fred had turned to face the front again, they made rude gestures and mouthed even ruder names at the back of his head.

At last, the royal party came across a few people, and how the Marshlanders stared! They fell to their knees like the shepherd in the Throne Room, and quite forgot to cheer or clap, but gaped as though they'd never seen anything like the king and the Royal Guard before – which, indeed, they hadn't, because while King Fred had visited all the major cities of Cornucopia after his coronation, nobody had thought it worth his while to visit the faraway Marshlands.

'Simple people, yes, but rather touching, aren't they?' the king called gaily to his men, as some ragged children gasped at the magnificent horses. They'd never seen animals so glossy and well fed in their lives.

'And where are we supposed to stay tonight?' Flapoon muttered to Spittleworth, eyeing the tumbledown stone cottages. 'No taverns here!'

'Well, there's one comfort, at least,' Spittleworth whispered back. 'He'll have to rough it like the rest of us, and we'll see how much he likes it.'

They rode on through the afternoon and at last, as the sun began to sink, they caught sight of the marsh where the Ickabog was supposed to live: a wide stretch of darkness studded with strange rock formations.

'Your Majesty!' called Major Beamish. 'I suggest we set up camp now and explore the marsh in the morning! As Your Majesty knows, the marsh can be treacherous! Fogs come suddenly here. We'd do best to approach it by daylight!'

'Nonsense!' said Fred, who was bouncing up and down in his saddle like an excited schoolboy. 'We can't stop now, when it's in sight, Beamish!'

The king had given his order, so the party rode on until, at last, when the moon had risen and was sliding in and out behind inky clouds, they reached the edge of the marsh. It was the eeriest place any of them had ever seen, wild and empty and desolate. A chilly breeze made the rushes whisper, but otherwise it was dead and silent.

'As you see, sire,' said Lord Spittleworth after a while, 'the ground is very boggy. Sheep and men alike would be sucked under if they wandered out too far. Then, the feeble-minded might take these giant rocks and boulders for monsters in the dark. The rustling of these weeds might even be taken for the hissing of some creature.'

'Yes, true, very true,' said King Fred, but his eyes still roamed over the dark marsh, as though he expected the Ickabog to pop up from behind a rock.

'Shall we pitch camp then, sire?' asked Lord Flapoon, who'd saved some cold pies from Baronstown and was eager for his supper.

'We can't expect to find even an imaginary monster in the dark,' pointed out Spittleworth.

'True, true,' repeated King Fred regretfully. 'Let us – good gracious, how foggy it has become!'

And sure enough, as they'd stood looking out across the marsh, a thick white fog had rolled over them so swiftly and silently that none of them had noticed it.

*Fred slept that night in a brass bed with a duck-down mattress, after a hearty meal of toasted cheese and chocolate fondue.*

*By Erica, age 12 years, Australia*

# CHAPTER 12

# The King's Lost Sword

Within seconds, it was as though each of the king's party was wearing a thick white blindfold. The fog was so dense they couldn't see their own hands in front of their faces. The mist smelled of the foul marsh, of brackish water and ooze. The soft ground seemed to shift beneath their feet as many of the men turned unwisely on the spot. Trying to catch sight of each other, they lost all sense of direction. Each man felt adrift in a blinding white sea, and Major Beamish was one of the few to keep his head.

'Have a care!' he called. 'The ground is treacherous. Stay still, don't attempt to move!'

But King Fred, who was suddenly feeling rather scared, paid no attention. He set off at once in what he thought was the direction of Major Beamish, but within a few steps he felt himself sinking into the icy marsh.

'Help!' he cried, as the freezing marsh water flooded over the tops of his shining boots. 'Help! Beamish, where are you? I'm sinking!'

There was an immediate clamour of panicked voices and jangling armour. The guards all hurried off in every direction, trying to find the king, bumping into each other and slipping over, but the floundering king's voice drowned out every other.

'I've lost my boots! Why doesn't somebody help me? *Where are you all?*'

The lords Spittleworth and Flapoon were the only two people who'd followed Beamish's advice and remained quite still in the places they'd occupied when the fog had rolled over them. Spittleworth was clutching a fold of Flapoon's ample pantaloons and Flapoon was holding tight to the skirt of Spittleworth's riding coat. Neither of them made the smallest attempt to help Fred, but waited, shivering, for calm to be restored.

'At least if the fool gets swallowed by the bog, we'll be able to go home,' Spittleworth muttered to Flapoon.

The confusion deepened. Several of the Royal Guard had now got stuck in the bog as they tried to find the king. The air was full of squelches, clanks, and shouts. Major Beamish was bellowing in a vain attempt to restore some kind of order, and the king's voice seemed to be receding into the blind night, becoming ever fainter, as though he was blundering away from them.

And then, out of the heart of the darkness, came an awful terror-struck shriek.

*'BEAMISH, HELP ME, I CAN SEE THE MONSTER!'*

'I'm coming, Your Majesty!' cried Major Beamish. 'Keep shouting, sire, I'll find you!'

*'HELP! HELP ME, BEAMISH!'* shouted King Fred.

'What's happened to the idiot?' Flapoon asked Spittleworth, but before Spittleworth could answer, the fog around the two lords thinned as quickly as it had arrived, so that they stood together in a little clearing, able to see each other, but still surrounded on all sides by high walls of thick white mist. The voices of the king, of Beamish and of the other soldiers were becoming fainter and fainter.

'Don't move yet,' Spittleworth cautioned Flapoon. 'Once the fog thins a little bit more, we'll be able to find the horses and we can retreat to a safe—'

At that precise moment, a slimy black figure burst out of the wall of fog and launched itself at the two lords. Flapoon let out a high-pitched scream and Spittleworth lashed out at the creature, missing only because it flopped to the ground, weeping. It was then that Spittleworth realised the gibbering, panting slime monster was, in fact, King Fred the Fearless.

'Thank heavens we've found you, Your Majesty, we've been searching everywhere!' cried Spittleworth.

'Ick – Ick – Ick—' whimpered the king.

'He's got hiccoughs,' said Flapoon. 'Give him a fright.'

'Ick – Ick – Ickabog!' moaned Fred. 'I s-s-saw it! A gigantic monster – it nearly caught me!'

'I beg Your Majesty's pardon?' asked Spittleworth.

'The m-monster is real!' gulped Fred. 'I'm lucky to b-be alive! To the horses! We must flee, and quickly!'

King Fred tried to hoist himself up by climbing Spittleworth's leg, but Spittleworth stepped swiftly aside to avoid getting covered in slime, instead aiming a consoling pat at the top of Fred's head, which was the cleanest part of him.

'Er – there, there, Your Majesty. You've had a most distressing experience, falling in the marsh. As we were saying earlier, the boulders do indeed assume monstrous forms in this thick fog—'

'Dash it, Spittleworth, I know what I saw!' shouted the king, staggering to his feet unaided. 'Tall as two horses, it was, and with eyes like huge lamps! I drew my sword, but my hands were so slimy it slipped from my grasp, so there was nothing for it but to pull my feet out of my stuck boots, and crawl away!'

Just then a fourth man made his way into their little clearing in the fog: Captain Roach, father of Roderick, who was Major Beamish's second-in-command – a big, burly man with jet-black moustaches. What Captain Roach was really like, we are about to find out. All you need to know now is that the king was very glad to see him, because he was the largest member of the Royal Guard.

'Did you see any sign of the Ickabog, Roach?' whimpered Fred.

'No, Your Majesty,' he said, with a respectful bow, 'all I've seen is fog and mud. I'm glad to know Your Majesty is safe, at any rate. You gentlemen stay here, and I'll round up the troops.'

Roach made to leave, but King Fred yelped. 'No, you stay here with me, Roach, in case the monster comes this way! You've still got a rifle, haven't you? Excellent – I lost my sword and my boots, you see. My very best dress sword, with the jewelled hilt!'

Though he felt much safer with Captain Roach beside him, the trembling king was otherwise as cold and scared as he could ever remember being. He also had a nasty feeling that nobody believed he'd really seen the Ickabog, a feeling that increased when he caught sight of Spittleworth rolling his eyes at Flapoon.

The king's pride was stung.

'Spittleworth, Flapoon,' he said, 'I want my sword and my boots back! They're over there somewhere,' he added, waving his arm at the encircling fog.

'Would – would it not be better to wait until the fog has cleared, Your Majesty?' asked Spittleworth nervously.

'I want my sword!' snapped King Fred. 'It was my grandfather's and it's very valuable! Go and find it, both of you. I shall wait here with Captain Roach. And don't come back empty-handed.'

*A slimy black figure burst out of the wall of fog and... flopped to the ground, weeping. It was... in fact, King Fred the Fearless.*

*By Joel, age 11 years, United Kingdom*

# CHAPTER 13

# The Accident

The two lords had no choice but to leave the king and Captain Roach in their little clearing in the fog and proceed onto the marsh. Spittleworth took the lead, feeling his way with his feet for the firmest bits of ground. Flapoon followed close behind, still holding tightly to the hem of Spittleworth's coat and sinking deeply with every footstep because he was so heavy. The fog was clammy on their skin and rendered them almost completely blind. In spite of Spittleworth's best efforts, the two lords' boots were soon full to the brim with fetid water.

'That blasted nincompoop!' muttered Spittleworth as they squelched along. 'That blithering buffoon! This is all his fault, the mouse-brained moron!'

'It'll serve him right if that sword's lost for good,' said Flapoon, now nearly waist-deep in marsh.

'We'd better hope it isn't, or we'll be here all night,' said Spittleworth. 'Oh, curse this fog!'

They struggled onwards. The mist would thin for a few steps, then close again. Boulders loomed suddenly out of nowhere like ghostly elephants, and the rustling reeds sounded just like snakes. Though Spittleworth and Flapoon knew perfectly well that there was no such thing as an Ickabog, their insides didn't seem quite so sure.

'Let go of me!' Spittleworth growled at Flapoon, whose constant tugging was making him think of monstrous claws or jaws fastened on the back of his coat.

Flapoon let go, but he too had been infected by a nonsensical fear, so he loosened his blunderbuss from its holster and held it ready.

'What's that?' he whispered to Spittleworth, as an odd noise reached them out of the darkness ahead.

Both lords froze, the better to listen.

A low growling and scrabbling was coming out of the fog. It conjured an awful vision in both men's minds, of a monster feasting on the body of one of the Royal Guard.

'Who's there?' Spittleworth called, in a high-pitched voice.

Somewhere in the distance, Major Beamish shouted back:

'Is that you, Lord Spittleworth?'

'Yes,' shouted Spittleworth. 'We can hear something strange, Beamish! Can you?'

It seemed to the two lords that the odd growling and scrabbling grew louder.

Then the fog shifted. A monstrous black silhouette with gleaming white eyes was revealed right in front of them, and it emitted a long yowl.

With a deafening, crashing boom that seemed to shake the marsh, Flapoon let off his blunderbuss. The startled cries of their fellow men echoed across the hidden landscape, and then, as though Flapoon's shot had frightened it, the fog parted like curtains before the two lords, giving them a clear view of what lay ahead.

The moon slid out from behind a cloud at that moment and they saw a vast granite boulder with a mass of thorny branches at its base. Tangled up in these brambles was a terrified, skinny dog, whimpering and scrabbling to free itself, its eyes flashing in the reflected moonlight.

A little beyond the giant boulder, face down in the bog, lay Major Beamish.

'What's going on?' shouted several voices out of the fog. 'Who fired?'

Neither Spittleworth nor Flapoon answered. Spittleworth waded as quickly as he could towards Major Beamish. A swift examination was enough: the major was stone-dead, shot through the heart by Flapoon in the dark.

'My God, my God, what shall we do?' bleated Flapoon, arriving at Spittleworth's side.

'Quiet!' whispered Spittleworth.

He was thinking harder and faster than he'd thought in the whole of his crafty, conniving life. His eyes moved slowly from Flapoon and the gun, to the shepherd's trapped dog, to the king's boots and jewelled sword, which he now noticed, half-buried in the bog just a few feet away from the giant boulder.

Spittleworth waded through the marsh to pick up the king's sword and used it to slash apart the brambles imprisoning the dog. Then, giving the poor animal a hearty kick, he sent it yelping away into the fog.

'Listen carefully,' murmured Spittleworth, returning to Flapoon, but before he could explain his plan, another large figure emerged from the fog: Captain Roach.

'The king sent me,' panted the captain. 'He's terrified. What happ—'

Then Roach saw Major Beamish lying dead on the ground.

Spittleworth realised immediately that Roach must be let in on the plan and that, in fact, he'd be very useful.

'Say nothing, Roach,' said Spittleworth, 'while I tell you what has happened.

'The Ickabog has killed our brave Major Beamish. In view of this tragic death, we shall need a new major, and of course, that will be you, Roach, for you're second-in-command. I shall recommend a large pay rise for you, because you were so valiant – listen closely, Roach – so *very* valiant in chasing after the dreadful Ickabog, as it ran away into the fog. You see, the Ickabog was devouring the poor major's body when Lord

Flapoon and I came upon it. Frightened by Lord Flapoon's blunderbuss, which he sensibly discharged into the air, the monster dropped Beamish's body and fled. You bravely gave chase, trying to recover the king's sword, which was half-buried in the monster's thick hide – but you weren't able to recover it, Roach. So sad for the poor king. I believe the priceless sword was his grandfather's, but I suppose it's now lost forever in the Ickabog's lair.'

So saying, Spittleworth pressed the sword into Roach's large hands. The newly promoted major looked down at its jewelled hilt, and a cruel and crafty smile to match Spittleworth's own spread over his face.

'Yes, a great pity that I wasn't able to recover the sword, my lord,' he said, sliding it out of sight beneath his tunic. 'Now, let's wrap up the poor major's body, because it would be dreadful for the other men to see the marks of the monster's fangs upon him.'

'How sensitive of you, Major Roach,' said Lord Spittleworth, and the two men swiftly took off their cloaks and wrapped up the body while Flapoon watched, heartily relieved that nobody need know he'd accidentally killed Beamish.

'Could you remind me what the Ickabog looked like, Lord Spittleworth?' asked Roach, when Major Beamish's body was well hidden. 'For the three of us saw it together and will, of course, have received identical impressions.'

'Very true,' said Lord Spittleworth. 'Well, according to the king, the beast is as tall as two horses, with eyes like lamps.'

'In fact,' said Flapoon, pointing, 'it looks a lot like this large boulder, with a dog's eyes gleaming at the base.'

'Tall as two horses, with eyes like lamps,' repeated Roach. 'Very well, my lords. If you'll assist me to put Beamish over my shoulder, I'll carry him to the king and we can explain how the major met his death.'

# CHAPTER 14

# Lord Spittleworth's Plan

When the fog cleared at last, it revealed a very different party of men to those who'd arrived at the edge of the marsh an hour earlier.

Quite apart from their shock at the sudden death of Major Beamish, a few of the Royal Guard were confused by the explanation they'd been given. Here were the two lords, the king, and the hastily promoted Major Roach, all swearing that they'd come face-to-face with a monster that all but the most foolish had dismissed for years as a fairy tale. Could it really be true that beneath the tightly wrapped cloaks, Beamish's body bore the tooth and claw marks of the Ickabog?

'Are you calling me a liar?' Major Roach growled into the face of a young private.

'Are you calling *the king* a liar?' barked Lord Flapoon.

The private didn't dare question the word of the king, so he shook his head. Captain Goodfellow, who'd been a particular friend of Major Beamish's, said nothing. However, there was such an angry and suspicious look on Goodfellow's face that Roach ordered him to go and pitch the tents on the most solid bit of ground he could find, and be quick about it, because the dangerous fog might yet return.

In spite of the fact that he had a straw mattress, and that blankets were taken from the soldiers to ensure his comfort, King Fred had never spent a more unpleasant night. He was tired, dirty, wet, and, above all, frightened.

'What if the Ickabog comes looking for us, Spittleworth?' the king whispered in the dark. 'What if it tracks us by our scent? It's already had a taste of poor Beamish. What if it comes looking for the rest of the body?'

Spittleworth attempted to soothe the king.

'Do not fear, Your Majesty, Roach has ordered Captain Goodfellow to keep watch outside your tent. Whoever else gets eaten, you will be the last.'

It was too dark for the king to see Spittleworth grinning. Far from wanting to reassure the king, Spittleworth hoped to fan the king's fears. His entire plan rested on a king who not only believed in an Ickabog, but who was scared it might leave the marsh to chase him.

The following morning, the king's party set off back to Jeroboam. Spittleworth had sent a message ahead to tell the Mayor of Jeroboam that there had been a nasty accident at the marsh, so the king didn't want any trumpets or corks greeting him. Thus, when the king's party arrived, the city was silent. Townsfolk pressing their faces to their windows, or peeking around their doors, were shocked to see the king so dirty and miserable, but not nearly as shocked as they were to see a body wrapped in cloaks, tied to Major Beamish's steel-grey horse.

When they reached the inn, Spittleworth took the landlord aside.

'We require some cold, secure place, perhaps a cellar, where we can store a body for the night, and I shall need to keep the key myself.'

'What happened, my lord?' asked the innkeeper, as Roach carried Beamish down the stone steps into the cellar.

'I shall tell you the truth, my good man, seeing as you have looked after us so well, but it must go no further,' said Spittleworth in a low, serious voice. 'The Ickabog is real and has savagely killed one of our men. You understand, I'm sure, why this must not be widely broadcast. There would be instant panic. The king is returning with all speed to the palace, where he and his advisors – myself, of course, included – will begin work at once on a set of measures to secure our country's safety.'

'The Ickabog? Real?' said the landlord, in astonishment and fear.

'Real and vengeful and vicious,' said Spittleworth. 'But, as I say, this must go no further. Widespread alarm will benefit nobody.'

In fact, widespread alarm was precisely what Spittleworth wanted, because it was essential for the next phase of his plan. Just as he'd expected, the landlord waited only until his guests had gone to bed, then rushed to tell his wife, who ran to tell the neighbours, and by the time the king's party set off for Kurdsburg the following morning, they left behind them a city where panic was fermenting as busily as the wine.

Spittleworth sent a message ahead to Kurdsburg, warning the cheesemaking city not to make a fuss of the king either, so it too was dark and silent when the royal party entered its streets. The faces at the windows were already scared. It so happened that a merchant from Jeroboam, with an especially fast horse, had carried the rumour about the Ickabog to Kurdsburg an hour previously.

Once again, Spittleworth requested the use of a cellar for Major Beamish's body, and once again confided to the landlord that the Ickabog had killed one of the king's men. Having seen Beamish's body safely locked up, Spittleworth went upstairs to bed.

He was just rubbing ointment into the blisters on his bottom when he received an urgent summons to go and see the king. Smirking, Spittleworth pulled on his pantaloons, winked at Flapoon, who was enjoying a cheese and pickle sandwich, picked up his candle and proceeded along the corridor to King Fred's room.

The king was huddled in bed wearing his silk nightcap, and as soon as Spittleworth closed the bedroom door, Fred said:

'Spittleworth, I keep hearing whispers about the Ickabog. The stable boys were talking, and even the maid who just passed by my bedroom door. Why is this? How can they know what happened?'

'Alas, Your Majesty,' sighed Spittleworth, 'I'd hoped to conceal the truth from you until we were safely back at the palace, but I should have known that Your Majesty is too shrewd to be fooled. Since we left the marsh, sire, the Ickabog has, as Your Majesty feared, become much more aggressive.'

'Oh, no!' whimpered the king.

'I'm afraid so, sire. But after all, attacking it was bound to make it more dangerous.'

'But who attacked it?' said Fred.

'Why, you did, Your Majesty,' said Spittleworth. 'Roach tells me your sword was embedded in the monster's neck when it ran— I'm sorry, Your Majesty, did you speak?'

The king had, in fact, let out a sort of hum, but after a second or two, he shook his head. He'd considered correcting Spittleworth – he was sure he'd told the story differently – but his horrible experience in the fog sounded much better the way Spittleworth told it now: that he'd stood his ground and fought the Ickabog, rather than simply dropping his sword and running away.

'But this is awful, Spittleworth,' whispered the king. 'What will become of us all, if the monster has become more ferocious?'

'Never fear, Your Majesty,' said Spittleworth, approaching the king's bed, the candlelight illuminating his long nose and his cruel smile from below. 'I intend to make it my life's work to protect you and the kingdom from the Ickabog.'

'Th-thank you, Spittleworth. You are a true friend,' said the king, deeply moved, and he fumbled to extract a hand from the eiderdown, and clasped that of the cunning lord.

*Smirking, Spittleworth pulled on his pantaloons… picked up his candle and proceeded along the corridor to King Fred's room.*

*By Sienna, age 9 years, New Zealand*

# CHAPTER 15

# The King Returns

By the time the king set out for Chouxville the following morning, rumours that the Ickabog had killed a man had not only travelled over the bridge into Baronstown, they'd even trickled down to the capital, courtesy of a cluster of cheesemongers, who'd set out before dawn.

However, Chouxville was not only the furthest away from the northern marsh, it also held itself to be far better informed and educated than the other Cornucopian towns, so when the wave of panic reached the capital, it met an upswell of disbelief.

The city's taverns and markets rang with excited arguments. Sceptics laughed at the preposterous idea of the Ickabog existing, while others said that people who'd never been to the Marshlands ought not to pretend to be experts.

The Ickabog rumours had gained a lot of colour as they travelled south. Some people said that the Ickabog had killed three men, others that it had merely torn off somebody's nose.

In the City-Within-The-City, however, discussion was seasoned with a little pinch of anxiety. The wives, children, and friends of the Royal Guard were worried about the soldiers, but they reassured each other that if any of the men had been killed, their families would have been informed by messenger. This was the comfort that Mrs Beamish gave Bert, when he came looking for her in the palace kitchens, having been scared by the rumours circulating among the schoolchildren.

'The king would have told us if anything had happened to Daddy,' she told Bert. 'Here, now, I've got you a little treat.'

Mrs Beamish had prepared Hopes-of-Heaven for the king's return, and she now gave one that wasn't quite symmetrical to Bert. He gasped (because he only ever had Hopes-of-Heaven on his birthday), and bit into the little cake. At once, his eyes filled with happy tears, as paradise wafted up through the roof of his mouth and melted all his cares away. He thought excitedly of his father coming home in his smart uniform, and how he, Bert, would be centre of attention at school tomorrow, because he'd know exactly what had happened to the king's men in the faraway Marshlands.

Dusk was settling over Chouxville when at last the king's party rode into view. This time, Spittleworth hadn't sent a messenger to tell people to stay inside. He wanted the king to feel the full force of Chouxville's panic and fear when they saw His Majesty returning to his palace with the body of one of the Royal Guard.

The people of Chouxville saw the drawn, miserable faces of the returning men, and watched in silence as the party approached. Then they spotted the wrapped-up body slung over the steel-grey horse, and gasps spread through the crowd like flames. Up through the narrow cobbled streets of Chouxville the king's party moved, and men removed their hats and women curtsied, and they hardly knew whether they were paying their respects to the king or the dead man.

Daisy Dovetail was one of the first to realise who was missing. Peering between the legs of grown-ups, she recognised Major Beamish's horse. Instantly forgetting that she and Bert hadn't talked to each other since their fight of the previous week, Daisy pulled free of her father's hand and began to run, forcing her way through the crowds, her brown pigtails flying. She had to reach Bert before he saw the body on the horse. She had to warn him. But the people were so tightly packed that, fast as Daisy moved, she couldn't keep pace with the horses.

Bert and Mrs Beamish, who were standing outside their cottage in the shadow of the palace walls, knew there was something wrong because of the crowd's gasps. Although Mrs Beamish felt somewhat anxious, she was still sure that she was about to see her handsome husband, because the king would have sent word if he'd been hurt.

So when the procession rounded the corner, Mrs Beamish's eyes slid from face to face, expecting to see the major's. And when she realised that there were no more faces left, the colour drained slowly from her own. Then her gaze fell upon the body strapped to Major Beamish's steel-grey horse, and, still holding Bert's hand, she fainted clean away.

# CHAPTER 16

# Bert Says Goodbye

Spittleworth noticed a commotion beside the palace walls and strained to see what was going on. When he spotted the woman on the ground, and heard the cries of shock and pity, he suddenly realised that he'd left a loose end that might yet trip him up: the widow! As he rode past the little knot of people in the crowd who were fanning Mrs Beamish's face, Spittleworth knew that his longed-for bath must be postponed, and his crafty brain began to race again.

Once the king's party was safely in the courtyard, and servants had hurried to assist Fred from his horse, Spittleworth pulled Major Roach aside.

'The widow, Beamish's widow!' he muttered. 'Why didn't you send her word about his death?'

'It never occurred to me, my lord,' said Roach truthfully. He'd been too busy thinking about the jewelled sword all the way home: how best to sell it, and whether it would be better to break it up into pieces so that nobody recognised it.

'Curse you, Roach, must I think of everything?' snarled Spittleworth. 'Go now, take Beamish's body out of those filthy cloaks, cover it with a Cornucopian flag, and lay him out in the Blue Parlour. Put guards on the door and then bring Mrs Beamish to me in the Throne Room.

'Also, give the order that these soldiers must not go home or talk to their families until I've spoken to them. It's essential that we all tell the same story! Now hurry, fool, hurry – Beamish's widow could ruin everything!'

Spittleworth pushed his way past soldiers and stable boys to where Flapoon was being lifted off his horse.

'Keep the king away from the Throne Room and the Blue Parlour,' Spittleworth whispered in Flapoon's ear. 'Encourage him to go to bed!'

Flapoon nodded and Spittleworth hurried away through the dimly lit palace corridors, casting off his dusty riding coat as he went, and bellowing at the servants to fetch him fresh clothes.

Once in the deserted Throne Room, Spittleworth pulled on his clean jacket, and ordered a maid to light a single lamp and bring him a glass of wine. Then he waited. At last, there came a knock on the door.

'Enter!' shouted Spittleworth, and in came Major Roach, accompanied by a white-faced Mrs Beamish, and young Bert.

'My dear Mrs Beamish... my *very* dear Mrs Beamish,' said Spittleworth, striding towards her and clasping her free hand. 'The king has asked me to tell you how deeply sorry he is. I add my own condolences. What a tragedy... what an awful tragedy.'

'Wh-why did nobody send word?' sobbed Mrs Beamish. 'Wh-why did we have to find out by seeing his poor – his poor body?'

She swayed a little, and Roach hurried to fetch a small golden chair. The maid, who was called Hetty, arrived with wine for Spittleworth, and while she was pouring it, Spittleworth said:

'Dear lady, we did in fact send word. We sent a messenger – didn't we, Roach?'

'That's right,' said Roach. 'We sent a young lad called...'

But here, Roach got stuck. He was a man of very little imagination.

'Nobby,' said Spittleworth, saying the first name that came into his head. 'Little Nobby... Buttons,' he added, because the flickering lamplight had just illuminated one of Roach's golden buttons. 'Yes, little Nobby Buttons volunteered, and off he galloped. What could have become of him? Roach,' said Spittleworth, 'we must send out a search party, at once, to see whether any trace of Nobby Buttons can be found.'

'At once, my lord,' said Roach, bowing deeply, and he left.

'How… how did my husband die?' whispered Mrs Beamish.

'Well, madam,' said Spittleworth, speaking carefully, for he knew that the story he told now would become the official version, and that he'd have to stick by it, forevermore. 'As you may have heard, we journeyed to the Marshlands, because we'd received word that the Ickabog had carried off a dog. Shortly after our arrival, I regret to say that our entire party was attacked by the monster.

'It lunged for the king first, but he fought most bravely, sinking his sword into the monster's neck. To the tough-skinned Ickabog, however, 'twas but a wasp sting. Enraged, it sought further victims, and though Major Beamish put up a most heroic struggle, I regret to say that he laid down his life for the king.

'Then Lord Flapoon had the excellent notion of firing his blunderbuss, which scared the Ickabog away. We brought poor Beamish out of the marsh, asked for a volunteer to take news of his death to his family. Dear little Nobby Buttons said he'd do it, and he leapt up onto his horse, and until we reached Chouxville, I never doubted that he'd arrived and given you warning of this dreadful tragedy.'

'Can I – can I see my husband?' wept Mrs Beamish.

'Of course, of course,' said Spittleworth. 'He's in the Blue Parlour.'

He led Mrs Beamish and Bert, who was still clutching his mother's hand, to the doors of the parlour, where he paused.

'I regret,' he said, 'that we cannot remove the flag covering him. His injuries would be far too distressing for you to see… the fang and claw marks, you know…'

Mrs Beamish swayed yet again and Bert grabbed hold of her, to keep her upright. Now Lord Flapoon walked up to the group, holding a tray of pies.

'King's in bed,' he said thickly to Spittleworth. 'Oh, hello,' he added, looking at Mrs Beamish, who was one of the few servants whose name he knew, because she baked the pastries. 'Sorry about the major,' said Flapoon, spraying Mrs Beamish and Bert with crumbs of pie crust. 'Always liked him.'

He walked away, leaving Spittleworth to open the door of the Blue Parlour to let Mrs Beamish and Bert inside. There lay the body of Major Beamish, concealed beneath the Cornucopian flag.

'Can't I at least kiss him one last time?' sobbed Mrs Beamish.

'Quite impossible, I'm afraid,' said Spittleworth. 'His face is half gone.'

'His hand, Mother,' said Bert, speaking for the first time. 'I'm sure his hand will be all right.'

And before Spittleworth could stop the boy, Bert reached beneath the flag for his father's hand, which was quite unmarked.

Mrs Beamish knelt down and kissed the hand over and over again, until it shone with tears as though made of porcelain. Then Bert helped her to her feet and the two of them left the Blue Parlour without another word.

*'Well, madam,' said Spittleworth, speaking carefully, for he knew that the story he told now would become the official version.*

*By Indrashis, age 7 years, India*

# CHAPTER 17

# Goodfellow Makes a Stand

Having watched the Beamishes out of sight, Spittleworth hurried off to the Guard's Room, where he found Roach keeping watch over the rest of the Royal Guard. The walls of the room were hung with swords and a portrait of King Fred, whose eyes seemed to watch everything that was happening.

'They're growing restless, my lord,' muttered Roach. 'They want to go home to their families and get to bed.'

'And so they shall, once we've had a little chat,' said Spittleworth, moving to face the weary and travel-stained soldiers.

'Has anyone got any questions about what happened back in the Marshlands?' he asked the men.

The soldiers looked at each other. Some of them stole furtive glances at Roach, who'd retreated against the wall, and was polishing a rifle. Then Captain Goodfellow raised his hand, along with two other soldiers.

'Why was Beamish's body wrapped up before any of us could look at it?' asked Captain Goodfellow.

'I want to know where that bullet went, that we heard being fired,' said the second soldier.

'How come only four people saw this monster, if it's so huge?' asked the third, to general nods and muttered agreement.

'All excellent questions,' replied Spittleworth smoothly. 'Let me explain.'

And he repeated the story of the attack that he'd told Mrs Beamish.

The soldiers who'd asked questions remained unsatisfied.

'I still reckon it's funny that a huge monster was out there and none of us saw it,' said the third.

'If Beamish was half-eaten, why wasn't there more blood?' asked the second.

'And who, in the name of all that's Holy,' said Captain Goodfellow, 'is Nobby Buttons?'

'How d'you know about Nobby Buttons?' blurted Spittleworth, without thinking.

'On my way here from the stables, I bumped into one of the maids, Hetty,' said Goodfellow. 'She served you your wine, my lord. According to her, you've just been telling Beamish's poor wife about a member of the Royal Guard called Nobby Buttons. According to you, Nobby Buttons was sent with a message to Beamish's wife, telling her he'd been killed.

'But I don't remember a Nobby Buttons. I've never met anyone called Nobby Buttons. So I ask you, my lord, how can that be? How can a man ride with us, and camp with us, and take orders from Your Lordship right in front of us, without any of us ever clapping eyes on him?'

Spittleworth's first thought was that he'd have to do something about that eavesdropping maid. Luckily, Goodfellow had given him her name. Then he said in a dangerous voice:

'What gives you the right to speak for everybody, Captain Goodfellow? Perhaps some of these men have better memories than you do. Perhaps they remember poor Nobby Buttons clearly. Dear little Nobby, in whose memory the king will add a fat bag of gold to everybody's pay this week. Proud, brave Nobby, whose sacrifice – for I fear the monster has eaten him, as well as Beamish – will mean a pay rise for all his comrades-in-arms. Noble Nobby Buttons, whose closest friends are surely marked for speedy promotion.'

Another silence followed Spittleworth's words, and this silence had a cold, heavy quality. Now the whole Royal Guard understood the choice facing them. They weighed in their minds the huge influence Spittleworth was known to have over the king, and the fact that Major Roach was now caressing the barrel of his rifle in a menacing manner, and they remembered the sudden death of their former leader, Major Beamish. They also considered the promise of more gold, and speedy promotion, if they agreed to believe in the Ickabog, and in Private Nobby Buttons.

Goodfellow stood up so suddenly that his chair clattered to the floor.

'There never was a Nobby Buttons, and I'm damned if there's an Ickabog, and I won't be party to a lie!'

The other two men who'd asked questions stood up as well, but the rest of the Royal Guard remained seated, silent, and watchful.

'Very well,' said Spittleworth. 'You three are under arrest for the filthy crime of treason. As I'm sure your comrades remember, you ran away when the Ickabog appeared. You forgot your duty to protect the king and thought only of saving your own cowardly hides! The penalty is death by firing squad.'

He chose eight soldiers to take the three men away, and even though the three honest soldiers struggled very hard, they were outnumbered and overwhelmed, and in no time at all they'd been dragged out of the Guard's Room.

'Very good,' said Spittleworth to the few soldiers remaining. 'Very good indeed. There will be pay rises all round, and I shall remember your names when it comes to promotions. Now, don't forget to tell your families exactly what happened in the Marshlands. It might bode ill for your wives, your parents, and your children if they're heard to question the existence of the Ickabog, or of Nobby Buttons.

'You may now return home.'

## CHAPTER 18

# End of an Advisor

No sooner had the guardsmen got to their feet to return home, than Lord Flapoon came bursting into the room, looking worried.

'What now?' groaned Spittleworth, who very much wanted his bath and bed.

'The – Chief – Advisor!' panted Flapoon.

And sure enough, Herringbone, the Chief Advisor, now appeared, wearing his dressing gown and an expression of outrage.

'I demand an explanation, my lord!' he cried. 'What stories are these that reach my ears? The Ickabog, real? Major Beamish, dead? And I've just passed three of the king's soldiers being dragged away under sentence of death! I have, of course, instructed that they be taken to the dungeons to await trial instead!'

'I can explain everything, Chief Advisor,' said Spittleworth with a bow, and for the third time that evening, he related the tale of the Ickabog attacking the king and killing Beamish, and then the mysterious disappearance of Nobby Buttons who, Spittleworth feared, had also fallen prey to the monster.

Herringbone, who'd always deplored the influence of Spittleworth and Flapoon on the king, waited for Spittleworth to finish his farrago of lies with the air of a wily old fox who waits at a rabbit hole for his dinner.

'A fascinating tale,' he said, when Spittleworth had finished. 'But I hereby relieve you of any further responsibility in the matter, Lord

Spittleworth. The advisors will take charge now. There are laws and protocols in Cornucopia to deal with emergencies such as these.

'Firstly, the men in the dungeons will be given a proper trial, so that we can hear their version of events. Secondly, the lists of the king's soldiers must be searched, to find the family of this Nobby Buttons, and inform them of his death. Thirdly, Major Beamish's body must be closely examined by the king's physicians, so that we may learn more about the monster that killed him.'

Spittleworth opened his mouth very wide, but nothing came out. He saw his whole glorious scheme collapsing on top of him, and himself trapped beneath it, imprisoned by his own cleverness.

Then Major Roach, who was standing behind the Chief Advisor, slowly put down his rifle and took a sword from the wall. A look like a flash of light on dark water passed between Roach and Spittleworth, who said:

'I think, Herringbone, that you are ripe for retirement.'

Steel flashed, and the tip of Roach's sword appeared out of the Chief Advisor's belly. The soldiers gasped, but the Chief Advisor didn't utter a word. He simply knelt, then toppled over, dead.

Spittleworth looked around at the soldiers who'd agreed to believe in the Ickabog. He liked seeing the fear on every face. He could feel his own power.

'Did everybody hear the Chief Advisor appointing me to his job before he retired?' he asked softly.

The soldiers all nodded. They'd just stood by and watched murder, and felt too deeply involved to protest. All they cared about now was escaping this room alive, and protecting their families.

'Very well, then,' said Spittleworth. 'The king believes the Ickabog is real, and I stand with the king. I am the new Chief Advisor, and I will be devising a plan to protect the kingdom. All who are loyal to the king will find their lives run very much as before. Any who stand against the king will suffer the penalty of cowards and traitors: imprisonment – or death.

'Now, I need one of you gentlemen to assist Major Roach in burying the body of our dear Chief Advisor – and be sure and put him where he won't be found. The rest of you are free to return to your families and inform them of the danger threatening our beloved Cornucopia.'

# CHAPTER 19

# Lady Eslanda

Spittleworth now marched off towards the dungeons. With Herringbone gone, there was nothing to stop him killing the three honest soldiers. He intended to shoot them himself. There would be time enough to invent a story afterwards – possibly he could place their bodies in the vault where the crown jewels were kept, and pretend they'd been trying to steal them.

However, just as Spittleworth put his hand on the door to the dungeons, a quiet voice spoke out of the darkness behind him.

'Good evening, Lord Spittleworth.'

He turned and saw Lady Eslanda, raven-haired and serious, stepping down from a dark spiral staircase.

'You're awake late, my lady,' said Spittleworth, with a bow.

'Yes,' said Lady Eslanda, whose heart was beating very fast. 'I – I couldn't sleep. I thought I'd take a little stroll.'

This was a fib. In fact, Eslanda had been fast asleep in her bed when she was woken by a frantic knocking on her bedroom door. Opening it, she found Hetty standing there: the maid who'd served Spittleworth his wine, and heard his lies about Nobby Buttons.

Hetty had been so curious about what Spittleworth was up to after his story about Nobby Buttons, that she'd crept along to the Guard's Room and, by pressing her ear to the door, heard everything that was going on inside. Hetty ran and hid when the three honest soldiers were dragged away, then sped upstairs to wake Lady Eslanda. She wanted to help the men who were about to be shot. The maid had no idea that Eslanda was secretly in love with Captain Goodfellow. She simply liked Lady Eslanda best of all the ladies at court, and knew her to be kind and clever.

Lady Eslanda hastily pressed some gold into Hetty's hands and advised her to leave the palace that night, because she was afraid the maid now might be in grave danger. Then Lady Eslanda dressed herself with trembling hands, seized a lantern, and hurried down the spiral staircase beside her bedroom. However, before she reached the bottom of the stairs she heard voices. Blowing out her lantern, Eslanda listened as Herringbone gave the order for Captain Goodfellow and his friends to be taken to the dungeons instead of being shot. She'd been hiding on the stairs ever since, because she had a feeling the danger threatening the men might not yet have passed – and here, sure enough, was Lord Spittleworth, heading for the dungeons with a pistol.

'Is the Chief Advisor anywhere about?' Lady Eslanda asked. 'I thought I heard his voice earlier.'

'Herringbone has retired,' said Spittleworth. 'You see standing before you the new Chief Advisor, my lady.'

'Oh, congratulations!' said Eslanda, pretending to be pleased, although she was horrified. 'So it will be you who oversees the trial of the three soldiers in the dungeons, will it?'

'You're very well informed, Lady Eslanda,' said Spittleworth, eyeing her closely. 'How did you know there are three soldiers in the dungeons?'

'I happened to hear Herringbone mention them,' said Lady Eslanda. 'They're well-respected men, it seems. He was saying how important it will be for them to have a fair trial. I know King Fred will agree, because he cares deeply about his own popularity – as he should, for if a king is to be effective, he must be loved.'

Lady Eslanda did a good job of pretending that she was thinking only of the king's popularity, and I think nine out of ten people would have believed her. Unfortunately, Spittleworth heard the tremor in her voice, and suspected that she must be in love with one of these men, to hurry downstairs in the dead of night, in hope of saving their lives.

'I wonder,' he said, watching her closely, 'which of them it is whom you care about so much?'

Lady Eslanda would have stopped herself blushing if she could, but unfortunately, she couldn't.

'I don't think it can be Ogden,' mused Spittleworth, 'because he's a very plain man, and in any case, he already has a wife. Might it be Wagstaff? He's an amusing fellow, but prone to boils. No,' said Lord Spittleworth softly, 'I think it must be handsome Captain Goodfellow who makes you blush, Lady Eslanda. But would you really stoop so low? His parents were cheesemakers, you know.'

'It makes no difference to me whether a man is a cheesemaker or a king, so long as he behaves with honour,' said Eslanda. 'And the king will be dishonoured, if those soldiers are shot without trial, and so I'll tell him, when he wakes.'

Lady Eslanda then turned, trembling, and climbed the spiral staircase. She had no idea whether she'd said enough to save the soldiers' lives, so she spent a sleepless night.

Spittleworth remained standing in the chilly passage until his feet were so cold he could barely feel them. He was trying to decide what to do.

On the one hand, he really did want to get rid of these soldiers, who knew far too much.

On the other, he feared Lady Eslanda was right: people would blame the king if the men were shot without trial. Then Fred would be angry at Spittleworth, and might even take the job of Chief Advisor away from him. If that happened, all the dreams of power and riches that Spittleworth had enjoyed on the journey back from the Marshlands would be dashed.

So Spittleworth turned away from the dungeon door and headed to his bed. He was deeply offended by the idea that Lady Eslanda, whom he'd once hoped to marry, preferred the son of cheesemakers. As he blew out his candle, Spittleworth decided that she would pay, one day, for that insult.

*Hetty had… crept along to the Guard's Room and, by pressing her ear to the door, heard everything that was going on inside.*

*By Meghashree, age 8 years, India*

# CHAPTER 20

# Medals for Beamish and Buttons

When King Fred woke next morning and was informed that his Chief Advisor had retired at this critical moment in the country's history, he was furious. It came as a great relief to know that Lord Spittleworth would be taking over, because Fred knew that Spittleworth understood the grave danger facing the kingdom.

Though feeling safer now that he was back in his palace, with its high walls and cannon-mounted turrets, its portcullis and its moat, Fred was unable to shake off the shock of his trip. He stayed shut up in his private apartments, and had all his meals brought to him on golden trays. Instead of going hunting, he paced up and down on his thick carpets, reliving his awful adventure in the north and meeting only his two best friends, who were careful to keep his fears alive.

On the third day after their return from the Marshlands, Spittleworth entered the king's private apartments with a sombre face, and announced that the soldiers who'd been sent back to the marsh to find out what happened to Private Nobby Buttons had discovered nothing but his bloodstained shoes, a single horseshoe, and a few well-gnawed bones.

The king turned white and sat down hard on a satin sofa.

'Oh, how dreadful, how dreadful… Private Buttons… Remind me, which one was he?'

'Young man, freckles, only son of a widowed mother,' said Spittleworth. 'The newest recruit to the Royal Guard, and such a promising boy. Tragic, really. And the worst of it is, between Beamish and Buttons, the Ickabog has developed a taste for human flesh – *precisely* as Your Majesty predicted. It is really astonishing, if I may say so, how Your Majesty grasped the danger from the first.'

'B-but what is to be done, Spittleworth? If the monster is hungry for more human prey…'

'Leave it all to me, Your Majesty,' said Spittleworth soothingly. 'I'm Chief Advisor, you know, and I'm at work day and night to keep the kingdom safe.'

'I'm so glad Herringbone appointed you his successor, Spittleworth,' said Fred. 'What would I do without you?'

'Tish, pish, Your Majesty, 'tis an honour to serve so gracious a king.

'Now, we ought to discuss tomorrow's funerals. We're intending to bury what's left of Buttons next to Major Beamish. It is to be a state occasion, you know, with plenty of pomp and ceremony, and I think it would be a very nice touch if you could present the Medal for Outstanding Bravery Against the Deadly Ickabog to relatives of the dead men.'

'Oh, is there a medal?' said Fred.

'Certainly there is, sire, and that reminds me – you haven't yet received your own.'

From an inner pocket, Spittleworth pulled out a most gorgeous gold medal, almost as large as a saucer. Embossed upon the medal was a monster with gleaming ruby eyes, which was being fought by a handsome, muscular man wearing a crown. The whole thing was suspended from a scarlet velvet ribbon.

'Mine?' said the king, wide-eyed.

'But of course, sire!' said Spittleworth. 'Did Your Majesty not plunge your sword into the monster's loathsome neck? We all remember it happening, sire!'

King Fred fingered the heavy gold medal. Though he said nothing, he was undergoing a silent struggle.

Fred's honesty had piped up, in a small, clear voice: *It didn't happen like that. You know it didn't. You saw the Ickabog in the fog, you dropped your sword and you ran away. You never stabbed it. You were never near enough!*

But Fred's cowardice blustered louder than his honesty: *You've already agreed with Spittleworth that that's what happened! What a fool you'll look if you admit you ran away!*

And Fred's vanity spoke loudest of all: *After all, I was the one who led the hunt for the Ickabog! I was the one who saw it first! I deserve this medal, and it will stand out beautifully against that black funeral suit.*

So Fred said:

'Yes, Spittleworth, it all happened just as you said. Naturally, one doesn't like to boast.'

'Your Majesty's modesty is legendary,' said Spittleworth, bowing low to hide his smirk.

The following day was declared a national day of mourning in honour of the Ickabog's victims. Crowds lined the streets to watch Major Beamish and Private Buttons's coffins pass on wagons drawn by plumed black horses.

King Fred rode behind the coffins on a jet-black horse, with the Medal for Outstanding Bravery Against the Deadly Ickabog bouncing on his chest and reflecting the sunlight so brightly that it hurt the eyes of the crowd. Behind the king walked Mrs Beamish and Bert, also dressed in black, and behind them came a howling old woman in a ginger wig, who'd been introduced to them as Mrs Buttons, Nobby's mother.

'Oh, my Nobby,' she wailed as she walked. 'Oh, down with the awful Ickabog, who killed my poor Nobby!'

The coffins were lowered into graves and the national anthem was played by the king's buglers. Buttons's coffin was particularly heavy, because it had been filled with bricks. The odd-looking Mrs Buttons wailed and cursed the Ickabog again while ten sweating men lowered her son's coffin into the ground. Mrs Beamish and Bert stood quietly weeping.

Then King Fred called the grieving relatives forward to receive their men's medals. Spittleworth hadn't been prepared to spend as much money on Beamish and the imaginary Buttons as he'd spent on the king, so their medals were made of silver rather than gold. However, it made an affecting ceremony, especially as Mrs Buttons was so overcome that she fell to the ground and kissed the king's boots.

Mrs Beamish and Bert walked home from the funeral and the crowds parted respectfully to let them pass. Only once did Mrs Beamish pause, and that was when her old friend Mr Dovetail stepped out of the crowd to tell her how sorry he was. The two embraced. Daisy wanted to say something to Bert, but the whole crowd was staring, and she couldn't even catch his eye, because he was scowling at his feet. Before she knew it, her father had released Mrs Beamish, and Daisy watched her best friend and his mother walk out of sight.

Once they were back in their cottage, Mrs Beamish threw herself face down on her bed where she sobbed and sobbed. Bert tried to comfort her, but nothing worked, so he took his father's medal into his own bedroom and placed it on the mantelpiece.

Only when he stood back to look at it did he realise that he'd placed his father's medal right beside the wooden Ickabog that Mr Dovetail had carved for him so long ago. Until this moment, Bert hadn't connected the toy Ickabog with the way his father had died.

Now he lifted the wooden model from its shelf, placed it on the floor, picked up a poker, and smashed the toy Ickabog to splinters. Then he picked up the remnants of the shattered toy and threw them into the fire. As he watched the flames leap higher and higher, he vowed that one day, when he was old enough, he'd hunt down the Ickabog, and revenge himself upon the monster that had killed his father.

# CHAPTER 21

# Professor Fraudysham

The morning after the funerals, Spittleworth knocked on the door of the king's apartments again and entered, carrying a lot of scrolls, which he let fall onto the table where the king sat.

'Spittleworth,' said Fred, who was still wearing his Medal for Outstanding Bravery Against the Deadly Ickabog, and had dressed in a scarlet suit, the better to show it off, 'these cakes aren't as good as usual.'

'Oh, I'm sorry to hear that, Your Majesty,' said Spittleworth. 'I thought it right for the widow Beamish to take a few days off work. These are the work of the under pastry chef.'

'Well, they're chewy,' said Fred, dropping half his Folderol Fancy back on his plate. 'And what are all these scrolls?'

'These, sire, are suggestions for improving the kingdom's defences against the Ickabog,' said Spittleworth.

'Excellent, excellent,' said King Fred, moving the cakes and the teapot aside to make more room, as Spittleworth pulled up a chair.

'The very first thing to be done, Your Majesty, was to find out as much as we could about the Ickabog itself, the better to discover how to defeat it.'

'Well, yes, but *how*, Spittleworth? The monster is a mystery! Everyone's thought it a fantasy all these years!'

'That, forgive me, is where Your Majesty is wrong,' said Spittleworth. 'By dint of ceaseless searching, I've managed to find the foremost Ickabog expert in all of Cornucopia. Lord Flapoon is waiting with him in the hall. With Your Majesty's permission—'

'Bring him in, bring him in, do!' said Fred excitedly.

So Spittleworth left the room and returned shortly afterwards with Lord Flapoon and a little old man with snowy white hair and spectacles so thick that his eyes had vanished almost into nothingness.

'This, sire, is Professor Fraudysham,' said Flapoon, as the mole-like little man made a deep bow to the king. 'What he doesn't know about Ickabogs isn't worth knowing!'

'How is it that I've never heard of you before, Professor Fraudysham?' asked the king, who was thinking that if he'd known the Ickabog was real enough to have its own expert, he'd never have gone looking for it in the first place.

'I live a retired life, Your Majesty,' said Professor Fraudysham, with a second bow. 'So few people believe in the Ickabog that I've formed the habit of keeping my knowledge to myself.'

King Fred was satisfied with this answer, which was a relief to Spittleworth, because Professor Fraudysham was no more real than Private Nobby Buttons or, indeed, old Widow Buttons in her ginger wig, who'd howled at Nobby's funeral. The truth was that beneath the wigs and the glasses, Professor Fraudysham and Widow Buttons were the same person: Lord Spittleworth's butler, who was called Otto Scrumble, and looked after Lord Spittleworth's estate while he lived at the palace. Like his master, Scrumble would do anything for gold, and had agreed to impersonate both the widow and the professor for a hundred ducats.

'So, what can you tell us about the Ickabog, Professor Fraudysham?' asked the king.

'Well, let's see,' said the pretend professor, who'd been told by Spittleworth what he ought to say. 'It's as tall as two horses—'

'If not taller,' interrupted Fred, whose nightmares had featured a gigantic Ickabog ever since he'd returned from the Marshlands.

'If, as Your Majesty says, not taller,' agreed Fraudysham. 'I should estimate that a medium-sized Ickabog would be as tall as two horses, whereas a large specimen might reach the size of – let's see—'

'Two elephants,' suggested the king.

'Two elephants,' agreed Fraudysham. 'And with eyes like lamps—'

'Or glowing balls of fire,' suggested the king.

'The very image I was about to employ, sire!' said Fraudysham.

'And can the monster really speak in a human tongue?' asked Fred, in whose nightmares the monster whispered, '*The king… I want the king… Where are you, little king?*' as it crept through the dark streets towards the palace.

'Yes, indeed,' said Fraudysham, with another low bow. 'We believe the Ickabog learnt to speak Human by taking people prisoner. Before disembowelling and eating its victims, we believe it forces them to give it English lessons.'

'Suffering Saints, what savagery!' whispered Fred, who'd turned pale.

'Moreover,' said Fraudysham, 'the Ickabog has a long and vengeful memory. If outwitted by a victim – as you outwitted it, sire, by escaping its deadly clutches – it has sometimes sneaked out of the marsh under cover of darkness, and claimed its victim while he or she slept.'

Whiter than the snowy icing on his half-eaten Folderol Fancy, Fred croaked:

'What's to be done? I'm doomed!'

'Nonsense, Your Majesty,' said Spittleworth bracingly. 'I've devised a whole raft of measures for your protection.'

So saying, Spittleworth took hold of one of the scrolls he'd brought with him and unrolled it. There, covering most of the table, was a coloured picture of a monster that resembled a dragon. It was huge and ugly, with thick black scales, gleaming white eyes, a tail that ended in a poisonous spike, a fanged mouth large enough to swallow a man, and long, razor-sharp claws.

'There are several problems to be overcome, when defending against an Ickabog,' said Professor Fraudysham, now taking out a short stick and pointing in turn to the fangs, the claws, and the poisonous tail. 'But the most difficult challenge is that killing an Ickabog causes two new Ickabogs to emerge from the corpse of the first.'

'Surely not?' said Fred faintly.

'Oh, yes, Your Majesty,' said Fraudysham. 'I've made a lifelong study of the monster, and I can assure you that my findings are quite correct.'

'Your Majesty might remember that many of the old tales of the Ickabog make mention of this curious fact,' interjected Spittleworth, who really needed the king to believe in this particular trait of the Ickabog, because most of his plan relied on it.

'But it seems so – so unlikely!' said Fred weakly.

'It *does* seem unlikely on the face of it, doesn't it, sire?' said Spittleworth, with another bow. 'In truth, it's one of those extraordinary, unbelievable ideas that only the very cleverest people can grasp, whereas common folk – *stupid* folk, sire – giggle and laugh at the notion.'

Fred looked from Spittleworth to Flapoon to Professor Fraudysham; all three men seemed to be waiting for him to prove how clever he was, and naturally he didn't want to seem stupid, so he said: 'Yes... well, if the professor says it, that's good enough for me... but if the monster turns into two monsters every time it dies, how do we kill it?'

'Well, in the first phase of our plan, we don't,' said Spittleworth.

'We don't?' said Fred, crestfallen.

Spittleworth now unrolled a second scroll, which showed a map of Cornucopia. The northernmost tip had a drawing of a gigantic Ickabog on it. All around the edge of the wide marsh stood a hundred little stick figures, holding swords. Fred looked closely to see whether any of them was wearing a crown, and was relieved to see that none were.

'As you can see, Your Majesty, our first proposal is a special Ickabog Defence Brigade. These men will patrol the edge of the Marshlands, to ensure that the Ickabog can't leave the marsh. We estimate the cost of such a brigade, including uniforms, weapons, horses, wages, training, board, lodging, sick pay, danger money, birthday presents, and medals to be around ten thousand gold ducats.'

'Ten thousand ducats?' repeated King Fred. 'That's a lot of gold. However, when it comes to protecting me – I mean to say, when it comes to protecting Cornucopia—'

'Ten thousand ducats a month is a small price to pay,' finished Spittleworth.

'Ten thousand *a month*!' yelped Fred.

'Yes, sire,' said Spittleworth. 'If we're to truly defend the kingdom, the expense will be considerable. However, if Your Majesty feels we could manage with fewer weapons—'

'No, no, I didn't say that—'

'Naturally, we don't expect Your Majesty to bear the expense alone,' continued Spittleworth.

'You don't?' said Fred, suddenly hopeful.

'Oh, no, sire, that would be grossly unfair. After all, the entire country will benefit from the Ickabog Defence Brigade. I suggest we impose an Ickabog tax. We'll ask every household in Cornucopia to pay one gold ducat a month. Of course, this will mean the recruitment and training of many new tax collectors, but if we raise the amount to two ducats, we'll cover the cost of them too.'

'Admirable, Spittleworth!' said King Fred. 'What a brain you have! Why, two ducats a month – people will barely notice the loss.'

*There, covering most of the table, was a... picture of a monster... with thick black scales... and long, razor-sharp claws.*

*By Charlotte, age 8 years, Republic of Ireland*

# CHAPTER 22

# The House with No Flags

And so a monthly tax of two gold ducats was imposed on every household in Cornucopia, to protect the country from the Ickabog. Tax collectors soon became a common sight on the streets of Cornucopia. They had large, staring white eyes like lamps painted on the backs of their black uniforms. These were supposed to remind everybody of what the tax was for, but people whispered in the taverns that they were Lord Spittleworth's eyes, watching to make sure everybody paid up.

Once they'd collected enough gold, Spittleworth decided to raise a statue to the memory of one of the Ickabog's victims, to remind people what a savage beast it was. At first Spittleworth planned a statue of Major Beamish, but his spies in the taverns of Chouxville reported that it was Private Buttons's story that had really captured the public imagination. Brave young Buttons, who'd volunteered to gallop off into the night with the news of his major's death, only to end up in the Ickabog's jaws himself, was generally felt to be a tragic, noble figure deserving of a handsome statue. Major Beamish, on the other hand, seemed merely to have died by accident, blundering unwisely across the foggy marsh in the dark. In fact, the drinkers of Chouxville felt quite resentful towards Beamish, as the man who'd forced Nobby Buttons to risk his life.

Happy to bow to the public mood, Spittleworth had a statue of Nobby Buttons made, and placed it in the middle of the largest public square in Chouxville. Seated on a magnificent charger, with his bronze cloak flying out behind him and a look of determination on his boyish face, Buttons was forever frozen in the act of galloping back to the City-Within-The-City. It became fashionable to lay flowers around the statue's base every Sunday. One rather plain young woman, who laid flowers every day of the week, claimed she'd been Nobby Buttons's girlfriend.

Spittleworth also decided to spend some gold on a scheme to keep the king diverted, because Fred was still too scared to go hunting, in case the Ickabog had sneaked south somehow and pounced on him in the forest. Bored of entertaining Fred, Spittleworth and Flapoon had come up with a plan.

'We need a portrait of you fighting the Ickabog, sire! The nation demands it!'

'Does it really?' said the king, fiddling with his buttons, which that day were made of emeralds. Fred remembered the ambition he'd formed, the morning he'd first tried on battledress, of being painted killing the Ickabog. He liked this idea of Spittleworth's very much, so he spent the next two weeks choosing and being fitted for a new uniform, because the old one was much stained by the marsh, and having a replacement jewelled sword made. Then Spittleworth hired the best portrait painter in Cornucopia, Malik Motley, and Fred began posing for weeks on end, for a portrait large enough to cover an entire wall of the Throne Room. Behind Motley sat fifty lesser artists, all copying his work, so as to have smaller versions of the painting ready to deliver to every city, town, and village in Cornucopia.

While he was being painted, the king amused Motley and the other artists by telling them the story of his famous fight with the monster, and the more he told the story, the more he found himself convinced of its truth. All of this kept Fred happily occupied, leaving Spittleworth and Flapoon free to run the country, and to divide up the trunks of gold left over each month, which were sent in the dead of night to the two lords' estates in the country.

But what, you might ask, of the eleven other advisors, who'd worked under Herringbone? Didn't they think it odd that the Chief Advisor had resigned in the middle of the night, and never been seen again? Didn't they ask questions, when they woke up to find Spittleworth in Herringbone's place? And, most importantly of all: did they believe in the Ickabog?

Well, those are excellent questions, and I'll answer them now.

They certainly muttered among themselves that Spittleworth shouldn't have been allowed to take over, without a proper vote. One or two of them even considered complaining to the king. However, they decided not to act, for the simple reason that they were scared.

You see, royal proclamations had now gone up in every town and village square in Cornucopia, all written by Spittleworth and signed by the king. It was treason to question the king's decisions, treason to suggest that the Ickabog might not be real, treason to question the need for the Ickabog tax, and treason not to pay your two ducats a month. There was also a reward of ten ducats if you reported someone for saying the Ickabog wasn't real.

The advisors were frightened of being accused of treason. They didn't want to be locked up in a dungeon. It really was much more pleasant to keep living in the lovely mansions which came with the job of advisor, and to continue wearing their special advisor robes, which meant they were allowed to go straight to the head of the queue in pastry shops.

So they approved all the expenses of the Ickabog Defence Brigade, who wore green uniforms, which Spittleworth said hid them better in the marsh weed. The Brigade soon became a common sight, parading through the streets of all of Cornucopia's major cities.

Some might wonder why the Brigade was riding through the streets waving at people, instead of remaining up in the north, where the monster was supposed to be, but they kept their thoughts to themselves. Meanwhile, most of their fellow citizens competed with each other to demonstrate their passionate belief in the Ickabog. They propped up cheap copies of the painting of King Fred fighting the Ickabog in their windows, and hung wooden signs on their doors, which bore messages like **PROUD TO PAY THE ICKABOG TAX** and **DOWN WITH THE ICKABOG, UP WITH THE KING!** Some parents even taught their children to bow and curtsy to the tax collectors.

The Beamish house was decorated in so many anti-Ickabog banners that it was hard to see what the cottage beneath looked like. Bert had returned to school at last, but to Daisy's disappointment, he spent all his breaks with Roderick Roach, talking about the time when they would both join the Ickabog Defence Brigade and kill the monster. She'd never felt lonelier, and wondered whether Bert missed her at all.

Daisy's own house was the only one in the City-Within-The-City that was entirely free of flags and signs welcoming the Ickabog tax. Her father also kept Daisy inside whenever the Ickabog Defence Brigade rode past, rather than urging her to run into the garden and cheer, like the neighbours' children.

Lord Spittleworth noticed the absence of flags and signs on the tiny cottage beside the graveyard, and filed that knowledge away in the back of his cunning head, where he kept information that might one day prove useful.

# CHAPTER 23

# The Trial

I'm sure you haven't forgotten those three brave soldiers locked up in the dungeons, who'd refused to believe in either the Ickabog or in Nobby Buttons.

Well, Spittleworth hadn't forgotten them either. He'd been trying to think up ways to get rid of them, without being blamed for it, ever since the night he'd imprisoned them. His latest idea was to feed them poison in their soup, and pretend they'd died of natural causes. He was still trying to decide on the best poison to use, when some of the soldiers' relatives turned up at the palace gates, demanding to speak to the king. Even worse, Lady Eslanda was with them, and Spittleworth had the sneaking suspicion she'd arranged the whole thing.

Instead of taking them to the king, Spittleworth had the group shown into his splendid new Chief Advisor's office, where he invited them politely to sit down.

'We want to know when our boys are going to stand trial,' said Private Ogden's brother, who was a pig farmer from just outside Baronstown.

'You've had them locked up for months now,' said the mother of Private Wagstaff, who was a barmaid in a Jeroboam tavern.

'And we'd all like to know what they're charged with,' said Lady Eslanda.

'They're charged with treason,' said Spittleworth, wafting his scented handkerchief under his nose, with his eyes on the pig farmer.

The man was perfectly clean, but Spittleworth meant to make him feel small, and I'm sorry to say he succeeded.

'Treason?' repeated Mrs Wagstaff in astonishment. 'Why, you won't find more loyal subjects of the king anywhere in the land than those three!'

Spittleworth's crafty eyes moved between the worried relatives, who so clearly loved their brothers and sons very deeply, and Lady Eslanda, whose face was so anxious, and a brilliant idea flashed into his brain like a lightning strike. He didn't know why he hadn't thought of it before! He didn't need to poison the soldiers at all! What he needed was to ruin their reputations.

'Your men will be put on trial tomorrow,' he said, getting to his feet. 'The trial will take place in the largest square in Chouxville, because I want as many people as possible to hear what they have to say. Good day to you, ladies and gentlemen.'

And with a smirk and a bow, Spittleworth left the astonished relatives and proceeded down into the dungeons.

The three soldiers were a lot thinner than the last time he'd seen them, and as they hadn't been able to shave or keep very clean, they made a miserable picture.

'Good morning, gentlemen,' said Spittleworth briskly, while the drunken warder snoozed in a corner. 'Good news! You're to stand trial tomorrow.'

'And what exactly are we charged with?' asked Captain Goodfellow suspiciously.

'We've been through this already, Goodfellow,' said Spittleworth. 'You saw the monster on the marsh, and ran away instead of staying to protect your king. You then claimed the monster isn't real, to cover up your own cowardice. That's treason.'

'It's a filthy lie,' said Goodfellow, in a low voice. 'Do what you like to me, Spittleworth, but I'll tell the truth.'

The other two soldiers, Ogden and Wagstaff, nodded their agreement with the captain.

'You might not care what I do to *you*,' said Spittleworth, smiling, 'but what about your families? It would be awful, wouldn't it, Wagstaff, if that barmaid mother of yours slipped on her way down into the cellar, and cracked open her skull? Or, Ogden, if your pig-farming brother accidentally stabbed himself with his own scythe, and got eaten by his own pigs? Or,' whispered Spittleworth, moving closer to the bars, and staring into Goodfellow's eyes, 'if Lady Eslanda were to have a riding accident, and break her slender neck.'

You see, Spittleworth believed that Lady Eslanda was Captain Goodfellow's lover. It would never occur to him that a woman might try and protect a man to whom she'd never even spoken.

Captain Goodfellow wondered why on earth Lord Spittleworth was threatening him with the death of Lady Eslanda. True, he thought her the loveliest woman in the kingdom, but he'd always kept that to himself, because cheesemakers' sons didn't marry ladies of the court.

'What has Lady Eslanda to do with me?' he asked.

'Don't pretend, Goodfellow,' snapped the Chief Advisor. 'I've seen her blushes when your name is mentioned. Do you think me a fool? She has been doing all that she can to protect you and, I must admit, it is down to her that you're still alive. However, it is the lady Eslanda who'll pay the price if you tell any truth but mine tomorrow. She saved your life, Goodfellow: will you sacrifice hers?'

Goodfellow was speechless with shock. The idea that Lady Eslanda was in love with him was so marvellous that it almost eclipsed Spittleworth's threats. Then the captain realised that, in order to save Eslanda's life, he would have to publicly confess to treason the next day, which would surely kill her love for him stone-dead.

From the way the colour had drained out of the three men's faces, Spittleworth could see that his threats had done the trick.

'Take courage, gentlemen,' he said. 'I'm sure no awful accidents will happen to your loved ones, as long as you tell the truth tomorrow…'

So notices were pinned up all over the capital announcing the trial, and the following day, an enormous crowd packed itself into the largest square in Chouxville. Each of the three brave soldiers took it in turns to stand on a wooden platform, while their friends and families watched, and one by one they confessed that they'd met the Ickabog on the marsh, and had run away like cowards instead of defending the king.

The crowd booed the soldiers so loudly that it was hard to hear what the judge (Lord Spittleworth) was saying. However, all the time Spittleworth was reading out the sentence – life imprisonment in the palace dungeons – Captain Goodfellow stared directly into the eyes of Lady Eslanda, who sat watching, high in the stands, with the other ladies of the court. Sometimes, two people can tell each other more with a look than others could tell each other with a lifetime of words. I will not tell you everything that Lady Eslanda and Captain Goodfellow said with their eyes, but she knew, now, that the captain returned her feelings, and he learnt, even though he was going to prison for the rest of his life, that Lady Eslanda knew he was innocent.

The three prisoners were led from the platform in chains, while the crowd threw cabbages at them and then dispersed, chattering loudly. Many of them felt Lord Spittleworth should have put the traitors to death, and Spittleworth chuckled to himself as he returned to the palace, for it was always best, if possible, to seem a reasonable man.

Mr Dovetail had watched the trial from the back of the crowd. He hadn't booed the soldiers, nor had he brought Daisy with him, but had left her carving in his workshop. As Mr Dovetail walked home, lost in thought, he saw Wagstaff's weeping mother being followed along the street by a gang of youths, who were booing and throwing vegetables at her.

'You follow this woman any further, and you'll have me to deal with!' Mr Dovetail shouted at the gang, who, seeing the size of the carpenter, slunk away.

*The three soldiers were a lot thinner than the last time he'd seen them, and as they hadn't been able to shave or keep very clean, they made a miserable picture.*

*By Caitlyn, age 8 years, United Kingdom*

# CHAPTER 24

# The Bandalore

Daisy was about to turn eight years old, so she decided to invite Bert Beamish to tea.

A thick wall of ice seemed to have grown up between Daisy and Bert since his father had died. He was always with Roderick Roach, who was very proud to have the son of an Ickabog victim as a friend, but Daisy's coming birthday, which was three days before Bert's, would be a chance to find out whether they could repair their friendship. So she asked her father to write a note to Mrs Beamish, inviting her and her son to tea. To Daisy's delight, a note came back accepting the invitation, and even though Bert still didn't talk to her at school, she held out hope that everything would be made right on her birthday.

Although he was well paid as carpenter to the king, even Mr Dovetail had felt the pinch of paying the Ickabog tax, so he and Daisy had bought fewer pastries than usual, and Mr Dovetail stopped buying wine. However, in honour of Daisy's birthday, Mr Dovetail brought out his last bottle of Jeroboam wine, and Daisy collected all her savings and bought two expensive Hopes-of-Heaven for herself and Bert, because she knew they were his favourites.

The birthday tea didn't start well. Firstly, Mr Dovetail proposed a toast to Major Beamish, which made Mrs Beamish cry. Then the four of them sat down to eat, but nobody seemed able to think of anything to say, until Bert remembered that he'd bought Daisy a present.

Bert had seen a bandalore, which is what people called yo-yos at that time, in a toyshop window and bought it with all his saved pocket money. Daisy had never seen one before, and what with Bert teaching her to use it, and Daisy swiftly becoming better at it than Bert was, and Mrs Beamish and Mr Dovetail drinking Jeroboam sparkling wine, conversation began to flow much more easily.

The truth was that Bert had missed Daisy very much, but hadn't known how to make up with her, with Roderick Roach always watching. Soon, though, it felt as though the fight in the courtyard had never happened, and Daisy and Bert were snorting with laughter about their teacher's habit of digging for bogies in his nose when he thought none of the children were looking. The painful subjects of dead parents, or fights that got out of hand, or King Fred the Fearless, were all forgotten.

The children were wiser than the adults. Mr Dovetail hadn't tasted wine in a long time, and, unlike his daughter, he didn't stop to consider that discussing the monster that was supposed to have killed Major Beamish might be a bad idea. Daisy only realised what her father was doing when he raised his voice over the children's laughter.

'All I'm saying, Bertha,' Mr Dovetail was almost shouting, 'is where's the proof? I'd like to see proof, that's all!'

'You don't consider it proof, then, that my husband was killed?' said Mrs Beamish, whose kindly face suddenly looked dangerous. 'Or poor little Nobby Buttons?'

'Little Nobby Buttons?' repeated Mr Dovetail. '*Little Nobby Buttons?* Now you come to mention it, I'd like proof of little Nobby Buttons! Who was he? Where did he live? Where's that old widowed mother gone, who wore that ginger wig? Have you ever met a Buttons family in the City-Within-The-City? And if you press me,' said Mr Dovetail, brandishing his wine glass, 'if you *press* me, Bertha, I'll ask you this: why was Nobby

Buttons's coffin so heavy, when all that was left of him were his shoes and a shin bone?'

Daisy made a furious face to try and shut her father up, but he didn't notice. Taking another large gulp of wine, he said: 'It doesn't add up, Bertha! Doesn't add up! Who's to say – and this is just an idea, mind you – but who's to say poor Beamish didn't fall off his horse and break his neck, and Lord Spittleworth saw an opportunity to pretend the Ickabog killed him, and charge us all a lot of gold?'

Mrs Beamish rose slowly to her feet. She wasn't a tall woman, but in her anger, she seemed to tower awfully over Mr Dovetail.

'My husband,' she whispered in a voice so cold that Daisy felt goosebumps, 'was the best horseman in all of Cornucopia. My husband would no sooner have fallen off his horse than you'd chop off your leg with your axe, Dan Dovetail. Nothing short of a terrible monster could have killed my husband, and you ought to watch your tongue, because saying the Ickabog isn't real happens to be treason!'

'Treason!' jeered Mr Dovetail. 'Come off it, Bertha, you're not going to stand there and tell me you believe in this treason nonsense? Why, a few months ago, not believing in the Ickabog made you a sane man, not a traitor!'

'That was before we knew the Ickabog was real!' screeched Mrs Beamish. 'Bert – we're going home!'

'No – no – please don't go!' Daisy cried. She picked up a little box she'd stowed under her chair and ran out into the garden after the Beamishes.

'Bert, please! Look – I got us Hopes-of-Heaven, I spent all my pocket money on them!'

Daisy wasn't to know that when he saw Hopes-of-Heaven now, Bert was instantly reminded of the day he'd found out his father was dead. The very last Hope-of-Heaven he'd ever eaten had been in the king's kitchens, when his mother was promising him they'd have heard if anything had happened to Major Beamish.

All the same, Bert didn't mean to dash Daisy's gift to the ground. He meant only to push it away. Unluckily, Daisy lost her grip on the box, and the costly pastries fell into the flowerbed and were covered in earth.

Daisy burst into tears.

'Well, if all you care about is pastries!' shouted Bert, and he opened the garden gate and led his mother away.

Text in image:
Cornucopian Bakery
2x Hopes Of Heaven
$30 Ducats

Cornucopian Bakery

Hopes (
Heav

*Bert… meant only to push it away. Unluckily, Daisy lost her grip on the box,
and the costly pastries fell into the flowerbed and were covered in earth.*

*By Ella, age 12 years, Australia*

# CHAPTER 25

# Lord Spittleworth's Problem

Unfortunately for Lord Spittleworth, Mr Dovetail wasn't the only person who'd started voicing doubts about the Ickabog.

Cornucopia was growing slowly poorer. The rich merchants had no problem paying their Ickabog taxes. They gave the collectors two ducats a month, then increased the prices on their pastries, cheeses, hams, and wines to pay themselves back. However, two gold ducats a month was increasingly hard to find for the poorer folk, especially with food at the markets more expensive. Meanwhile, up in the Marshlands, children began to grow hollow-cheeked.

Spittleworth, who had spies in every city and village, began hearing word that people wanted to know what their gold was being spent on, and even to demand proof that the monster was still a danger.

Now, people said of the cities of Cornucopia that their inhabitants had different natures: Jeroboamers were supposed to be brawlers and dreamers, the Kurdsburgers peaceful and courteous, while the citizens of Chouxville were often said to be proud, even snooty. But the people of Baronstown were said to be plain speakers and honest dealers, and it was here that the first serious outbreak of disbelief in the Ickabog happened.

A butcher called Tubby Tenderloin called a meeting in the town hall. Tubby was careful not to say he didn't believe in the Ickabog, but he invited everyone at the meeting to sign a petition to the king, asking for evidence that the Ickabog tax was still necessary. As soon as this meeting was over, Spittleworth's spy, who had of course attended the meeting, jumped on his horse and rode south, arriving at the palace by midnight.

Woken by a footman, Spittleworth hurriedly summoned Lord Flapoon and Major Roach from their beds, and the two men joined Spittleworth in his bedroom to hear what the spy had to say. The spy told the story of the treasonous meeting, then unfurled a map on which he'd helpfully circled the houses of the ringleaders, including that of Tubby Tenderloin.

'Excellent work,' growled Roach. 'We'll have all of them arrested for treason and slung in jail. Simple!'

'It isn't simple at all,' said Spittleworth impatiently. 'There were two hundred people at this meeting, and we can't lock up two hundred people! We haven't got room, for one thing, and for another, everyone will just say it proves we can't show the Ickabog's real!'

'Then we'll shoot 'em,' said Flapoon, 'and wrap 'em up like we did Beamish, and leave 'em up by the marsh to be found, and people will think the Ickabog got 'em.'

'Is the Ickabog supposed to have a gun now?' snapped Spittleworth. 'And two hundred cloaks in which to wrap its victims?'

'Well, if you're going to sneer at our plans, my lord,' said Roach, 'why don't you come up with something clever yourself?'

But that was exactly what Spittleworth couldn't do. Cudgel his sneaky brains though he might, he couldn't think of any way to frighten the Cornucopians back into paying their taxes without complaint. What he needed was proof that the Ickabog really existed, but where was he to get it?

Pacing alone in front of his fire, after the others had gone back to bed, Spittleworth heard another tap on his bedroom door.

'What now?' he snapped.

Into the room slid the footman, Cankerby.

'What do you want? Out with it quickly, I'm busy!' said Spittleworth.

'If it pleases Your Lordship,' said Cankerby, 'I 'appened to be passing your room earlier, and I couldn't 'elp 'earing about that there treasonous meeting in Baronstown what you, Lord Flapoon and Major Roach was talking about.'

'Oh, couldn't you *help* it?' said Spittleworth, in a dangerous voice.

'I thought I should tell you, my lord: I've got evidence that there's a man 'ere in the City-Within-The-City what thinks the same way as those traitors in Baronstown,' said Cankerby. ''E wants proof, just like them butchers do. Sounded like treason to me, when I 'eard about it.'

'Well, of course it's treason!' said Spittleworth. 'Who dares say such things, in the very shadow of the palace? Which of the king's servants dares question the king's word?'

'Well… as to that…' said Cankerby, shuffling his feet. 'Some would say that's valuable information, some would—'

'You tell me who it is,' snarled Spittleworth, seizing the footman by the front of his jacket, 'and then I'll see whether you deserve payment! Their name – *give me their name!*'

'It's D-D-Dan Dovetail!' said the footman.

'Dovetail… Dovetail… I know that name,' said Spittleworth, releasing the footman, who staggered sideways and fell into an end table. 'Wasn't there a seamstress…?'

''Is wife, sir. She died,' said Cankerby, straightening up.

'Yes,' said Spittleworth slowly. 'He lives in that house by the graveyard, where they never fly a flag and without a single portrait of the king in the windows. How d'you know he's expressed these treasonous views?'

'I 'appened to over'ear Mrs Beamish telling the scullery maid what 'e said,' said Cankerby.

'You *happen* to hear a lot of things, don't you, Cankerby?' commented

Spittleworth, feeling in his waistcoat for some gold. 'Very well. Here are ten ducats for you.'

'Thank you very much, my lord,' said the footman, bowing low.

'Wait,' said Spittleworth, as Cankerby turned to go. 'What does he do, this Dovetail?'

What Spittleworth really wanted to know was whether the king would miss Mr Dovetail, if he disappeared.

'Dovetail, my lord? 'E's a carpenter,' said Cankerby, and he bowed himself out of the room.

'A carpenter,' repeated Spittleworth out loud. 'A *carpenter*…'

And as the door closed on Cankerby, another of Spittleworth's lightning strike ideas hit him, and so amazed was he at his own brilliance, he had to clutch the back of the sofa, because he felt he might topple over.

# CHAPTER 26

# A Job for Mr Dovetail

Daisy had gone to school, and Mr Dovetail was busy in his workshop next morning, when Major Roach knocked on the carpenter's door. Mr Dovetail knew Roach as the man who lived in his old house, and who'd replaced Major Beamish as head of the Royal Guard. The carpenter invited Roach inside, but the major declined.

'We've got an urgent job for you at the palace, Dovetail,' he said. 'A shaft on the king's carriage has broken and he needs it tomorrow.'

'Already?' said Mr Dovetail. 'I only mended that last month.'

'It was kicked,' said Major Roach, 'by one of the carriage horses. Will you come?'

'Of course,' said Mr Dovetail, who was hardly likely to turn down a job from the king. So he locked up his workshop and followed Roach through the sunlit streets of the City-Within-The-City, talking of this and that, until they reached the part of the royal stables where the carriages were kept. Half a dozen soldiers were loitering outside the door, and they all looked up when they saw Mr Dovetail and Major Roach approaching. One soldier had an empty flour sack in his hands, and another, a length of rope.

'Good morning,' said Mr Dovetail.

He made to walk past them, but before he knew what was happening, one soldier had thrown the flour sack over Mr Dovetail's head and two more had pinned his arms behind his back and tied his wrists together with the rope. Mr Dovetail was a strong man – he struggled and fought, but Roach muttered in his ear:

'Make one sound, and it'll be your daughter who pays the price.'

Mr Dovetail closed his mouth. He permitted the soldiers to march him inside the palace, though he couldn't see where he was going. He soon guessed, though, because they took him down two steep flights of stairs and then onto a third, which was made of slippery stone. When he felt a chill on his flesh, he suspected that he was in the dungeons, and he knew it for sure when he heard the turning of an iron key, and the clanking of bars.

The soldiers threw Mr Dovetail onto the cold stone floor. Somebody pulled off his hood.

The surroundings were almost completely dark, and at first, Mr Dovetail couldn't make out anything around him. Then one of the soldiers lit a torch, and Mr Dovetail found himself staring at a pair of highly polished boots. He looked up. Standing over him was a smiling Lord Spittleworth.

'Good morning, Dovetail,' said Spittleworth. 'I have a little job for you. If you do it well, you'll be home with your daughter before you know it. Refuse – or do a poor job – and you'll never see her again. Do we understand each other?'

Six soldiers and Major Roach were lined up against the cell wall, all of them holding swords.

'Yes, my lord,' said Mr Dovetail in a low voice. 'I understand.'

'Excellent,' said Spittleworth. Moving aside, he revealed an enormous piece of wood, a section of a fallen tree as big as a pony. Beside the wood was a small table, bearing a set of carpenter's tools.

'I want you to carve me a gigantic foot, Dovetail, a monstrous foot, with razor-sharp claws. On top of the foot, I want a long handle, so that a man on horseback can press the foot into soft ground, to make an imprint. Do you understand your task, carpenter?'

Mr Dovetail and Lord Spittleworth looked deep into each other's eyes. Of course, Mr Dovetail understood exactly what was going on. He was being told to fake proof of the Ickabog's existence. What terrified Mr Dovetail was that he couldn't imagine why Spittleworth would ever let him go, after he'd created the fake monster's foot, in case he talked about what he'd done.

'Do you swear, my lord,' said Mr Dovetail quietly, 'do you *swear* that if I do this, my daughter won't be harmed? And that I'll be permitted to go home to her?'

'Of course, Dovetail,' said Spittleworth lightly, already moving to the door of the cell. 'The quicker you complete the task, the sooner you'll see your daughter again.

'Now, every night, we'll collect these tools from you, and every morning they'll be brought back to you, because we can't have prisoners keeping the means to dig themselves out, can we? Good luck, Dovetail, and work hard. I look forward to seeing my foot!'

And with that, Roach cut the rope binding Mr Dovetail's wrists, and rammed the torch he was carrying into a bracket on the wall. Then Spittleworth, Roach, and the other soldiers left the cell. The iron door closed with a clang, a key turned in the lock, and Mr Dovetail was left alone with the enormous piece of wood, his chisels, and his knives.

# CHAPTER 27

# Kidnapped

When Daisy arrived home from school that afternoon, playing with her bandalore as she went, she headed as usual to her father's workshop to tell him about her day. However, to her surprise, she found the workshop locked up. Assuming that Mr Dovetail had finished work early and was back in the cottage, she walked in through the front door with her schoolbooks under her arm.

Daisy stopped dead in the doorway, staring around. All the furniture was gone, as were the pictures on the walls, the rug on the floor, the lamps, and even the stove.

She opened her mouth to call her father, but in that instant, a sack was thrown over her head and a hand clamped over her mouth. Her schoolbooks and her bandalore fell with a series of thuds to the floor. Daisy was lifted off her feet, struggling wildly, then carried out of the house, and slung into the back of a wagon.

'If you make a noise,' said a rough voice in her ear, 'we'll kill your father.'

Daisy, who'd drawn breath into her lungs to scream, let it out quietly instead. She felt the wagon lurch, and heard the jingling of a harness and trotting hooves as they began to move. By the turn that the wagon took, Daisy knew that they were heading out of the City-Within-The-City, and by the sounds of market traders and other horses, she realised they were moving into wider Chouxville. Though more frightened than she'd ever been in her life, Daisy nevertheless forced herself to concentrate on every turn, every sound, and every smell, so she could get some idea of where she was being taken.

After a while, the horse's hooves were no longer falling on cobblestones, but on an earthy track, and the sugar-sweet air of Chouxville was gone, replaced by the green, loamy smell of the countryside.

The man who'd kidnapped Daisy was a large, rough member of the Ickabog Defence Brigade called Private Prodd. Spittleworth had told Prodd to 'get rid of the little Dovetail girl', and Prodd had understood Spittleworth to mean that he was to kill her. (Prodd was quite right to think this. Spittleworth had selected Prodd for the job of murdering Daisy because Prodd was fond of using his fists and seemed not to care whom he hurt.)

However, as he drove through the countryside, passing woods and forests where he might easily strangle Daisy and bury her body, it slowly dawned on Private Prodd that he wasn't going to be able to do it. He happened to have a little niece around Daisy's age, of whom he was very fond. In fact, every time he imagined himself strangling Daisy, he seemed to see his niece Rosie in his mind's eye, pleading for her life. So instead of turning off the dirt track into the woods, Prodd drove the wagon onwards, racking his brains as to what to do with Daisy.

Inside the flour sack, Daisy smelled the sausages of Baronstown mingling with the cheese fumes of Kurdsburg, and wondered which of the two she was being taken to. Her father had occasionally taken her to buy cheese and meat in these famous cities. She believed that if she could somehow give the driver the slip when he lifted her down from the wagon, she'd be able to make her way back to Chouxville in a couple of days. Her frantic mind kept returning to her father, and where he was, and why all the furniture in their house had been removed, but she forced herself to concentrate on the journey the wagon was making instead, to be sure of finding her way home again.

However, hard as she listened out for the sound of the horse's hooves on the stone bridge over the Fluma that connected Baronstown and Kurdsburg, it never came, because instead of entering either city, Private Prodd passed them by. He'd just had a brainwave about what to do with Daisy. So, skirting the city of sausagemakers, he drove on north. Slowly, the meat and cheese smells disappeared from the air and night began to fall.

Private Prodd had remembered an old woman who lived on the outskirts of Jeroboam, which happened to be his hometown. Everyone called this old woman Ma Grunter. She took in orphans, and was paid one ducat a month for each child she had living with her. No boy or girl had ever succeeded in running away from Ma Grunter's house, and it was this that made Prodd decide to take Daisy there. The last thing he wanted was Daisy finding her way back home to Chouxville, because Spittleworth was likely to be furious that Prodd hadn't done what he was told.

Though so scared, cold, and uncomfortable in the back of the wagon, the rocking had lulled Daisy to sleep, but suddenly she jerked awake again. She could smell something different on the air now, something she didn't much like, and after a while she identified it as wine fumes, which she recognised from the rare occasions when Mr Dovetail had a drink. They must be approaching Jeroboam, a city she'd never visited. Through the small holes in the sack she could see daybreak. The wagon was soon jolting over cobblestones again, and after a while it came to a halt.

At once, Daisy tried to wriggle out of the back of the wagon onto the ground, but before she'd hit the street, Private Prodd seized her. Then he carried her, struggling, to the door of Ma Grunter's, which he pounded with a heavy fist.

'All right, all right, I'm coming,' came a high, cracked voice from inside the house.

There came the noise of many bolts and chains being removed and Ma Grunter was revealed in the doorway, leaning heavily on a silver-topped cane – though, of course, Daisy, being still in the sack, couldn't see her.

'New child for you, Ma,' said Prodd, carrying the wriggling sack into Ma Grunter's hallway, which smelled of boiled cabbage and cheap wine.

Now, you might think Ma Grunter would be alarmed to see a child in a sack carried into her house, but in fact, the kidnapped children of so-called traitors had found their way to her before. She didn't care what a child's story was; all she cared about was the one ducat a month the authorities paid her for keeping them. The more children she packed into her tumbledown hovel, the more wine she could afford, which was really all she cared about. So she held out her hand and croaked, 'Five ducat placement fee,' – which was what she always asked for, if she could tell somebody really wanted to get rid of a child.

Prodd scowled, handed over five ducats, and left without another word. Ma Grunter slammed the door behind him.

As he climbed back onto his wagon, Prodd heard the rattle of Ma Grunter's chains and the scraping of her locks. Even if it had cost him half his month's pay, Prodd was glad to have got rid of the problem of Daisy Dovetail, and he drove off as fast as he could, back to the capital.

*In that instant, a sack was thrown over her head and... Daisy was lifted off her feet, struggling wildly, then carried out of the house.*

*By Charlie, age 10 years, United Kingdom*

# CHAPTER 28

# Ma Grunter

Having made sure her front door was secure, Ma Grunter pulled the sack off her new charge.

Blinking in the sudden light, Daisy found herself in a narrow, rather dirty hallway, face-to-face with a very ugly old woman who was dressed all in black, a large brown wart with hairs growing out of it on the tip of her nose.

'John!' the old woman croaked, without taking her eyes off Daisy, and a boy much bigger and older than Daisy with a blunt, scowling face came shuffling into the hall, cracking his knuckles. 'Go and tell the Janes upstairs to put another mattress in their room.'

'Make one of the little brats do it,' grunted John. 'I 'aven't 'ad breakfast.'

Ma Grunter suddenly swung her heavy, silver-handled cane at the boy's head. Daisy expected to hear a horrible thud of silver on bone, but the boy ducked the cane neatly, as though he'd had a lot of practice, cracked his knuckles again and said sullenly: 'Orl right, orl right.' He disappeared up some rickety stairs.

'What's your name?' said Ma Grunter, turning back to Daisy.

'Daisy,' said Daisy.

'No, it isn't,' said Ma Grunter. 'Your name is Jane.'

Daisy would soon find out that Ma Grunter did the same thing to every single child who arrived in her house. Every girl was rechristened

Jane, and every boy was renamed John. The way the child reacted to being given a new name told Ma Grunter exactly what she needed to know about how hard it was going to be to break that child's spirit.

Of course, the very tiny children who came to Ma Grunter simply agreed that their name was John or Jane, and quickly forgot that they'd been called anything else. Homeless children and lost children, who could tell that being John or Jane was the price of having a roof over their heads, were also quick to agree to the change.

But every so often Ma Grunter met a child who wouldn't accept their new name without a fight, and she knew, before Daisy even opened her mouth, that the girl was going to be one of them. There was a nasty, proud look about the newcomer, and, while skinny, she looked strong, standing there in her overalls with her fists clenched.

'My name,' said Daisy, 'is Daisy Dovetail. I was named after my mother's favourite flower.'

'Your mother is dead,' said Ma Grunter, because she always told the children in her care that their parents were dead. It was best if the little wretches didn't think there was anybody to run away to.

'That's true,' said Daisy, her heart hammering very fast. 'My mother *is* dead.'

'And so is your father,' said Ma Grunter.

The horrible old woman seemed to swim before Daisy's eyes. She'd had nothing to eat since the previous lunchtime and had spent a night of terror on Prodd's wagon. Nevertheless, she said in a cold, clear voice: 'My father's alive. I'm Daisy Dovetail, and my father lives in Chouxville.'

She had to believe her father was still there. She couldn't let herself doubt it, because if her father was dead, then all light would disappear from the world, forever.

'No, he isn't,' said Ma Grunter, raising her cane. 'Your father's as dead as a doornail and your name is Jane.'

'My name—' began Daisy, but with a sudden *whoosh*, Ma Grunter's cane came swinging at her head. Daisy ducked as she'd seen the big boy do, but the cane swung back again, and this time it hit Daisy painfully on the ear, and knocked her sideways.

'Let's try that again,' said Ma Grunter. 'Repeat after me. "My father is dead and my name is Jane."'

'I won't,' shouted Daisy, and before the cane could swing back at her, she'd darted under Ma Grunter's arm and run off into the house, hoping that the back door might not have bolts on it. In the kitchen she found two skinny, frightened-looking children, a boy and a girl, ladling a dirty green liquid into bowls, and a door with just as many chains and padlocks on it as the other. Daisy turned and ran back to the hall, dodged Ma Grunter and her cane, then sped upstairs, where more thin, pale children were cleaning and making beds with threadbare sheets. Ma Grunter was already climbing the stairs behind her.

'Say it,' croaked Ma Grunter. 'Say, "My father is dead and my name is Jane."'

'My father's alive and my name is Daisy!' shouted Daisy, now spotting a hatch in the ceiling that she suspected led to an attic. Snatching a feather duster out of the hand of a scared girl, she poked the hatch open. A rope ladder fell, which Daisy climbed, pulling it up after her and slamming the attic door, so that Ma Grunter and her cane couldn't reach her. She could hear the old woman cackling below, and ordering a boy to stand guard over the hatch, to make sure Daisy didn't come out.

Later, Daisy would discover that the children gave each other extra names, so they knew which John or Jane they were talking about. The big boy now standing guard over the attic hatch was the same one Daisy had seen downstairs. His nickname among the other children was Basher John, for the way he bullied the smaller children. Basher John was by way of being a deputy for Ma Grunter, and now he called up to Daisy,

telling her children had died of starvation in that attic and that she'd find
their skeletons if she looked hard enough.

The ceiling of Ma Grunter's attic was so low that Daisy had to
crouch. It was also very dirty, but there was a small hole in the roof
through which a shaft of sunlight fell. Daisy wriggled over to this and
put her eye to it. Now she could see the skyline of Jeroboam. Unlike
Chouxville, where the buildings were mostly sugar-white, this was a
city of dark-grey stone. Two men were reeling along the street below,
bellowing a popular drinking song.

> '*I drank a single bottle and the Ickabog's a lie,*
> *I drank another bottle, and I thought I heard it sigh,*
> *And now I've drunk another, I can see it slinking by,*
> *The Ickabog is coming, so let's drink before we die!*'

Daisy sat with her eye pressed against the spyhole for an hour, until Ma
Grunter came and banged on the hatch with her cane.

'What is your name?'

'Daisy Dovetail!' bellowed Daisy.

And every hour afterwards, the question came, and the answer
remained the same.

However, as the hours wore by, Daisy began to feel light-headed with
hunger. Every time she shouted 'Daisy Dovetail' back at Ma Grunter, her
voice was weaker. At last, she saw through her spyhole in the attic that
it was becoming dark. She was very thirsty now, and she had to face the
fact that, if she kept refusing to say her name was Jane, there really might
be a skeleton in the attic for Basher John to frighten other children with.

So the next time Ma Grunter banged on the attic hatch with her
cane and asked what Daisy's name was, she answered, 'Jane.'

'And is your father alive?' asked Ma Grunter.

Daisy crossed her fingers and said:

'No.'

'Very good,' said Ma Grunter, pulling open the hatch, so that the rope ladder fell down. 'Come down here, Jane.'

When Daisy was standing beside her again, the old lady cuffed her around the ear. 'That's for being a nasty, lying, filthy little brat. Now go and drink your soup, wash up the bowl, then get to bed.'

Daisy gulped down a small bowl of cabbage soup, which was the nastiest thing she'd ever eaten, washed the bowl in the greasy barrel that Ma Grunter kept for doing dishes, then went back upstairs. There was a spare mattress on the floor of the girls' bedroom, so she crept inside while all the other girls watched her, and got under the threadbare blanket, fully dressed, because the room was very cold.

Daisy found herself looking into the kind blue eyes of a girl her own age, with a gaunt face.

'You lasted much longer than most,' whispered the girl. She had an accent Daisy had never heard before. Later, Daisy would learn that the girl was a Marshlander.

'What's your name?' Daisy whispered. 'Your *real* name?'

The girl considered Daisy with those huge, forget-me-not eyes.

'We're not allowed to say.'

'I promise I won't tell,' whispered Daisy.

The girl stared at her. Just when Daisy thought she wasn't going to answer, the girl whispered:

'Martha.'

'Pleased to meet you, Martha,' whispered Daisy. 'I'm Daisy Dovetail and my father's still alive.'

*Daisy found herself… face-to-face with a very ugly old woman who was dressed all in black, a large brown wart with hairs growing out of it on the tip of her nose.*

*By Jordyn, age 8 years, Australia*

# CHAPTER 29

# Mrs Beamish Worries

Back in Chouxville, Spittleworth made sure the story was circulated that the Dovetail family had packed up in the middle of the night, and moved to the neighbouring country of Pluritania. Daisy's former teacher told her old classmates, and Cankerby the footman informed all the palace servants.

After he got home from school that day, Bert went and lay on his bed, staring up at the ceiling. He was thinking back to the days when he'd been a small, plump boy whom the other children called 'Butterball', and how Daisy had always stuck up for him. He remembered their long-ago fight in the palace courtyard, and the expression on Daisy's face when he'd accidentally knocked her Hopes-of-Heaven to the ground on her birthday.

Then Bert considered the way he spent his break times these days. At first, Bert had sort of liked being friends with Roderick Roach, because Roderick used to bully him and he was glad he'd stopped, but if he was truly honest with himself, Bert didn't really enjoy the same things that Roderick did: for instance, trying to hit stray dogs with catapults, or finding live frogs to hide in the girls' satchels. In fact, the more he remembered the fun he used to have with Daisy, the more he thought about how his face ached from fake-smiling at the end of a day with Roderick, and the more Bert regretted that he'd never tried to repair his and Daisy's friendship. But it was too late, now. Daisy was gone forever: gone to Pluritania.

While Bert was lying on his bed, Mrs Beamish sat alone in the kitchen. She felt almost as bad as her son.

Ever since she'd done it, Mrs Beamish had regretted telling the scullery maid what Mr Dovetail had said about the Ickabog not being real. She'd been so angry at the suggestion that her husband might have fallen off his horse she hadn't realised she was reporting treason, until the words were out of her mouth and it was too late to call them back. She really hadn't wanted to get such an old friend into trouble, so she'd begged the scullery maid to forget what she'd said, and Mabel had agreed.

Relieved, Mrs Beamish had turned around to take a large batch of Maidens' Dreams out of the oven, then spotted Cankerby, the footman, skulking in the corner. Cankerby was known to everyone who worked at the palace as a sneak and a tattletale. He had a knack of arriving noiselessly in rooms, and peeping unnoticed through keyholes. Mrs Beamish didn't dare ask Cankerby how long he'd been standing there, but now, sitting alone at her own kitchen table, a terrible fear gripped her heart. Had news of Mr Dovetail's treason been carried by Cankerby to Lord Spittleworth? Was it possible that Mr Dovetail had gone, not to Pluritania, but to prison?

The longer she thought about it, the more frightened she became, until finally, Mrs Beamish called out to Bert that she was going for an evening stroll, and hurried from the house.

There were still children playing in the streets, and Mrs Beamish wound her way in and out of them until she reached the small cottage that lay between the City-Within-The-City gates and the graveyard. The windows were dark and the workshop locked up, but when Mrs Beamish gave the front door a gentle push, it opened.

All the furniture was gone, right down to the pictures on the walls.

Mrs Beamish let out a long, slow sigh of relief. If they'd slung Mr Dovetail in jail, they'd hardly have put all his furniture in there with him. It really did look as though he'd packed up and taken Daisy off to Pluritania. Mrs Beamish felt a little easier in her mind as she walked back through the City-Within-The-City.

Some little girls were jumping rope in the road up ahead, chanting a rhyme now repeated in playgrounds all over the kingdom.

> *'Ickabog, Ickabog, he'll get you if you stop,*
> *Ickabog, Ickabog, so skip until you flop,*
> *Never look back if you feel squeamish,*
> *'Cause he's caught a soldier called Major—'*

One of the little girls turning the rope for her friend spotted Mrs Beamish, let out a squeal and dropped her end. The other little girls turned too and, seeing the pastry chef, all of them turned red. One let out a terrified giggle and another burst into tears.

'It's all right, girls,' said Mrs Beamish, trying to smile. 'It doesn't matter.'

The children remained quite still as she passed them, until suddenly Mrs Beamish turned to look again at the girl who'd dropped the end of the skipping rope.

'Where,' asked Mrs Beamish, 'did you get that dress?'

The scarlet-faced little girl looked down at it, then back up at Mrs Beamish.

'My daddy gave it to me, missus,' said the girl. 'When he come home from work yesterday. And he gave my brother a bandalore.'

After staring at the dress for a few more seconds, Mrs Beamish turned slowly away and walked on home. She told herself she must be mistaken, but she was sure she could remember Daisy Dovetail wearing a beautiful little dress exactly like that – sunshine yellow, with daisies embroidered around the neck and cuffs – back when her mother was alive, and made all Daisy's clothes.

# CHAPTER 30

# The Foot

A month passed. Deep in the dungeons, Mr Dovetail worked in a kind of frenzy. He had to finish the monstrous wooden foot, so he could see Daisy again. He'd forced himself to believe that Spittleworth would keep his word, and let him leave the dungeon after he'd completed his task, even though a voice in his head kept saying, *They'll never let you go after this. Never.*

To drive out fear, Mr Dovetail started singing the national anthem, over and over again:

> *'Coooorn – ucopia, give praises to the king,*
> *Coooorn – ucopia, lift up your voice and sing…'*

His constant singing annoyed the other prisoners even more than the sound of his chisel and hammer. The now thin and ragged Captain Goodfellow begged him to stop, but Mr Dovetail paid no attention. He'd become a little delirious. He had a confused idea that if he showed himself a faithful subject of the king, Spittleworth might think him less of a danger, and release him. So the carpenter's cell rang with the banging and scraping of his tools and the national anthem, and slowly but surely, a monstrous clawed foot took shape, with a long handle out of the top, so that a man on horseback could press it deep into soft ground.

When at last the wooden foot was finished, Spittleworth, Flapoon, and Major Roach came down into the dungeons to inspect it.

'Yes,' said Spittleworth slowly, examining the foot from every angle. 'Very good indeed. What do you think, Roach?'

'I think that'll do very nicely, my lord,' replied the major.

'You've done well, Dovetail,' Spittleworth told the carpenter. 'I'll tell the warder to give you extra rations tonight.'

'But you said I'd go free when I finished,' said Mr Dovetail, falling to his knees, pale and exhausted. 'Please, my lord. Please. I have to see my daughter… *please.*'

Mr Dovetail reached for Lord Spittleworth's bony hand, but Spittleworth snatched it back.

'Don't touch me, traitor. You should be grateful I didn't have you put to death. I may yet, if this foot doesn't do the trick – so if I were you, I'd pray my plan works.'

# CHAPTER 31

# Disappearance of a Butcher

That night, under cover of darkness, a party of horsemen dressed all in black rode out from Chouxville, headed by Major Roach. Hidden beneath a large bit of sacking on a wagon in their midst was the gigantic wooden foot, with its carved scales and long sharp claws.

At last they reached the outskirts of Baronstown. Now the riders – members of the Ickabog Defence Brigade whom Spittleworth had chosen for the job – slipped from their horses and covered the animals' hooves with sacking to muffle the noise and the shape of their prints. Then they lifted the giant foot off the wagon, remounted, and carried it between them to the house where Tubby Tenderloin the butcher lived with his wife, which was luckily a little distance from its neighbours.

Several of the soldiers now tied up their horses, stole up to Tubby's back door and forced entry, while the rest pressed the giant foot into the mud around his back gate.

Five minutes after the soldiers arrived, they carried Tubby and his wife, who had no children, out of their house, bound and gagged, then threw them onto the wagon. I may as well tell you now that Tubby and his wife were about to be killed, their bodies buried in the woods, in exactly the way Private Prodd had been supposed to dispose of Daisy. Spittleworth only kept alive those people for whom he had a use: Mr Dovetail might need to repair the Ickabog foot if it got damaged, and Captain Goodfellow and his friends might need to be dragged out again some day, to repeat their lies about the Ickabog. Spittleworth couldn't imagine ever needing a treasonous sausagemaker, though, so he'd ordered his murder. As for poor Mrs Tenderloin, Spittleworth barely considered her at all, but I'd like you to know that she was a very kind person, who babysat her friends' children and sang in the local choir.

Once the Tenderloins had been taken away, the remaining soldiers entered the house and smashed up the furniture as though a giant creature had wrecked it, while the rest of the men broke down the back fence and pressed the giant foot into the soft soil around Tubby's chicken coop, so that it appeared the prowling monster had also attacked the birds. One of the soldiers even stripped off his socks and boots, and made bare footprints in the soft earth, as though Tubby had rushed outside to protect his chickens. Finally, the same man cut off the head of one of the hens and made sure plenty of blood and feathers was spread around, before breaking down the side of the coop to allow the rest of the chickens to escape.

After pressing the giant foot many more times onto the mud outside Tubby's house, so the monster appeared to have run away onto solid ground, the soldiers heaved Mr Dovetail's creation back onto the wagon beside the soon-to-be-murdered butcher and his wife, remounted their horses, and disappeared into the night.

# CHAPTER 32

# A Flaw in the Plan

When Mr and Mrs Tenderloin's neighbours woke up the next day and found chickens all over the road, they hurried to tell Tubby his birds had escaped. Imagine the neighbours' horror when they found the enormous footprints, the blood and the feathers, the broken-down back door, and no sign of either husband or wife.

Before an hour had passed, a huge crowd had congregated around Tubby's empty house, all examining the monstrous footprints, the smashed-in door, and the wrecked furniture. Panic set in, and within a few hours, news of the Ickabog's raid on a Baronstown butcher's house was spreading north, south, east, and west. Town criers rang their bells in the city squares, and within a couple of days, only the Marshlanders would be ignorant of the fact that the Ickabog had slunk south overnight and carried off two people.

Spittleworth's Baronstown spy, who'd been mingling with the crowds all day to observe their reactions, sent word to his master that his plan had worked magnificently. However, in the early evening, just as the spy was thinking of heading off to the tavern for a celebratory sausage roll and a pint of beer, he noticed a group of men whispering together as they examined one of the Ickabog's giant footprints. The spy sidled over.

'Terrifying, isn't it?' the spy asked them. 'The size of its feet! The length of its claws!'

One of Tubby's neighbours straightened up, frowning.

'It's hopping,' he said.

'Excuse me?' said the spy.

'It's *hopping*,' repeated the neighbour. 'Look. It's the same left foot, over and over again. Either the Ickabog's hopping, or...'

The man didn't finish his sentence, but the look on his face alarmed the spy. Instead of heading for the tavern, he mounted his horse again, and galloped off towards the palace.

*Imagine the neighbours' horror when they found…*
*the blood and the feathers.*

*By Aria, age 7 years, India*

# CHAPTER 33

# King Fred is Worried

Little knowing of the new threat to their schemes, Spittleworth and Flapoon had just sat down to one of their usual sumptuous late-night dinners with the king. Fred was most alarmed to hear of the Ickabog's attack on Baronstown, because it meant that the monster had strayed closer to the palace than ever before.

'Ghastly business,' said Flapoon, lifting an entire black pudding onto his plate.

'Shocking, really,' said Spittleworth, carving himself a slice of pheasant.

'What I don't understand,' fretted Fred, 'is how it slipped through the blockade!'

For, of course, the king had been told that a division of the Ickabog Defence Brigade was permanently camped round the edge of the marsh, to stop the Ickabog escaping into the rest of the country. Spittleworth, who'd been expecting Fred to raise this point, had his explanation ready.

'I regret to say that two soldiers fell asleep on watch, Your Majesty. Taken unawares by the Ickabog, they were eaten whole.'

'Suffering Saints!' said Fred, horrified.

'Having broken through the line,' continued Spittleworth, 'the monster headed south. We believe it was attracted to Baronstown because of the smell of meat. While there, it gobbled up some chickens, as well as the butcher and his wife.'

'Dreadful, dreadful,' said Fred with a shudder, pushing his plate away from him. 'And then it slunk off back home to the marsh, did it?'

'So our trackers tell us, sire,' said Spittleworth, 'but now that it's tasted a butcher full of Baronstown sausage, we must prepare for it trying to break through the soldiers' lines regularly – which is why I think we should double the number of men stationed there, sire. Sadly, that will mean doubling the Ickabog tax.'

Luckily for them, Fred was watching Spittleworth, so he didn't see Flapoon smirk.

'Yes... I *suppose* that makes sense,' said the king.

He got to his feet and began roaming restlessly around the dining room. The lamplight made his costume, which today was of sky-blue silk with aquamarine buttons, shine beautifully. As he paused to admire himself in the mirror, Fred's expression clouded.

'Spittleworth,' he said, 'the people do still *like* me, don't they?'

'How can Your Majesty ask such a thing?' said Spittleworth, with a gasp. 'You're the most beloved king in the whole of Cornucopia's history!'

'It's just that... riding back from hunting yesterday, I couldn't help thinking that people didn't seem quite as happy as usual to see me,' said King Fred. 'There were hardly any cheers, and only one flag.'

'Give me their names and addresses,' said Flapoon through a mouthful of black pudding, and he groped in his pockets for a pencil.

'I don't know their names and addresses, Flapoon,' said Fred, who was now playing with a tassel on the curtains. 'They were just people, you know, passing by. But it upset me, rather, and then, when I got back to the palace, I heard that the Day of Petition has been cancelled.'

'Ah,' said Spittleworth, 'yes, I was going to explain that to Your Majesty...'

'There's no need,' said Fred. 'Lady Eslanda has already spoken to me about it.'

'*What?*' said Spittleworth, glaring at Flapoon. He'd given his friend strict instructions never to let Lady Eslanda near the king, because he was worried what she might tell him. Flapoon scowled and shrugged. Really, Spittleworth couldn't expect him to be at the king's side every minute of the day. A man needed the bathroom occasionally, after all.

'Lady Eslanda told me that people are complaining that the Ickabog tax is too high. She says rumours are flying that there aren't even any troops stationed in the north!'

'Piffle and poppycock,' said Spittleworth, though in fact it was perfectly true that there were no troops stationed in the north, and also true that there'd been even more complaints about the Ickabog tax, which was why he'd cancelled the Day of Petition. The last thing he wanted was for Fred to hear that he was losing popularity. He might take it into his foolish head to lower the taxes or, even worse, send people to investigate the imaginary camp in the north.

'There are times, obviously, when two regiments swap over,' said Spittleworth, thinking that he'd have to station some soldiers near the marsh now, to stop busybodies asking questions. 'Possibly some foolish Marshlander saw a regiment riding away, and imagined that there was nobody left up there... Why don't we *triple* the Ickabog tax, sire?' asked Spittleworth, thinking that this would serve the complainers right. 'After all, the monster *did* break through the lines last night! Then there can never again be any danger of a scarcity of men on the edge of the Marshlands and everyone will be happy.'

'Yes,' said King Fred uneasily. 'Yes, that does make sense. I mean, if the monster can kill four people and some chickens in a single night...'

At this moment, Cankerby the footman entered the dining room and, with a low bow, whispered to Spittleworth that the Baronstown spy had just arrived with urgent news from the sausage-making city.

'Your Majesty,' said Spittleworth smoothly, 'I must leave you. Nothing to worry about! A minor issue with my, ah, horse.'

# CHAPTER 34

# Three More Feet

'This had better be worth my while,' snapped Spittleworth five minutes later, as he entered the Blue Parlour, where the spy was waiting.

'Your – Lordship,' said the breathless man, 'they're saying – the monster's – hopping.'

'They're saying *what*?'

'Hopping, my lord – *hopping*!' he panted. 'They've noticed – all the prints – are made by the same – left – foot!'

Spittleworth stood speechless. It had never occurred to him that the common folk might be clever enough to spot a thing like that. Indeed, he, who'd never had to look after a living creature in his life, not even his own horse, hadn't stopped to consider the fact that a creature's feet might not all make the same prints in the ground.

'Must I think of everything?' bellowed Spittleworth, and he stormed out of the parlour and off to the Guard's Room, where he found Major Roach drinking wine and playing cards with some friends. The major leapt to his feet at the sight of Spittleworth, who beckoned him to come outside.

'I want you to assemble the Ickabog Defence Brigade immediately, Roach,' Spittleworth told the major, in a low voice. 'You're to ride north, and be sure to make plenty of noise as you go. I want everyone from Chouxville to Jeroboam to see you passing by. Then, once you're up there, spread out, and mount a guard over the border of the marsh.'

'But—' began Major Roach, who'd got used to a life of ease and plenty at the palace, with occasional rides around Chouxville in full uniform.

'I don't want "buts", I want action!' shouted Spittleworth. 'Rumours are flying that there's nobody stationed in the north! Go, now, and make sure you wake up as many people as possible as you go – but leave me two men, Roach. Just two. I have another small job for them.'

So the grumpy Roach ran off to assemble his troops, and Spittleworth proceeded alone to the dungeons.

The first thing he heard when he got there was the sound of Mr Dovetail, who was still singing the national anthem.

'Be quiet!' bellowed Spittleworth, drawing his sword and gesturing to the warder to let him into Mr Dovetail's cell.

The carpenter appeared quite different to the last time Lord Spittleworth had seen him. Since learning that he wasn't to be let out of the dungeon to see Daisy, a wild look had appeared in Mr Dovetail's eye. Of course, he hadn't been able to shave for weeks either, and his hair had grown rather long.

'I said, be quiet!' barked Spittleworth, because the carpenter, who didn't seem able to help himself, was still humming the national anthem. 'I need another three feet, d'you hear me? One more left foot, and two right. Do you understand me, carpenter?'

Mr Dovetail stopped humming.

'If I carve them, will you let me out to see my daughter, my lord?' he asked in a hoarse voice.

Spittleworth smiled. It was clear to him that the man was going slowly mad, because only a madman would imagine he'd be let out after making another three Ickabog feet.

'Of course I will,' said Spittleworth. 'I shall have the wood delivered to you first thing tomorrow morning. Work hard, carpenter. When you're finished, I'll let you out to see your daughter.'

When Spittleworth emerged from the dungeons, he found two soldiers waiting for him, just as he'd requested. Spittleworth led these men up to his private apartments, made sure Cankerby the footman wasn't skulking about, locked the door, and turned to give the men their instructions.

'There will be fifty ducats for each of you, if you succeed in this job,' he said, and the soldiers looked excited.

'You are to follow the lady Eslanda, morning, noon, and night, you understand me? She must not know you are following her. You will wait for a moment when she is quite alone, so that you can kidnap her without anyone hearing or seeing anything. If she escapes, or if you are seen, I shall deny that I gave you this order, and put you to death.'

'What do we do with her once we've got her?' asked one of the soldiers, who no longer looked excited, but very scared.

'Hmm,' said Spittleworth, turning to look out of the window while he considered what best to do with Eslanda. 'Well, a lady of the court isn't the same as a butcher. The Ickabog can't enter the palace and eat her... No, I think it best,' said Spittleworth, a slow smile spreading over his crafty face, 'if you take Lady Eslanda to my estate in the country. Send word when you've got her there, and I'll join you.'

*Since learning that he wasn't to be let out of the dungeon to see Daisy, a wild look had appeared in Mr Dovetail's eye... and his hair had grown rather long.*

*By Divymaan, age 10 years, India*

# CHAPTER 35

# Lord Spittleworth's Proposal

A few days later, Lady Eslanda was walking alone in the palace rose garden when the two soldiers hiding in a bush spotted their chance. They seized her, gagged her, bound her hands, and drove her away to Spittleworth's estate in the country. Then they sent a message to Spittleworth, and waited for him to join them.

Spittleworth promptly summoned Lady Eslanda's maid, Millicent. By threatening to murder Millicent's little sister, he forced her to deliver messages to all Lady Eslanda's friends, telling them that her mistress had decided to become a nun.

Lady Eslanda's friends were all shocked by this news. She'd never mentioned wanting to become a nun to any of them. In fact, several of them were suspicious that Lord Spittleworth had had something to do with her sudden disappearance. However, I'm sad to tell you that Spittleworth was now so widely feared, that apart from whispering their suspicions to each other, Eslanda's friends did nothing to either find her, or ask Spittleworth what he knew. Perhaps even worse was the fact that none of them tried to help Millicent, who was caught by soldiers trying to flee the City-Within-The-City, and imprisoned in the dungeons.

Next, Spittleworth had set out for his country estate, where he arrived late the following evening. After giving each of Eslanda's kidnappers fifty ducats, and reminding them that if they talked, he'd have them executed, Spittleworth smoothed his thin moustaches in a mirror, then went to find

Lady Eslanda, who was sitting in his rather dusty library, reading a book by candlelight.

'Good evening, my lady,' said Spittleworth, sweeping her a bow.

Lady Eslanda looked at him in silence.

'I have good news for you,' continued Spittleworth, smiling. 'You are to become the wife of the Chief Advisor.'

'I'd sooner die,' said Lady Eslanda pleasantly, and, turning a page in her book, she continued to read.

'Come, come,' said Spittleworth. 'As you can see, my house really needs a woman's tender care. You'll be far happier here, making yourself useful, than pining over the cheesemakers' son, who in any case, is likely to starve to death any day now.'

Lady Eslanda, who'd expected Spittleworth to mention Captain Goodfellow, had been preparing for this moment ever since arriving in the cold and dirty house. So she said, with neither a blush nor a tear:

'I stopped caring for Captain Goodfellow a long time ago, Lord Spittleworth. The sight of him confessing to treason disgusted me. I could never love a treacherous man – which is why I could never love you.'

She said it so convincingly that Spittleworth believed her. He tried a different threat, and told her he'd kill her parents if she didn't marry him, but Lady Eslanda reminded him that she, like Captain Goodfellow, was an orphan. Then Spittleworth said he'd take away all the jewellery her mother had left her, but she shrugged and said she preferred books anyway. Finally, Spittleworth threatened to kill her, and Lady Eslanda suggested he get on with it, because that would be far better than listening to him talk.

Spittleworth was enraged. He'd become used to having his own way in everything, and here was something he couldn't have, and it only made him want it all the more. Finally, he said that if she liked books so much, he'd lock her up inside the library forever. He'd have bars fitted on all the windows, and Scrumble the butler would bring her food three times a day, but she would only ever leave the room to go to the bathroom – unless she agreed to marry him.

'Then I shall die in this room,' said Lady Eslanda calmly, 'or, perhaps – who knows? – in the bathroom.'

As he couldn't get another word out of her, the furious Chief Advisor left.

*A few days later, Lady Eslanda was walking alone in the palace rose garden.*

---

*By Sofia, age 12 years, Australia*

# CHAPTER 36

# Cornucopia Hungry

A year passed… then two… then three, four, and five.

The tiny kingdom of Cornucopia, which had once been the envy of its neighbours for its magically rich soil, for the skill of its cheesemakers, winemakers, and pastry chefs, and for the happiness of its people, had changed almost beyond recognition.

True, Chouxville was carrying on more or less as it always had. Spittleworth didn't want the king to notice that anything had changed, so he spent plenty of gold in the capital to keep things running as they always had, especially in the City-Within-The-City. Up in the northern cities, though, people were struggling. More and more businesses – shops, taverns, blacksmiths, wheelwrights, farms, and vineyards – were closing down. The Ickabog tax was pushing people into poverty, and as if that wasn't bad enough, everyone feared being the next to receive a visit from the Ickabog – or whatever it was that broke down doors and left monster-like tracks around houses and farms.

People who voiced doubts about whether the Ickabog was really behind these attacks were usually next to receive a visit from the Dark Footers. That was the name Spittleworth and Roach had given to the squads of men who murdered unbelievers in the night, leaving footprints around their victims' houses.

Occasionally, though, the Ickabog doubters lived in the middle of a city, where it was difficult to fake an attack without the neighbours seeing. In this case, Spittleworth would hold a trial, and by threatening their families, as he had with Goodfellow and his friends, he made the accused agree that they'd committed treason.

Increasing numbers of trials meant Spittleworth had to oversee the building of more jails. He also needed more orphanages. Why did he need orphanages, you ask?

Well, in the first place, quite a number of parents were being killed or imprisoned. As everyone was now finding it difficult to feed their own families, they weren't able to take in the abandoned children.

In the second place, poor people were dying of hunger. As parents usually fed their children rather than themselves, children were often the last of the family left alive.

And in the third place, some heartbroken, homeless families were giving up their children to orphanages, because it was the only way they could make sure their children would have food and shelter.

I wonder whether you remember the palace maid, Hetty, who so bravely warned Lady Eslanda that Captain Goodfellow and his friends were about to be executed?

Well, Hetty used Lady Eslanda's gold to take a coach home to her father's vineyard, just outside Jeroboam. A year later, she married a man called Hopkins, and gave birth to twins, a boy and a girl.

However, the effort of paying the Ickabog tax was too much for the Hopkins family. They lost their little grocery store, and Hetty's parents couldn't help them, because shortly after losing their vineyard, they'd starved to death. Homeless now, their children crying with hunger, Hetty and her husband walked in desperation to Ma Grunter's orphanage. The twins were torn, sobbing, from their mother's arms. The door slammed, the bolts banged home, and poor Hetty Hopkins and her husband walked away, crying no less hard than their children, and praying that Ma Grunter would keep them alive.

# CHAPTER 37

# Daisy and the Moon

Ma Grunter's orphanage had changed a great deal since Daisy Dovetail had been taken there in a sack. The broken-down hovel was now an enormous stone building, with bars on the windows, locks on every door, and space for a hundred children.

Daisy was still there, grown much taller and thinner, but still wearing the overalls in which she'd been kidnapped. She'd sewn lengths onto the arms and legs so they still fit, and patched them carefully when they tore. They were the last thing she had of her home and her father, and so she kept wearing them instead of making herself dresses out of the sacks the cabbages came in, as Martha and the other big girls did.

Daisy had held onto the idea that her father was still alive for several long years after her kidnap. She was a clever girl, and had always known her father didn't believe in the Ickabog, so she forced herself to believe that he was in a cell somewhere, looking up through the barred window at the same moon she watched every night, before she fell asleep.

Then one night, in her sixth year at Ma Grunter's, after tucking the Hopkins twins in for the night, and promising them they'd see their mummy and daddy again soon, Daisy lay down beside Martha and looked up at the pale gold disc in the sky as usual, and realised she no longer believed her father was alive. That hope had left her heart like a bird fleeing a ransacked nest, and though tears leaked out of her eyes, she told herself that her father was in a better place now, up there in the glorious heavens with her mother. She tried to find comfort in the idea that, being no longer earthbound, her parents could live anywhere, including in her own heart, and that she must keep their memories alive inside her, like a flame. Still, it was hard to have parents who lived inside you, when all you really wanted was for them to come back, and hug you.

Unlike many of the orphanage children, Daisy retained a clear memory of her parents. The memory of their love sustained her, and every day she helped look after the little ones in the orphanage, and made sure they had the hugs and kindness she was missing herself.

Yet it wasn't only the thought of her mother and father that enabled Daisy to carry on. She had a strange feeling that she was meant to do something important – something that would change not only her own life, but the fortunes of Cornucopia. She'd never told anyone about this strange feeling, not even her best friend, Martha. After all, who'd believe that a penniless girl locked up in an orphanage could save the country? Yet the strange belief burned stubbornly inside her, like a flame that refused to go out.

*She told herself that her father was in a better place now, up there in the glorious heavens with her mother.*

By Sakina, age 12 years, United Kingdom

# CHAPTER 38

# Lord Spittleworth Comes to Call

Ma Grunter was one of the few Cornucopians who'd grown richer and richer in the last few years. She'd crammed her hovel with children and babies until the place was at bursting point, then demanded gold from the two lords who now ruled the kingdom, to enlarge her tumbledown house. These days the orphanage was a thriving business, which meant that Ma Grunter was able to dine on delicacies that only the richest could afford. Most of her gold paid for bottles of finest Jeroboam wine, and I'm sorry to say that when drunk, Ma Grunter was very cruel indeed. The children inside the orphanage sported many cuts and bruises, because of Ma Grunter's drunken temper.

Some of her charges didn't last long on a diet of cabbage soup and cruelty. While endless hungry children poured in at the front door, a little cemetery at the back of the building became fuller and fuller. Ma Grunter didn't care. All the Johns and Janes of the orphanage were alike to her, their faces sad and pinched, their only worth the gold she got for taking them in.

But in the seventh year of Lord Spittleworth's rule over Cornucopia, when he received yet another request for gold from Ma Grunter's orphanage, the Chief Advisor decided to go and inspect the place, before he gave the old woman more funds. Ma Grunter dressed up in her best black silk dress to greet His Lordship, and was careful not to let him smell wine on her breath.

'Poor little mites, ain't they, Your Lordship?' she asked him, as he looked around at all the thin, scared children, with his scented handkerchief held to his nostrils. Ma Grunter stooped down to pick up one tiny Marshlander, whose belly was swollen from hunger. 'You see 'ow much they needs Your Lordship's 'elp.'

'Yes, yes, clearly,' said Spittleworth, his handkerchief clamped to his face. He didn't like children, especially children as dirty as these, but he knew many Cornucopians were stupidly fond of brats, so it was a bad idea to let too many of them die. 'Very well, further funds are approved, Ma Grunter.'

As he turned to leave, the lord noticed a pale girl standing beside the door, holding a baby in each arm. She wore patched overalls which had been let out and lengthened. There was something about the girl that set her apart from the other children. Spittleworth even had the strange notion that he'd seen somebody like her before. Unlike the other brats, she didn't seem at all impressed by his sweeping Chief Advisor's robes, nor by the jangling medals he'd awarded himself for being Regimental Colonel of the Ickabog Defence Brigade.

'What's your name, girl?' Spittleworth asked, halting beside Daisy, and lowering his scented handkerchief.

'Jane, my lord. We're all called Jane here, you know,' said Daisy, examining Spittleworth with cool, serious eyes. She remembered him from the palace courtyard where she'd once played, how he and Flapoon would scare the children into silence as they walked past, scowling.

'Why don't you curtsy? I am the king's Chief Advisor.'

'A Chief Advisor isn't a king,' said the girl.

'What's that she's saying?' croaked Ma Grunter, hobbling over to see that Daisy wasn't making trouble. Of all the children in her orphanage,

Daisy Dovetail was the one Ma Grunter liked least. The girl's spirit had never quite been broken, although Ma Grunter had tried her hardest to do it. 'What are you saying, Ugly Jane?' she asked. Daisy wasn't ugly in the slightest, but this name was one of the ways Ma Grunter tried to break her spirit.

'She's explaining why she doesn't curtsy to me,' said Spittleworth, still staring into Daisy's dark eyes, and wondering where he'd seen them before.

In fact, he'd seen them in the face of the carpenter he visited regularly in the dungeons, but as Mr Dovetail was now quite insane, with long white hair and beard, and this girl looked intelligent and calm, Spittleworth didn't make the connection between them.

'Ugly Jane's always been impertinent,' said Ma Grunter, inwardly vowing to punish Daisy as soon as Lord Spittleworth had gone. 'One of these days I'll turn her out, my lord, and she can see how she likes begging on the streets, instead of sheltering under my roof and eating my food.'

'*How* I'd miss cabbage soup,' said Daisy, in a cold, hard voice. 'Did you know that's what we eat here, my lord? Cabbage soup, three times a day?'

'Very nourishing, I'm sure,' said Lord Spittleworth.

'Though, sometimes, as a special treat,' said Daisy, 'we get Orphanage Cakes. Do you know what those are, my lord?'

'No,' said Spittleworth, against his will. There was something about this girl... *What was it?*

'They're made of spoiled ingredients,' said Daisy, her dark eyes boring into his. 'Bad eggs, mouldy flour, scraps of things that have been in the cupboard too long... People haven't got any other food to spare for us, so they mix up the things they don't want and leave them on the front steps. Sometimes the Orphanage Cakes make the children sick, but they eat them anyway, because they're so hungry.'

Spittleworth wasn't really listening to Daisy's words, but to her accent. Though she'd now spent so long in Jeroboam, her voice still carried traces of Chouxville.

'Where do you come from, girl?' he asked.

The other children had fallen silent now, all of them watching the lord talking to Daisy. Though Ma Grunter hated her, Daisy was a great favourite among the younger children, because she protected them from Ma Grunter and Basher John, and never stole their dry crusts, unlike some of the other big children. She'd also been known to sneak them bread and cheese from Ma Grunter's private stores, although that was a risky business, and sometimes led to Daisy being beaten by Basher John.

'I come from Cornucopia, my lord,' said Daisy. 'You might have heard of it. It's a country that used to exist, where nobody was ever poor or hungry.'

'That's enough,' snarled Lord Spittleworth and, turning to Ma Grunter, he said, 'I agree with you, madam. This child seems ungrateful for your kindness. Perhaps she ought to be left to fend for herself, out in the world.'

With that, Lord Spittleworth swept out of the orphanage, slamming the door behind him. As soon as he had gone, Ma Grunter swung her cane at Daisy, but long practice enabled Daisy to duck out of harm's way. The old woman shuffled away, swishing her cane before her, making all the little ones scatter, then slammed the door of her comfortable parlour behind her. The children heard the popping of a cork.

Later, after they'd climbed into their neighbouring beds that night, Martha suddenly said to Daisy:

'You know, Daisy, it isn't true, what you said to the Chief Advisor.'

'Which bit, Martha?' whispered Daisy.

'It isn't true that everyone was well fed and happy in the old days.

My family never had enough in the Marshlands.'

'I'm sorry,' said Daisy quietly. 'I forgot.'

'Of course,' sighed the sleepy Martha, 'the Ickabog kept stealing our sheep.'

Daisy wriggled deeper under her thin blanket, trying to keep warm. In all their time together, she'd never managed to convince Martha that the Ickabog wasn't real. Tonight, though, Daisy wished that she too believed in a monster in the marsh, rather than in the human wickedness she'd seen staring out of Lord Spittleworth's eyes.

# CHAPTER 39

# Bert and the Ickabog Defence Brigade

We now return to Chouxville, where some important things are about to happen.

I'm sure you remember the day of Major Beamish's funeral, when little Bert returned home, smashed apart his Ickabog toy with the poker, and vowed that when he grew up, he'd hunt down the Ickabog and take revenge upon the monster that killed his father.

Well, Bert was about to turn fifteen. This might not seem very old to you, but in those days it was big enough to become a soldier, and Bert had heard that the Brigade was expanding. So one Monday morning, without telling his mother what he was planning, Bert set off from their little cottage at the usual time, but instead of going to school, he stuffed his schoolbooks into the garden hedge where he could retrieve them later, then headed for the palace, where he intended to apply to join the Brigade. Under his shirt, for luck, he wore the silver medal his father had won for outstanding bravery against the Ickabog.

Bert hadn't gone far when he saw a commotion ahead of him in the road. A small crowd was clustered around a mail coach. As he was far too busy trying to think of good answers to the questions Major Roach was sure to ask him, Bert walked past the mail coach without paying much attention.

What Bert didn't realise was that the arrival of that mail coach was going to have some very important consequences, which would send him on a dangerous adventure. Let's allow Bert to walk on without us for a moment or two, so I can tell you about the coach.

Ever since Lady Eslanda had informed King Fred that Cornucopia was unhappy about the Ickabog tax, Spittleworth and Flapoon had taken steps to make sure he never heard news from outside the capital again. As Chouxville remained quite rich and bustling, the king, who never left the capital any more, assumed the rest of the country must be the same. In fact, the other Cornucopian cities were all full of beggars and boarded-up shops, because the two lords and Roach had stolen so much gold from the people. To ensure the king never got wind of all this, Lord Spittleworth, who read all the king's mail in any case, had hired gangs of highwaymen lately to stop any letters entering Chouxville. The only people who knew this were Major Roach, because he'd hired the highwaymen, and Cankerby the footman, who'd been lurking outside the Guard's Room door when the plan was hatched.

Spittleworth's plan had worked well so far, but today, just before dawn, some of the highwaymen had bungled the job. They'd ambushed the coach as usual, dragging the poor driver from his seat, but before they could steal the mail sacks, the frightened horses had bolted. When the highwaymen fired their guns after the horses they merely galloped all the faster, so that the mail coach soon entered Chouxville, where it careered through the streets, finally coming to rest in the City-Within-The-City. There a blacksmith succeeded in seizing the reins and bringing the horses to a halt. Soon, the servants of the king were tearing open long-awaited letters from their families in the north. We'll find out more about those letters later, because it's now time to rejoin Bert, who'd just reached the palace gates.

'Please,' Bert said to the guard, 'I want to join the Ickabog Defence Brigade.'

The guard took Bert's name and told him to wait, then carried the message to Major Roach. However, when he reached the door of the Guard's Room, the soldier paused, because he could hear shouting. He knocked, and the voices fell silent at once.

'Enter!' barked Roach.

The guard obeyed, and found himself face-to-face with three men: Major Roach, who looked extremely angry, Lord Flapoon, whose face was scarlet above his striped silk dressing gown, and Cankerby the footman, who, with his usual good timing, had been walking to work when the mail coach came galloping into town, and had hastened to tell Flapoon that letters had managed to make their way past the highwaymen. On hearing this news, Flapoon had stormed downstairs from his bedroom into the Guard's Room to blame Roach for the highwaymen's failure, and a shouting match erupted. Neither man wanted to be blamed by Spittleworth when he returned from his inspection of Ma Grunter's and heard what had happened.

'Major,' said the soldier, saluting both men, 'there's a boy at the gate, sir, name of Bert Beamish. Wants to know if he can join the Ickabog Defence Brigade.'

'Tell him to go away,' barked Flapoon. 'We're busy!'

'Do *not* tell the Beamish boy to go away!' snapped Roach. 'Bring him to me immediately. Cankerby, leave us!'

'I was hoping,' began Cankerby, in his weaselly way, 'that you gentlemen might want to reward me for—'

'Any idiot can see a mail coach speed past them!' said Flapoon. 'If you'd wanted a reward, you should've hopped on board and driven it straight back out of the city again!'

So the disappointed footman slunk out, and the guard went to fetch Bert.

'What are you bothering with this boy for?' Flapoon demanded of Roach, once they were alone. 'We have to solve this problem of the mail!'

'He isn't just any boy,' said Roach. 'He's the son of a national hero. You remember Major Beamish, my lord. You shot him.'

'All right, all right, there's no need to go on about it,' said Flapoon irritably. 'We've all made a tidy bit of gold out of it, haven't we? What do you suppose his son wants – compensation?'

But before Major Roach could answer, in walked Bert, looking nervous and eager.

'Good morning, Beamish,' said Major Roach, who'd known Bert a long time, because of his friendship with Roderick. 'What can I do for you?'

'Please, Major,' said Bert, 'please, I want to join the Ickabog Defence Brigade. I heard you're needing more men.'

'Ah,' said Major Roach. 'I see. And what makes you want to do that?'

'I want to kill the monster that killed my father,' said Bert.

There was a short silence, in which Major Roach wished he was as good as Lord Spittleworth at thinking up lies and excuses. He glanced towards Lord Flapoon for help, but none came, although Roach could tell that Flapoon too had spotted the danger. The last thing the Ickabog Defence Brigade needed was somebody who actually wanted to find an Ickabog.

'There are tests,' said Roach, playing for time. 'We don't let just anybody join. Can you ride?'

'Oh, yes, sir,' said Bert truthfully. 'I taught myself.'

'Can you use a sword?'

'I'm sure I could pick it up fast enough,' said Bert.

'Can you shoot?'

'Yes, sir, I can hit a bottle from the end of the paddock!'

'Hmm,' said Roach. 'Yes. But the problem is, Beamish – you see, the problem is, you might be too—'

'Foolish,' said Flapoon cruelly. He really wanted this boy gone, so that he and Roach could think up a solution to this problem of the mail coach.

Bert's face flooded with colour. 'Wh-what?'

'Your schoolmistress told me,' lied Flapoon. He'd never spoken to the schoolmistress in his life. 'She says you're a bit of a dunce. Nothing that should hold you back in any line of work other than soldiering, but dangerous to have a dunce on the battlefield.'

'My – my marks are all right,' said poor Bert, trying to stop his voice from shaking. 'Miss Monk never told me she thinks I'm—'

'Of course she hasn't *told* you,' said Flapoon. 'Only a *fool* would think a nice woman like that would tell a fool he's a fool. Learn to make pastries like your mother, boy, and forget about the Ickabog, that's my advice.'

Bert was horribly afraid his eyes had filled with tears. Scowling in his effort to keep from crying, he said:

'I – I'd welcome the chance to prove I'm not – not a fool, Major.'

Roach wouldn't have put matters as rudely as Flapoon, but after all, the important thing was to stop the boy joining the Brigade, so Roach said: 'Sorry, Beamish, but I don't think you're cut out for soldiering. However, as Lord Flapoon suggests—'

'Thank you for your time, Major,' said Bert in a rush. 'I'm sorry to have troubled you.'

And with a low bow, he left the Guard's Room.

Once outside, Bert broke into a run. He felt very small and humiliated. The last thing he wanted to do was return to school, not after hearing what his teacher really thought of him. So, assuming that his mother would have left for work in the palace kitchens, he ran all the way home, barely noticing the knots of people now standing on street corners, talking about the letters in their hands.

When Bert entered the house, he found Mrs Beamish was still standing in the kitchen, staring at a letter of her own.

'Bert!' she said, startled by the sudden appearance of her son. 'What are you doing home?'

'Toothache,' Bert invented on the spot.

'Oh, you poor thing… Bert, we've had a letter from Cousin Harold,' said Mrs Beamish, holding it up. 'He says he's worried he's going to lose his tavern – that marvellous inn he built up from nothing! He's written to ask me whether I might be able to get him a job working for the king… I don't understand what can have happened. Harold says he and the family are actually going hungry!'

'It'll be the Ickabog, won't it?' said Bert. 'Jeroboam's the city nearest the Marshlands. People have probably stopped visiting taverns at night, in case they meet the monster on the way!'

'Yes,' said Mrs Beamish, looking troubled, 'yes, maybe that's why… Gracious me, I'm late for work!' Setting Cousin Harold's letter down on the table, she said, 'Put some oil of cloves on that tooth, love,' and, giving her son a quick kiss, she hurried out of the door.

Once his mother had gone, Bert went and flung himself face down on his bed, and sobbed with rage and disappointment.

Meanwhile, anxiety and anger were spreading through the streets of the capital. Chouxville had at last found out that their relatives in the north were so poor they were starving and homeless. When Lord Spittleworth returned to the city that night, he found serious trouble brewing.

*Bert didn't realise… that the arrival of that mail coach was going to have…*
*important consequences, which would send him on a dangerous adventure.*

---

*By Morgan, age 12 years, New Zealand*

# CHAPTER 40

# Bert Finds a Clue

When he heard that a mail coach had reached the heart of Chouxville, Spittleworth seized a heavy wooden chair and threw it at Major Roach's head. Roach, who was far stronger than Spittleworth, batted the chair aside easily enough, but his hand flew to the hilt of his sword and for a few seconds, the two men stood with teeth bared in the gloom of the Guard's Room, while Flapoon and the spies watched, open-mouthed.

'You will send a party of Dark Footers to the outskirts of Chouxville tonight,' Spittleworth ordered Roach. 'You will fake a raid – we must *terrify* these people. They must understand that the tax is necessary, that any hardship their relatives are suffering is the fault of the Ickabog, not mine or the king's. Go, and undo the harm you've done!'

The furious major left the room, privately thinking of all the ways he'd like to hurt Spittleworth, if given ten minutes alone with him.

'And you,' said Spittleworth to his spies, 'will report to me tomorrow whether Major Roach has done his work well enough. If the city's still whispering about starvation and penniless relations, well then, we'll have to see how Major Roach likes the dungeons.'

So a group of Major Roach's Dark Footers waited until the capital slept, then set out for the first time to make Chouxville believe that the Ickabog had come calling. They selected a cottage on the very edge of town that stood a little apart from its neighbours. The men who were most skilful at breaking into houses entered the cottage, where, it pains me to say, they killed the little old lady who lived there, who, you might like to know, had written several beautifully illustrated books about the fish that lived in the River Fluma. Once her body had been carried away to be buried somewhere remote, a group of men pressed four of Mr Dovetail's finest carved feet into the ground around the fish expert's house, smashed up her furniture and her fish tanks and let her specimens die, gasping, on the floor.

Next morning, Spittleworth's spies reported that the plan seemed to have worked. Chouxville, so long avoided by the fearsome Ickabog, had at last been attacked. As the Dark Footers had now perfected the art of making the tracks look natural, and breaking down doors as though a gigantic monster had smashed them in, and using pointed metal tools to mimic tooth marks on wood, the Chouxville residents who flocked to see the poor old woman's house were entirely taken in.

Young Bert Beamish stayed at the scene even after his mother had left to start cooking their supper. He was treasuring up every detail of the beast's footprints and its fang marks, the better to imagine what it would look like when at last he came face-to-face with the evil creature that had killed his father, because he'd by no means abandoned his ambition to avenge him.

When Bert was sure he had every detail of the monster's prints memorised, he walked home, burning with fury, and shut himself up in his bedroom, where he took down his father's Medal for Outstanding Bravery Against the Deadly Ickabog, and the tiny medal the king had given him after he'd fought Daisy Dovetail. The smaller medal made Bert feel sad these days. He'd never had a friend as good as Daisy since she'd left for Pluritania, but at least, he thought, she and her father were beyond the reach of the evil Ickabog.

Angry tears started in Bert's eyes. He'd so wanted to join the Ickabog Defence Brigade! He *knew* he'd be a good soldier. He wouldn't even care if he died in the fight! Of course, it would be extremely upsetting for his mother if the Ickabog killed her son as well as her husband, but on the other hand, Bert would be a hero, like his father!

Lost in thoughts of revenge and glory, Bert made to replace the two medals on the mantelpiece when the smaller of them slipped through his fingers and rolled away under the bed. Bert lay down and groped for it, but couldn't reach. He wriggled further under his bed and found it at last in the furthermost, dustiest corner, along with something sharp that seemed to have been there a very long time, because it was cobwebby.

Bert pulled both the medal and the sharp thing out from the corner and sat up, now rather dusty himself, to examine the unknown object.

By the light of his candle, he saw a tiny, perfectly carved Ickabog foot, the last remaining piece of the toy carved so long ago by Mr Dovetail. Bert had thought he'd burned up every last bit of the toy, but this foot must have flown under the bed when he'd smashed up the rest of the Ickabog with his poker.

He was on the point of tossing the foot onto his bedroom fire when Bert suddenly changed his mind, and began to examine it more closely.

# CHAPTER 41

# Mrs Beamish's Plan

'Mother,' said Bert.

Mrs Beamish had been sitting at the kitchen table, mending a hole in one of Bert's sweaters and pausing occasionally to wipe her eyes. The Ickabog's attack on their Chouxville neighbour had brought back awful memories of the death of Major Beamish, and she'd just been thinking about that night when she'd kissed his poor, cold hand in the Blue Parlour at the palace, while the rest of him was hidden by the Cornucopian flag.

'Mother, look,' said Bert, in a strange voice, and he set down in front of her the tiny, clawed wooden foot he'd found beneath his bed.

Mrs Beamish picked it up and examined it through the spectacles she wore when sewing by candlelight.

'Why, it's part of that little toy you used to have,' said Bert's mother. 'Your toy Icka…'

But Mrs Beamish didn't finish the word. Still staring at the carved foot, she remembered the monstrous footprints she and Bert had seen earlier that day, in the soft ground around the house of the vanished old lady. Although much, much bigger, the shape of that foot was identical to this, as were the angles of the toes, the scales, and the long claws.

For several minutes, the only sound was the sputtering of the candle, as Mrs Beamish turned the little wooden foot in her trembling fingers.

It was as though a door had flown open inside her mind, a door she'd been keeping blocked and barricaded for a very long time. Ever since her husband had died, Mrs Beamish had refused to admit a single doubt or suspicion about the Ickabog. Loyal to the king, trusting in Spittleworth, she'd believed the people who claimed the Ickabog wasn't real were traitors.

But now the uncomfortable memories she'd tried to shut out came flooding in upon her. She remembered telling the scullery maid all about Mr Dovetail's treasonous speech about the Ickabog, and turning to see Cankerby the footman listening in the shadows. She remembered how soon afterwards the Dovetails had disappeared. She remembered the little girl who'd been skipping, wearing one of Daisy Dovetail's old dresses, and the bandalore she'd claimed her brother had been given on the same day. She thought of her cousin Harold starving, and the strange absence of mail from the north that she and all her neighbours had noticed over the past few months. She thought, too, of the sudden disappearance of Lady Eslanda, which many had puzzled over. These, and a hundred other odd happenings, added themselves together in Mrs Beamish's mind as she gazed at the little wooden foot, and together they formed a monstrous outline that frightened her far more than the Ickabog. What, she asked herself, had really happened to her husband up on that marsh? Why hadn't she been allowed to look beneath the Cornucopian flag covering his body? Horrible thoughts now tumbled on top of each other as Mrs Beamish turned to look at her son, and saw her suspicions reflected in his face.

'The king can't know,' she whispered. 'He can't. He's a good man.'

Even if everything else she'd believed might be wrong, Mrs Beamish couldn't bear to give up her belief in the goodness of King Fred the Fearless. He'd always been so kind to her and Bert.

Mrs Beamish stood up, the little wooden foot clutched tightly in her hand, and laid down Bert's half-darned sweater.

'I'm going to see the king,' she said, with a more determined look on her face than Bert had ever seen there.

'Now?' he asked, looking out into the darkness.

'Tonight,' said Mrs Beamish, 'while there's a chance neither of those lords are with him. He'll see me. He's always liked me.'

'I want to come too,' said Bert, because a strange feeling of foreboding had come over him.

'No,' said Mrs Beamish. She approached her son, put her hand on his shoulder, and looked up into his face. 'Listen to me, Bert. If I'm not back from the palace in one hour, you're to leave Chouxville. Head north to Jeroboam, find Cousin Harold and tell him everything.'

'But—' said Bert, suddenly afraid.

'Promise me you'll go if I'm not back in an hour,' said Mrs Beamish fiercely.

'I... I will,' said Bert, but the boy who'd earlier imagined dying a heroic death, and not caring how much it upset his mother, was suddenly terrified. 'Mother—'

She hugged him briefly. 'You're a clever boy. Never forget, you're a soldier's son, as well as a pastry chef's.'

Mrs Beamish walked quickly to the door and put on her shoes. After one last smile at Bert, she slipped out into the night.

# CHAPTER 42

# Behind the Curtain

The kitchens were dark and empty when Mrs Beamish let herself in from the courtyard. Moving on tiptoe, she peeked around corners as she went, because she knew how Cankerby the footman liked to lurk in the shadows. Slowly and carefully, Mrs Beamish made her way towards the king's private apartments, holding the little wooden foot so tightly in her hand that its sharp claws dug into her palm.

At last she reached the scarlet-carpeted corridor leading to Fred's rooms. Now she could hear laughter coming from behind the doors. Mrs Beamish rightly guessed that Fred hadn't been told about the Ickabog attack on the outskirts of Chouxville, because she was sure he wouldn't be laughing if he had. However, somebody was clearly with the king, and she wanted to see Fred alone. As she stood there, wondering what was best to do, the door ahead opened.

With a gasp, Mrs Beamish dived behind a long velvet curtain and tried to stop it swaying. Spittleworth and Flapoon were laughing and joking with the king as they bade him goodnight.

'Excellent joke, Your Majesty, why, I think I've split my pantaloons!' guffawed Flapoon.

'We shall have to rechristen you King Fred the Funny, sire!' chuckled Spittleworth.

Mrs Beamish held her breath and tried to suck in her tummy. She heard the sound of Fred's door closing. The two lords stopped laughing at once.

'Blithering idiot,' said Flapoon in a low voice.

'I've met cleverer blobs of Kurdsburg cheese,' muttered Spittleworth.

'Can't you take a turn entertaining him tomorrow?' grumbled Flapoon.

'I'll be busy with the tax collectors until three,' said Spittleworth. 'But if—'

Both lords stopped talking. Their footsteps also ceased. Mrs Beamish was still holding her breath, her eyes closed, praying they hadn't noticed the bulge in the curtain.

'Well, goodnight, Spittleworth,' said Flapoon's voice.

'Yes, sleep well, Flapoon,' said Spittleworth.

Very softly, her heart beating very fast, Mrs Beamish let out her breath. It was all right. The two lords were going to bed... and yet she couldn't hear footsteps...

Then, so suddenly she had no time to draw breath into her lungs, the curtain was ripped back. Before she could cry out, Flapoon's large hand had closed over her mouth and Spittleworth had seized her wrists. The two lords dragged Mrs Beamish out of her hiding place and down the nearest set of stairs, and while she struggled and tried to shout, she couldn't make a sound through Flapoon's thick fingers, nor could she wriggle free. At last, they pulled her into that same Blue Parlour where she'd once kissed her dead husband's hand.

'Do not scream,' Spittleworth warned her, pulling out a short dagger he'd taken to wearing, even inside the palace, 'or the king will need a new pastry chef.'

He gestured to Flapoon to take his hand away from Mrs Beamish's mouth. The first thing she did was take a gasp of breath, because she felt like fainting.

'You made an outsized lump in that curtain, cook,' sneered

Spittleworth. 'Exactly what were you doing, lurking there, so close to the king, after the kitchens have closed?'

Mrs Beamish might have made up some silly lie, of course. She could have pretended she wanted to ask King Fred what kinds of cakes he'd like her to make tomorrow, but she knew the two lords wouldn't believe her. So instead she held out the hand clutching the Ickabog foot, and opened her fingers.

'I know,' she said quietly, 'what you're up to.'

The two lords moved closer and peered down at her palm, and the perfect, tiny replica of the huge feet the Dark Footers were using. Spittleworth and Flapoon looked at each other, and then at Mrs Beamish, and all the pastry chef could think, when she saw their expressions, was, *Run, Bert – run!*

*With a gasp, Mrs Beamish dived behind a long velvet curtain
and tried to stop it swaying.*

*By Orla, age 7 years, United Kingdom*

# CHAPTER 43

# Bert and the Guard

The candle on the table beside Bert burned slowly downwards while he watched the minute hand creep around the clock face. He told himself his mother would definitely come home soon. She'd walk in any minute, pick up his half-darned sweater as though she'd never dropped it, and tell him what had happened when she saw the king.

Then the minute hand seemed to speed up, when Bert would have done anything to make it slow down. Four minutes. Three minutes. Two minutes left.

Bert got to his feet and moved to the window. He looked up and down the dark street. There was no sign of his mother returning.

But wait! His heart leapt: he'd seen movement on the corner! For a few shining seconds, Bert was sure he was about to see Mrs Beamish step into the patch of moonlight, smiling as she caught sight of his anxious face at the window.

And then his heart seemed to drop like a brick into his stomach. It wasn't Mrs Beamish who was approaching, but Major Roach, accompanied by four large members of the Ickabog Defence Brigade, all carrying torches.

Bert leapt back from the window, snatched up the sweater from the table, and sprinted through to his bedroom. He grabbed his shoes and his father's medal, forced up the bedroom window, clambered out of it, then gently slid the window closed from outside. As he dropped down into the vegetable patch, he heard Major Roach banging on the front door, then a rough voice said: 'I'll check the back.'

Bert threw himself flat in the earth behind a row of beetroots, smeared his fair hair with soil and lay very still in the darkness.

Through his closed eyelids he saw flickering light. A soldier held his torch high in hopes of seeing Bert running away across other people's gardens. The soldier didn't notice the earthy shape of Bert concealed behind the beetroot leaves, which threw long, swaying shadows.

'Well, he hasn't got out this way,' shouted the soldier.

There was a crash, and Bert knew Roach had broken down the front door. He listened to the soldiers opening cupboards and wardrobes. Bert remained utterly still in the earth, because torchlight was still shining through his closed eyelids.

'Maybe he cleared out before his mother went to the palace?'

'Well, we've got to find him,' growled the familiar voice of Major Roach. 'He's the son of the Ickabog's first victim. If Bert Beamish starts telling the world the monster's a lie, people will listen. Spread out and search, he can't have got far. And if you catch him,' said Roach, as his men's heavy footsteps sounded across the Beamishes' wooden floorboards, 'kill him. We'll work out our stories later.'

Bert lay completely flat and still, listening to the men running away up and down the street, and then a cool part of Bert's brain said:

*Move.*

He put his father's medal around his neck, pulled on the half-darned sweater and snatched up his shoes, then began to crawl through the earth until he reached a neighbouring fence, where he tunnelled out enough dirt to let him wriggle beneath it. He kept crawling until he reached a cobbled street, but he could still hear the soldiers' voices echoing through the night as they banged on doors, demanding to search houses, asking people whether they'd seen Bert Beamish, the pastry chef's son.

He heard himself described as a dangerous traitor.

Bert took another handful of earth and smeared it over his face. Then he got to his feet and, crouching low, darted into a dark doorway across the street. A soldier ran past, but Bert was now so filthy that he was well camouflaged against the dark door, and the man noticed nothing. When the soldier had disappeared, Bert ran barefooted from doorway to doorway, carrying his shoes, hiding in shadowy alcoves and edging ever closer to the City-Within-The-City gates. However, when he drew near, he saw a guard keeping watch, and before Bert could think up a plan, he had to slide behind a statue of King Richard the Righteous, because Roach and another soldier were approaching.

'Have you seen Bert Beamish?' they shouted at the guard.

'What, the pastry chef's son?' asked the man.

Roach seized the front of the man's uniform and shook him as a terrier shakes a rabbit. 'Of course, the pastry chef's son! Have you let him through these gates? Tell me!'

'No, I haven't,' said the guard, 'and what's the boy done, to have you lot chasing him?'

'He's a traitor!' snarled Roach. 'And I'll personally shoot anyone who helps him, understood?'

'Understood,' said the guard. Roach released the man and he and his companion ran off again, their torches casting swinging pools of light on all the walls, until they were swallowed once more by the darkness.

Bert watched the guard straighten his uniform and shake his head. Bert hesitated, then, knowing this might cost him his life, crept out of his hiding place. So thoroughly had Bert camouflaged himself with all the earth, that the guard didn't realise anyone was beside him until he saw the whites of Bert's eyes in the moonlight, and he let out a yelp of terror.

'Please,' whispered Bert. 'Please… don't give me away. I need to get out of here.'

From beneath his sweater, he pulled his father's heavy silver medal, brushed earth from the surface, and showed the guard.

'I'll give you this – it's real silver! – if you just let me out through the gates, and don't tell anyone you've seen me. I'm not a traitor,' said Bert. 'I haven't betrayed anyone, I swear.'

The guard was an older man, with a stiff grey beard. He considered the earth-covered Bert for a moment or two before saying:

'Keep your medal, son.'

He opened the gate just wide enough for Bert to slide through.

'Thank you!' gasped Bert.

'Stick to the back roads,' advised the guard. 'And trust no one. Good luck.'

*Bert threw himself flat in the earth behind a row of beetroots, smeared his fair hair with soil and lay very still in the darkness.*

*By Mahli, age 12 years, Australia*

# CHAPTER 44

# Mrs Beamish Fights Back

While Bert was slipping out of the city gates, Mrs Beamish was being shunted into a cell in the dungeons by Lord Spittleworth. A cracked, reedy voice nearby sang the national anthem in time to hammer blows.

'Be quiet!' bellowed Spittleworth towards the wall. The singing stopped.

'When I finish this foot, my lord,' said the broken voice, 'will you let me out to see my daughter?'

'Yes, yes, you'll see your daughter,' Spittleworth called back, rolling his eyes. 'Now, be quiet, because I want to talk to your neighbour!'

'Well, before you get started, my lord,' said Mrs Beamish, 'I've got a few things I want to say to *you*.'

Spittleworth and Flapoon stared at the plump little woman. Never had they placed anyone in the dungeons who looked so proud and unconcerned at being slung in this dank, cold place. Spittleworth was reminded of Lady Eslanda, who was still shut up in his library, and still refusing to marry him. He'd never imagined a cook could look as haughty as a lady.

'Firstly,' said Mrs Beamish, 'if you kill me, the king will know. He'll notice I'm not making his pastries. He can taste the difference.'

'That's true,' said Spittleworth, with a cruel smile. 'However, as the king will believe that you've been killed by the Ickabog, he'll simply have to get used to his pastries tasting different, won't he?'

'My house lies in the shadow of the palace walls,' countered Mrs Beamish. 'It will be impossible to fake an Ickabog attack there without waking up a hundred witnesses.'

'That's easily solved,' said Spittleworth. 'We'll say you were foolish enough to take a night-time stroll down by the banks of the River Fluma, where the Ickabog was having a drink.'

'Which might have worked,' said Mrs Beamish, making up a story off the top of her head, 'if I hadn't left certain instructions, to be carried out if word gets out that I've been killed by the Ickabog.'

'What instructions, and whom have you given them to?' said Flapoon.

'Her son, I daresay,' said Spittleworth, 'but he'll soon be in our power. Make a note, Flapoon – we only kill the cook once we've killed her son.'

'In the meantime,' said Mrs Beamish, pretending she hadn't felt an icy stab of terror at the thought of Bert falling into Spittleworth's hands, 'you might as well equip this cell properly with a stove and all my regular implements, so I can keep making cakes for the king.'

'Yes... Why not?' said Spittleworth slowly. 'We all enjoy your pastries, Mrs Beamish. You may continue to cook for the king until your son is caught.'

'Good,' said Mrs Beamish, 'but I'm going to need assistance. I suggest I train up some of my fellow prisoners who can at least whisk the egg whites and line my baking trays.

'That will require you to feed the poor fellows a little more. I noticed as you marched me through here that some of them look like skeletons. I can't have them eating all my raw ingredients because they're starving.

'And lastly,' said Mrs Beamish, giving her cell a sweeping glance, 'I shall need a comfortable bed and some clean blankets if I'm to get enough sleep to produce cakes of the quality the king demands. It's his birthday coming up too. He'll be expecting something very special.'

Spittleworth eyed this most surprising captive for a moment or two, then said:

'Doesn't it alarm you, madam, to think that you and your child will soon be dead?'

'Oh, if there's one thing you learn at cookery school,' said Mrs Beamish, with a shrug, 'burned crusts and soggy bases happen to the best of us. Roll up your sleeves and start something else, I say. No point moaning over what you can't fix!'

As Spittleworth couldn't think of a good retort to this, he beckoned to Flapoon and the two lords left the cell, the door clanging shut behind them.

As soon as they'd gone, Mrs Beamish stopped pretending to be brave and dropped down onto the hard bed, which was the only piece of furniture in the cell. She was shaking all over and for a moment, she was afraid that she was going to have hysterics.

However, a woman didn't rise to be in charge of the king's kitchens, in a city of the finest pastry-makers on earth, without being able to manage her own nerves. Mrs Beamish took a deep, steadying breath and then, hearing the reedy voice next door break into the national anthem again, she pressed her ear to the wall, and began to listen for the place where the noise was coming into her cell. At last she found a crack near the ceiling. Standing on her bed, she called softly: 'Dan? Daniel Dovetail? I know that's you. This is Bertha, Bertha Beamish!'

But the broken voice only continued to sing. Mrs Beamish sank back down on her bed, wrapped her arms around herself, closed her eyes and prayed with every part of her aching heart that wherever Bert was, he was safe.

# CHAPTER 45

# Bert in Jeroboam

At first, Bert didn't realise that the whole of Cornucopia had been warned by Lord Spittleworth to watch out for him. Following the guard's advice at the city gates, he kept to country lanes and back roads. He'd never been as far north as Jeroboam, but by roughly following the course of the River Fluma, he knew he must be travelling in the right direction.

Hair matted and shoes clogged with mud, he walked across ploughed fields and slept in ditches. Not until he sneaked into Kurdsburg on the third night, to try and find something to eat, did he come face-to-face for the first time with a picture of himself on a *Wanted* poster, taped up in a cheesemonger's window. Luckily, the drawing of a neat, smiling young man looked nothing like the reflection of the grubby tramp he saw staring out of the dark glass beside it. Nevertheless, it was a shock to see that there was a reward of one hundred ducats on his head, dead or alive.

Bert hurried on through the dark streets, passing skinny dogs and boarded-up windows. Once or twice he came across other grubby, ragged people who were also foraging in bins. At last he managed to retrieve a lump of hard and slightly mouldy cheese before anyone else could grab it. After taking a drink of rainwater from a barrel behind a disused dairy, he hurried back out of Kurdsburg and returned to the country roads.

All the time he walked, Bert's thoughts kept scurrying back to his mother. *They won't kill her*, he told himself, over and over again. *They'll never kill her. She's the king's favourite servant. They wouldn't dare.* He had to block the possibility of his mother's death from his mind, because if he thought she'd gone, he knew he might not have the strength to get out of the next ditch he slept in.

Bert's feet soon blistered, because he was walking miles out of his way to avoid meeting other people. The next night, he stole the last few rotting apples from an orchard, and the night after that, he took the carcass of a chicken from somebody's dustbin, and gnawed off the last few scraps of meat. By the time he saw the dark grey outline of Jeroboam on the horizon, he'd had to steal a length of twine from a blacksmith's yard to use as a belt, because he'd lost so much weight that his trousers were falling down.

All through his journey, Bert told himself that if he could only find Cousin Harold, everything would be all right: he'd lay down his troubles at the feet of a grown-up, and Harold would sort everything out. Bert lurked outside the city walls until it was growing dark, then limped into the winemaking city, his blisters now hurting terribly, and headed for Harold's tavern.

There were no lights in the window and when Bert drew near, he saw why. The doors and windows had all been boarded up. The tavern had gone out of business and Harold and his family seemed to have left.

'Please,' the desperate Bert asked a passing woman, 'can you tell me where Harold's gone? Harold, who used to own this tavern?'

'Harold?' said the woman. 'Oh, he went south a week ago. He's got relatives down in Chouxville. He's hoping to get a job with the king.'

Stunned, Bert watched the woman walk away into the night. A chilly wind blew around him, and out of the corner of his eye he saw one of his own *Wanted* posters fluttering on a nearby lantern post. Exhausted, and with no idea what to do next, he imagined sitting down on this cold doorstep and simply waiting for the soldiers to find him.

It was then he felt the point of a sword at his back, and a voice in his ear said:

'*Got you.*'

*The doors and windows had all been boarded up. The tavern had gone out of business and Harold and his family seemed to have left.*

By Divyanshi, age 8 years, India

# CHAPTER 46

# The Tale of Roderick Roach

You might think Bert would be terrified at the sound of these words, but believe it or not, the voice filled him with relief. He'd recognised it, you see. So instead of putting up his hands, or pleading for his life, he turned around, and found himself looking at Roderick Roach.

'What are you smiling about?' growled Roderick, staring into Bert's filthy face.

'I know you're not going to stab me, Roddy,' said Bert quietly.

Even though Roderick was the one holding the sword, Bert could tell the other boy was far more scared than he was. The shivering Roderick was wearing a coat over his pyjamas and his feet were wrapped in bloodstained rags.

'Have you walked all the way from Chouxville like that?' asked Bert.

'That's none of your business!' spat Roderick, trying to look fierce, though his teeth were chattering. 'I'm taking you in, Beamish, you traitor!'

'No, you aren't,' said Bert and he pulled the sword out of Roderick's hand. At that, Roderick burst into tears.

'Come on,' said Bert kindly, and he put his arm round Roderick's shoulders and led him off down a side alley, away from the fluttering *Wanted* poster.

'Get off,' sobbed Roderick, shrugging away Bert's arm. 'Get off me! It's all your fault!'

'What's my fault?' asked Bert, as the two boys came to a halt beside some bins full of empty wine bottles.

'You ran away from my father!' said Roderick, wiping his eyes on his sleeve.

'Well, of course I did,' said Bert reasonably. 'He wanted to kill me.'

'But n – now *he's* been – been killed!' sobbed Roderick.

'Major Roach is dead?' said Bert, taken aback. 'How?'

'Sp – Spittleworth,' sobbed Roderick. 'He c – came t – to our house with soldiers when n – nobody could find you. He was so angry Father hadn't caught you – he grabbed a soldier's gun – and he...'

Roderick sat down on a dustbin and wept. A cold wind blew down the alleyway. This, Bert thought, showed just how dangerous Spittleworth was. If he could shoot dead his faithful head of the Royal Guard, nobody was safe.

'How did you know I'd come to Jeroboam?' Bert asked.

'C – Cankerby from the palace told me. I gave him five ducats. He remembered your mother talking about your cousin owning a tavern.'

'How many people d'you think Cankerby's told?' asked Bert, now worried.

'Plenty, probably,' said Roderick, mopping his face with his pyjama sleeve. 'He'll sell anyone information for gold.'

'That's rich, coming from you,' said Bert, getting angry. 'You were about to sell me for a hundred ducats!'

'I d – didn't want the g – gold,' said Roderick. 'It was for my m – mother and brothers. I thought I might be able to g – get them back if I turned you in. Spittleworth t – took them away. I escaped out of my bedroom window. That's why I'm in my pyjamas.'

'I escaped from my bedroom window too,' said Bert. 'But at least I had the sense to bring shoes. Come on, we'd better get out of here,' he added, pulling Roderick to his feet. 'We'll try and steal you some socks off a washing line on the way.'

But they'd taken barely a couple of steps when a man's voice spoke from behind them.

'Hands up! You two are coming with me!'

Both boys raised their hands and turned round. A man with a dirty, mean face had just emerged from the shadows, and was pointing a rifle at them. He wasn't in uniform and neither Bert nor Roderick recognised him, but Daisy Dovetail could have told them exactly who this was: Basher John, Ma Grunter's deputy, now a full-grown man.

Basher John took a few steps closer, squinting from one boy to the other. 'Yeah,' he said. 'You two'll do. Gimme that sword.'

With a rifle pointed at his chest, Bert had no choice but to hand it over. However, he wasn't quite as scared as he might have been, because Bert – whatever Flapoon might have told him – was actually a very clever boy. This dirty-looking man didn't seem to realise he'd just caught a fugitive worth one hundred gold ducats. He seemed to have been looking for *any* two boys, though why, Bert couldn't imagine. Roderick, on the other hand, had turned deathly pale. He knew Spittleworth had spies in every city, and was convinced they were both about to be handed over to the Chief Advisor, and that he, Roderick Roach, would be put to death for being in league with a traitor.

'Move,' said the blunt-faced man, gesturing them out of the alley with his rifle. With the gun at their backs, Bert and Roderick were forced away through the dark streets of Jeroboam until, finally, they reached the door of Ma Grunter's orphanage.

## CHAPTER 47

# Down in the Dungeons

The kitchen workers in the palace were most surprised to hear from Lord Spittleworth that Mrs Beamish had requested her own, separate kitchen, because she was so much more important than they were. Indeed, some of them were suspicious, because Mrs Beamish had never been stuck up, in all the years they'd known her. However, as her cakes and pastries were still appearing regularly at the king's table, they knew she was alive, wherever she was, and like many of their fellow countrymen, the servants decided it was safest not to ask questions.

Meanwhile, life in the palace dungeons had been utterly transformed. A stove had been fitted in Mrs Beamish's cell, her pots and pans had been brought down from the kitchens, and the prisoners in neighbouring cells had been trained up to help her perform the different tasks that went into producing the feather-light pastries that made her the best baker in the kingdom. She demanded the doubling of the prisoners' rations (to make sure they were strong enough to whisk and fold, to measure and weigh, to sift and pour) and a rat-catcher to clean the place of vermin, and a servant to run between the cells, handing out different implements through the bars.

The heat from the stove dried out the damp walls. Delicious smells replaced the stench of mould and dank water. Mrs Beamish insisted that each of the prisoners had to taste a finished cake, so that they understood the results of their efforts. Slowly, the dungeon started to be a place of activity, even of cheerfulness, and prisoners who'd been weak and starving before Mrs Beamish arrived were gradually fattening up. In this way she kept busy, and tried to distract herself from her worries about Bert.

All the time the rest of the prisoners baked, Mr Dovetail sang the national anthem, and kept carving giant Ickabog feet in the cell next door. His singing and banging had enraged the other prisoners before Mrs Beamish arrived, but now she encouraged everyone to join in with him. The sound of all the prisoners singing the national anthem drowned out the perpetual noises of his hammer and chisel, and the best of it was that when Spittleworth ran down into the dungeons to tell them to stop making such a racket, Mrs Beamish said innocently that surely it was treason, to stop people singing the national anthem? Spittleworth looked foolish at that, and all the prisoners bellowed with laughter. With a leap of joy, Mrs Beamish thought she heard a weak, wheezy chuckle from the cell next door.

Mrs Beamish might not have known much about madness, but she knew how to rescue things that seemed spoiled, like curdled sauces and falling soufflés. She believed Mr Dovetail's broken mind might yet be mended, if only he could be brought to understand that he wasn't alone, and to remember who he was. And so every now and then Mrs Beamish would suggest songs other than the national anthem, trying to jolt Mr Dovetail's poor mind onto a different course that might bring him back to himself.

And at last, to her amazement and joy, she heard him joining in with the Ickabog drinking song, which had been popular even in the days long before people thought the monster was real.

*'I drank a single bottle and the Ickabog's a lie,*
*I drank another bottle, and I thought I heard it sigh,*

*And now I've drunk another, I can see it slinking by,*
*The Ickabog is coming, so let's drink before we die!'*

Setting down the tray of cakes she'd just taken out of the stove, Mrs Beamish jumped up onto her bed, and spoke softly through the crack high in the wall.

'Daniel Dovetail, I heard you singing that silly song. It's Bertha Beamish here, your old friend. Remember me? We used to sing that a long time ago, when the children were tiny. My Bert, and your Daisy. D'you remember that, Dan?'

She waited for a response and in a little while, she thought she heard a sob.

You may think this strange, but Mrs Beamish was glad to hear Mr Dovetail cry, because tears can heal a mind, as well as laughter. And that night, and for many nights afterwards, Mrs Beamish talked softly to Mr Dovetail through the crack in the wall, and after a while he began to talk back. Mrs Beamish told Mr Dovetail how terribly she regretted telling the kitchen maid what he'd said about the Ickabog, and Mr Dovetail told her how wretched he'd felt, afterwards, for suggesting that Major Beamish had fallen off his horse. And each promised the other that their child was alive, because they had to believe it, or die.

A freezing chill was now stealing into the dungeons through its one high, tiny, barred window. The prisoners could tell a hard winter was approaching, yet the dungeon had become a place of hope and healing. Mrs Beamish demanded more blankets for all her helpers and kept her stove burning all night, determined that they would survive.

*A freezing chill was now stealing into the dungeons through its one high,
tiny, barred window.*

By Rowan, age 12 years, United Kingdom

## CHAPTER 48

# Bert and Daisy Find Each Other

The chill of winter was felt in Ma Grunter's orphanage too. Children in rags who are fed only on cabbage soup cannot withstand coughs and colds as easily as children who are well fed. The little cemetery at the back of the orphanage saw a steady stream of Johns and Janes who'd died for lack of food, and warmth, and love, and they were buried without anybody knowing their real names, although the other children mourned them.

The sudden spate of deaths was the reason Ma Grunter had sent Basher John out onto the streets of Jeroboam, to round up as many homeless children as he could find, to keep up her numbers. Inspectors came to visit three times a year to make sure she wasn't lying about how many children were in her care. She preferred to take in older children, if possible, because they were hardier than the little ones.

The gold she received for each child had now made Ma Grunter's private rooms in the orphanage some of the most luxurious in Cornucopia, with a blazing fire and deep velvet armchairs, thick silk rugs and a bed with soft woollen blankets. Her table was always provided with the finest food and wine. The starving children caught whiffs of heaven as Baronstown pies and Kurdsburg cheeses passed into Ma Grunter's apartment. She rarely left her rooms now except to greet the inspectors, leaving Basher John to manage the children.

Daisy Dovetail paid little attention to the two new boys when they first arrived. They were dirty and ragged, as were all newcomers, and Daisy and Martha were busy trying to keep as many of the smaller children alive as was possible. They went hungry themselves to make sure the little ones got enough to eat, and Daisy carried bruises from Basher John's cane because she often inserted herself between him and a smaller child he was trying to hit. If she thought about the new boys at all, it was to despise them for agreeing to be called John without putting up any sort of fight. She wasn't to know that it suited the two boys very well for nobody to know their real names.

A week after Bert and Roderick arrived at the orphanage, Daisy and her best friend Martha held a secret birthday party for Hetty Hopkins's twins. Many of the youngest children didn't know when their birthdays were, so Daisy picked a date for them, and always made sure it was celebrated, if only with a double portion of cabbage soup. She and Martha always encouraged the little ones to remember their real names too, although they taught them to call each other John and Jane in front of Basher John.

Daisy had a special treat for the twins. She'd actually managed to steal two real Chouxville pastries from a delivery for Ma Grunter several days before, and saved them for the twins' birthday, even though the smell of the pastries had tortured Daisy and it had been hard to resist eating them herself.

'Oh, it's lovely,' sighed the little girl through tears of joy.

'Lovely,' echoed her brother.

'Those came from Chouxville, which is the capital,' Daisy told them. She tried to teach the smaller children the things she remembered from her own interrupted schooldays, and often described the cities they'd never seen. Martha liked hearing about Kurdsburg, Baronstown, and

Chouxville too, because she'd never lived anywhere but the Marshlands and Ma Grunter's orphanage.

The twins had just swallowed the last crumbs of their pastries, when Basher John came bursting into the room. Daisy tried to hide the plate, on which was a trace of cream, but Basher John had spotted it.

'You,' he bellowed, approaching Daisy with the cane held up over his head, 'have been stealing again, Ugly Jane!' He was about to bring it down on her when he suddenly found it caught in mid-air. Bert had heard the shouting and gone to find out what was going on. Seeing that Basher John had cornered a skinny girl in much-patched overalls, Bert grabbed and held the cane on the way down.

'Don't you dare,' Bert told Basher John in a low growl. For the first time, Daisy heard the new boy's Chouxville accent, but he looked so different to the Bert she'd once known, so much older, so much harder-faced, that she didn't recognise him. As for Bert, who remembered Daisy as a little olive-skinned girl with brown pigtails, he had no idea he'd ever met the girl with the burning eyes before.

Basher John tried to pull his cane free of Bert's grip, but Roderick came to Bert's aid. There was a short fight, and for the first time in any of the children's memories, Basher John lost. Finally, vowing revenge, he left the room with a cut lip, and word spread in whispers around the orphanage that the two new boys had rescued Daisy and the twins, and that Basher John had slunk off looking stupid.

Later that evening, when all the orphanage children were settling down for bed, Bert and Daisy passed each other on an upstairs landing, and they paused, a little awkwardly, to talk to each other.

'Thank you very much,' said Daisy, 'for earlier.'

'You're welcome,' said Bert. 'Does he often behave like that?'

'Quite often,' said Daisy, with a little shrug. 'But the twins got their pastries. I'm very grateful.'

Bert now thought he saw something familiar in the shape of Daisy's face, and heard the trace of Chouxville in her voice. Then he looked down at the ancient, much-washed overalls, onto which Daisy had had to sew extra lengths to the legs.

'What's your name?' he asked.

Daisy glanced around to make sure they weren't being overheard.

'Daisy,' she said. 'But you must remember to call me Jane when Basher John's around.'

'Daisy,' gasped Bert. 'Daisy – *it's me! Bert Beamish!*'

Daisy's mouth fell open, and before they knew it, they were hugging and crying, as though they'd been transformed back into small children in those sunlit days in the palace courtyard, before Daisy's mother had died, and Bert's father had been killed, when Cornucopia had seemed the happiest place on earth.

# CHAPTER 49

# Escape from Ma Grunter's

Children generally stayed at Ma Grunter's orphanage until she threw them out onto the street. She received no gold for looking after grown men and women, and had allowed Basher John to stay only because he was useful to her. While they were still worth gold, Ma Grunter made sure no children escaped by keeping all doors securely locked and bolted. Only Basher John had keys, and the last boy who'd tried to steal them had spent months recovering from his injuries.

Daisy and Martha both knew the time was coming when they'd be thrown out, but they were less worried for themselves than for what would become of the little ones once they were gone. Bert and Roderick knew they'd have to leave around the same time, if not sooner. They weren't able to check and see whether *Wanted* posters with Bert's face on them were still stuck to the walls of Jeroboam, but it seemed unlikely they'd been taken down. The four lived in daily dread that Ma Grunter and Basher John would realise they had a valuable fugitive worth one hundred gold ducats under their roof.

In the meantime, Bert, Daisy, Martha, and Roderick met every night, while the other children were asleep, to share their stories and pool their knowledge about what was going on in Cornucopia. They held these meetings in the only place Basher John never went: the large cabbage cupboard in the kitchen.

Roderick, who'd been raised to make jokes about the Marshlanders, laughed at Martha's accent during the first of these meetings, but Daisy told him off so fiercely that he didn't do it again.

Huddled around a single candle as though it were a fire, amid mounds of tough, smelly cabbages, Daisy told the boys about her kidnap, Bert shared his fear that his father had died in some kind of accident, and Roderick explained about the way the Dark Footers faked attacks on towns to keep people believing in the Ickabog. He also told the others about how the mail was intercepted, how the two lords were stealing wagon-loads of gold from the country, and that hundreds of people had been killed, or, if they were useful to Spittleworth in some way, imprisoned.

However, each of the boys was hiding something, and I'll tell you what it was.

Roderick suspected that Major Beamish had been accidentally shot on the marsh all those years ago, but he hadn't told Bert that, because he was scared his friend would blame him for not telling him sooner.

Meanwhile, Bert, who was certain Mr Dovetail had carved the giant feet the Dark Footers were using, didn't tell Daisy so. You see, he was certain Mr Dovetail must have been killed after making them, and he didn't want to give Daisy false hope that he was still alive. As Roderick didn't know who'd carved the many sets of feet used by the Dark Footers, Daisy had no idea about her father's part in the attacks.

'But what about the soldiers?' Daisy asked Roderick, on the sixth night they met in the cabbage cupboard. 'The Ickabog Defence Brigade and the Royal Guard? Are they in on it?'

'I think they must be, a bit,' said Roderick. 'But only the very top people know everything – the two lords and my – and whoever's replaced my father.' He fell silent for a while.

'The soldiers must know there is no Ickabog,' said Bert, 'after all the time they've spent up in the Marshlands.'

'There *is* an Ickabog, though,' said Martha. Roddy didn't laugh, though he might have done if he'd just met her. Daisy ignored Martha, as she usually did, but Bert said kindly: 'I believed in it myself, until I realised what was really going on.'

The foursome went off to bed later that night, agreeing to meet again the following evening. Each was burning with the ambition to save the country, but they kept coming back to the fact that without weapons, they could hardly fight Spittleworth and his many soldiers.

However, when the girls arrived in the cabbage cupboard on the seventh night, Bert knew from their expressions that something bad had happened.

'Trouble,' whispered Daisy, as soon as Martha had closed the cupboard door. 'We heard Ma Grunter and Basher John talking, just before we went to bed. There's an orphanage inspector on the way. He'll be here tomorrow afternoon.'

The boys looked at each other, extremely worried. The last thing they wanted was for an outsider to recognise them as two fugitives.

'We have to leave,' said Bert to Roderick. 'Now. Tonight. Together, we can manage to get the keys from Basher John.'

'I'm game,' said Roderick, clenching his fists.

'Well, Martha and I are coming with you,' said Daisy. 'We've thought of a plan.'

'What plan?' asked Bert.

'I say the four of us head north, to the soldiers' camp in the Marshlands,' said Daisy. 'Martha knows the way, she can guide us. When we get there, we tell the soldiers everything Roderick's told us – about the Ickabog being fake—'

'It's real, though,' said Martha, but the other three ignored her.

'—and about the killings and all the gold Spittleworth and Flapoon are stealing from the country. We can't take on Spittleworth alone. There must be *some* good soldiers, who'd stop obeying him, and help us take the country back!'

'It's a good plan,' said Bert slowly, 'but I don't think you girls should come. It might be dangerous. Roderick and I will do it.'

'No, Bert,' said Daisy, her eyes almost feverish. 'With four of us, we double the number of soldiers we can talk to. Please don't argue. Unless something changes, soon, most of the children in this orphanage will be in that cemetery before the winter's over.'

It took a little more argument for Bert to agree that the two girls should come, because he privately worried that Daisy and Martha were too frail to make the journey, but at last he agreed.

'All right. You'd better grab your blankets off your beds, because it's going to be a long, cold walk. Roddy and I will deal with Basher John.'

So Bert and Roderick sneaked into Basher John's room. The fight was short and brutal. It was lucky Ma Grunter had drunk two whole bottles of wine with her dinner, because otherwise all the banging and shouting would definitely have woken her. Leaving Basher John bloody and bruised, Roderick stole his boots. Then, they locked him in his own room and the two boys sprinted to join the girls, who were waiting beside the front door. It took five long minutes to unfasten all the padlocks and loosen all the chains.

A blast of icy air met them as they opened the door. With one last glance back at the orphanage, threadbare blankets around their shoulders, Daisy, Bert, Martha, and Roderick slipped out onto the street and set off for the Marshlands through the first few flakes of snow.

# CHAPTER 50

# A Winter's Journey

No harder journey had been made, in all of Cornucopia's history, than the trek of those four young people to the Marshlands.

It was the bitterest winter the kingdom had seen for a hundred years, and by the time the dark outline of Jeroboam had vanished behind them, the snow was falling so thickly it dazzled their eyes with whiteness. Their thin, patched clothes and their torn blankets were no match for the freezing air, which bit at every part of them like tiny, sharp-toothed wolves.

If not for Martha, it would have been impossible to find their way, but she was familiar with the country north of Jeroboam and, in spite of the thick snow now covering every landmark, she recognised old trees she used to climb, odd-shaped rocks that had always been there, and ramshackle sheep sheds that had once belonged to neighbours. Even so, the further north they travelled, the more all of them wondered in their hearts whether the journey would kill them, though they never spoke the thought aloud. Each felt their body plead with them to stop, to lie down in the icy straw of some abandoned barn, and give up.

On the third night, Martha knew they were close, because she could smell the familiar ooze and brackish water of the marsh. All of them regained a little hope: they strained their eyes for any sign of torches and fires in the soldiers' encampment, and imagined they heard men talking, and the jingling of horses' harnesses, through the whistling wind. Every now and then they saw a glint in the distance, or heard a noise, but it was always just the moonlight reflecting on a frozen puddle, or a tree creaking in the blizzard.

At last they reached the edge of the wide expanse of rock, marsh, and rustling weed, and they realised there were no soldiers there at all.

The winter storms had caused a retreat. The commander, who was privately certain there was no Ickabog, had decided that he wasn't going to let his men freeze to death just to please Lord Spittleworth. So he'd given the order to head south, and if it hadn't been for the thick snow, which was still falling so fast it covered all tracks, the friends might have been able to see the soldiers' five-day-old footprints, going in the opposite direction.

'Look,' said Roderick, pointing as he shivered. 'They *were* here...'

A wagon had been abandoned in the snow because it had got stuck, and the soldiers wanted to escape the storm quickly. The foursome approached the wagon and saw food, food such as Bert, Daisy, and Roderick remembered only from their dreams, and which Martha had never seen in her life. Heaps of creamy Kurdsburg cheeses, piles of Chouxville pastries, sausages and venison pies of Baronstown, all sent to keep the camp commander and his soldiers happy, because there was no food to be had in the Marshlands.

Bert reached out numb fingers to try and take a pie, but a thick layer of ice now covered the food, and his fingers simply slid off.

He turned a hopeless face to Daisy, Martha, and Roderick, all of whose lips were now blue. Nobody said anything. They knew they were going to die of cold on the edge of the Ickabog's marsh and none of them really cared any longer. Daisy was so cold that to sleep forever seemed a wonderful idea. She barely felt the added chill as she sank slowly into the snow. Bert sank down and put his arms around her, but he too was feeling sleepy and strange. Martha leant up against Roderick, who tried to draw her under his blanket. Huddled together beside the wagon, all four were soon unconscious, and the snow crept up their bodies as the moon began to rise.

And then a vast shadow rippled over them. Two enormous arms covered in long green hair, like marsh weed, descended upon the four friends. As easily as if they were babies, the Ickabog scooped them up and bore them away across the marsh.

*A wagon had been abandoned in the snow because it had got stuck, and the soldiers wanted to escape the storm quickly.*

*By Eliana, age 11 years, New Zealand*

# CHAPTER 51

# Inside the Cave

Some hours later, Daisy woke up, but at first she didn't open her eyes. She couldn't remember being this cosy since childhood, when she'd slept beneath a patchwork quilt stitched by her mother, and woken every winter morning to the sound of a fire crackling in her grate. She could hear the fire crackling now, and smell venison pies heating in the oven, so she knew she must be dreaming that she was back at home with both her parents.

But the sound of flames and the smell of pie were so real it then occurred to Daisy that instead of dreaming, she might be in heaven. Perhaps she'd frozen to death on the edge of the marsh? Without moving her body, she opened her eyes and saw a flickering fire, and the rough-hewn walls of what seemed to be a very large cavern, and she realised she and her three companions were lying in a large nest of what seemed to be unspun sheep's wool.

There was a gigantic rock beside the fire, which was covered with long greenish-brown marsh weed. Daisy gazed at this rock until her eyes became accustomed to the semi-darkness. Only then did she realise that the rock, which was as tall as two horses, was looking back at her.

Even though the old stories said the Ickabog looked like a dragon, or a serpent, or a drifting ghoul, Daisy knew at once that this was the real thing. In panic, she closed her eyes again, reached out a hand through the soft mass of sheep's wool, found one of the others' backs, and poked it.

'What?' whispered Bert.

'Have you seen it?' whispered Daisy, eyes still tightly shut.

'Yes,' breathed Bert. 'Don't look at it.'

'I'm not,' said Daisy.

'I *told* you there was an Ickabog,' came Martha's terrified whisper.

'I think it's cooking pies,' whispered Roderick.

All four lay quite still, with their eyes closed, until the smell of venison pie became so deliciously overpowering that each of them felt it would be almost worth dying to jump up, snatch a pie and maybe wolf down a few mouthfuls before the Ickabog could kill them.

Then they heard the monster moving. Its long coarse hair rustled, and its heavy feet made loud muffled thumps. There was a clunk, as though the monster had laid down something heavy. Then a low, booming voice said:

'Eat them.'

All four opened their eyes.

You might think the fact that the Ickabog could speak their language would be a huge shock, but they were already so stunned that the monster was real, that it knew how to make fires and that it was cooking venison pies, that they barely stopped to consider that point. The Ickabog had placed a rough-hewn wooden platter of pies beside them on the floor, and they realised that it must have taken them from the frozen stock of food on the abandoned wagon.

Slowly and cautiously, the four friends moved into sitting positions, staring up into the large, mournful eyes of the Ickabog, which peered at them through the tangle of long, coarse, greenish hair that covered it from head to foot. Roughly shaped like a person, it had a truly enormous belly, and huge shaggy paws, each of which had a single sharp claw.

'What do you want with us?' asked Bert, bravely.

In its deep, booming voice the Ickabog replied:

'I'm going to eat you. But not yet.'

The Ickabog turned, picked up a pair of baskets, which were woven from strips of bark, and walked away to the mouth of the cave. Then, as though a sudden thought had struck it, the Ickabog turned back to them and said, 'Roar.'

It didn't actually roar. It simply said the word. The four humans stared at the Ickabog, which blinked, then turned round and walked out of the cave, a basket in each paw. Then a boulder as large as the cave mouth rumbled its way across the entrance, to keep the prisoners inside. They listened as the Ickabog's footsteps crunched through the snow outside, and died away.

*The Ickabog... peered at them through the tangle of long, coarse,*
*greenish hair that covered it from head to foot.*

*By Aron, age 7 years, India*

# CHAPTER 52

# Mushrooms

Never would Daisy and Martha forget the taste of those Baronstown pies, after the long years of cabbage soup at Ma Grunter's. Indeed, Martha burst into tears after the first bite, and said she'd never known food could be like this. All of them forgot about the Ickabog while eating. Once they'd finished the pies, they felt braver, and they got up to explore the Ickabog's cave by the light of the fire.

'Look,' said Daisy, who'd found drawings on the wall.

A hundred shaggy Ickabogs were being chased by stickmen with spears.

'See this one!' said Roderick, pointing at a drawing close to the mouth of the cave.

By the light of the Ickabog's fire, the foursome examined a picture of a lone Ickabog, standing face-to-face with a stick figure wearing a plumed helmet and holding a sword.

'That looks like the king,' whispered Daisy, pointing at the figure. 'You don't think he *really* saw the Ickabog that night, do you?'

The others couldn't answer, of course, but I can. I'll tell you the whole truth now, and I hope you won't be annoyed that I didn't before.

Fred really *did* catch a glimpse of the Ickabog in the thick marsh mist, that fatal night when Major Beamish was shot. I can also tell you that the following morning, the old shepherd who'd thought his dog had been eaten by the Ickabog heard a whining and scratching at the door, and realised that faithful Patch had come home again, because, of course, Spittleworth had set the dog free from the brambles in which he was trapped.

Before you judge the old shepherd too harshly for not letting the king know that Patch hadn't been eaten by the Ickabog after all, you should remember that he was weary after his long journey to Chouxville. In any case, the king wouldn't have cared. Once Fred had seen the monster through the mist, nothing and nobody would have persuaded him it wasn't real.

'I wonder,' said Martha, 'why the Ickabog didn't eat the king?'

'Maybe he really did fight it off, like the stories say?' asked Roderick doubtfully.

'You know, it's strange,' said Daisy, turning to look at the Ickabog's cave, 'that there aren't any bones in here, if the Ickabog eats people.'

'It must eat the bones too,' said Bert. His voice was shaking.

Now Daisy remembered that, of course, they must have been wrong in thinking that Major Beamish had died in an accident on the marsh. Clearly, the Ickabog had killed him, after all. She'd just reached for Bert's hand, to show him she knew how horrible it was for him to be in the lair of his father's killer, when they heard heavy footsteps outside again, and knew the monster had returned. All four dashed back to the soft pile of sheep's wool and sat down in it as though they'd never moved.

There was a loud rumble as the Ickabog rolled back the stone, letting in the wintry chill. It was still snowing hard outside, and the Ickabog had a lot of snow trapped in its hair. In one of its baskets it had a large number of mushrooms and some firewood. In the other, it had some frozen Chouxville pastries.

While the humans watched, the Ickabog built up the fire again, and placed the icy block of pastries on a flat stone beside it, where they slowly began to thaw. Then, while Daisy, Bert, Martha, and Roderick watched, the Ickabog began eating mushrooms. It had a curious way of doing so. It speared a few at a time on the single spike protruding from each paw, then picked them off delicately in its mouth, one by one, chewing them up with what looked like great enjoyment.

After a while, it seemed to become aware that the four humans were watching it.

'Roar,' it said again, and fell back to ignoring them, until it had eaten all the mushrooms, after which it carefully lifted the unfrozen Chouxville pastries off the warm rock, and offered them to the humans in its huge, hairy paws.

'It's trying to fatten us up!' said Martha in a terrified whisper, but nevertheless she seized a Folderol Fancy and the next second, her eyes were closed in ecstasy.

After the Ickabog and the humans had eaten, the Ickabog put its two baskets away tidily in a corner, poked up the fire, and moved to the mouth of the cave, where the snow continued to fall and the sun was beginning to set. With a strange noise you'd recognise if you've ever heard a bagpipe inflate before somebody starts to play it, the Ickabog drew in breath and began to sing in a language none of the humans could understand. The song echoed forth over the marsh as darkness fell. The four humans listened, and soon felt drowsy, and one by one they sank back into the nest of sheep's wool, and fell asleep.

*The Ickabog began eating mushrooms… It speared a few at a time on the single spike protruding from each paw, then picked them off delicately in its mouth.*

*By Elias, age 10 years, Republic of Ireland*

# CHAPTER 53

# The Mysterious Monster

It was several days before Daisy, Bert, Martha, and Roderick plucked up the courage to do anything other than eat the frozen food that the Ickabog brought them from the wagon, and watch the monster eat the mushrooms it foraged for itself. Whenever the Ickabog went out (always rolling the enormous boulder into the mouth of the cave, to stop them escaping) they discussed its strange ways, but in low voices, in case it was lurking on the other side of the boulder, listening.

One thing they argued about was whether the Ickabog was a boy or a girl. Daisy, Bert, and Roderick all thought it must be male, because of the booming depth of its voice, but Martha, who'd looked after sheep before her family had starved to death, thought the Ickabog was a girl.

'Its belly's growing,' she told them. 'I think it's going to have babies.'

The other thing the children discussed, of course, was exactly when the Ickabog was likely to eat them, and whether they were going to be able to fight it off when it tried.

'I think we've got a bit of time yet,' said Bert, looking at Daisy and Martha, who were still very skinny from their time at the orphanage. 'You two wouldn't make much of a meal.'

'If I got it round the back of the neck,' said Roderick, miming the action, 'and Bert hit it really hard in the stomach—'

'We'll never be able to overpower the Ickabog,' said Daisy. 'It can move a boulder as big as itself. We're nowhere near strong enough.'

'If only we had a weapon,' said Bert, standing up and kicking a stone across the cave.

'Don't you think it's odd,' said Daisy, 'that all we've seen the Ickabog eat is mushrooms? Don't you feel as though it's pretending to be fiercer than it really is?'

'It eats sheep,' said Martha. 'Where did all this wool come from, if it hasn't eaten sheep?'

'Maybe it just saved up wisps of wool caught on brambles?' suggested Daisy, picking up a bit of the soft, white fluff. 'I still don't understand why there aren't any bones in here, if it's in the habit of eating creatures.'

'What about that song it sings every night?' said Bert. 'It gives me the creeps. If you ask me, that's a battle song.'

'It scares me too,' agreed Martha.

'I wonder what it means?' said Daisy.

A few minutes later, the giant boulder at the mouth of the cave shifted again, and the Ickabog reappeared with its two baskets, one full of mushrooms as usual, and the other packed with frozen Kurdsburg cheeses.

Everyone ate without talking, as they always did, and after the Ickabog had tidied away its baskets and poked up the fire, it moved, as the sun was setting, to the mouth of the cave, ready to sing its strange song, in the language the humans couldn't understand.

Daisy stood up.

'What are you doing?' whispered Bert, grabbing her ankle. 'Sit down!'

'No,' said Daisy, pulling herself free. 'I want to talk to it.'

So she walked boldly to the mouth of the cave, and sat down beside the Ickabog.

*So she walked boldly to the mouth of the cave, and sat
down beside the Ickabog.*

*By Sai Prasad, age 11 years, India*

# CHAPTER 54

# The Song of the Ickabog

The Ickabog had just drawn breath, with its usual sound of an inflating bagpipe, when Daisy said:

'What language do you sing in, Ickabog?'

The Ickabog looked down at her, startled to find Daisy so close. At first, Daisy thought it wasn't going to answer, but at last it said in its slow, deep voice:

'Ickerish.'

'And what's the song about?'

'It's the story of Ickabogs – and of your kind too.'

'You mean, people?' asked Daisy.

'People, yes,' said the Ickabog. 'The two stories are one story, because people were Bornded out of Ickabogs.'

It drew in its breath to sing again, but Daisy asked: 'What does "Bornded" mean? Is it the same as born?'

'No,' said the Ickabog, looking down at her, 'Bornded is very different from being born. It's how new Ickabogs come to be.'

Daisy wanted to be polite, seeing how enormous the Ickabog was, so she said cautiously:

'That does sound a *bit* like being born.'

'Well, it isn't,' said the Ickabog, in its deep voice. 'Born and Bornded are very different things. When babies are Bornded, we who have Bornded them die.'

'Always?' asked Daisy, noticing how the Ickabog absent-mindedly rubbed its tummy as it spoke.

'Always,' said the Ickabog. 'That is the way of the Ickabog. To live with your children is one of the strangenesses of people.'

'But that's so sad,' said Daisy slowly. 'To die when your children are born.'

'It isn't sad at all,' said the Ickabog. 'The Bornding is a glorious thing! Our whole lives lead up to the Bornding. What we're doing and what we're feeling when our babies are Bornded gives them their natures. It is very important to have a good Bornding.'

'I don't understand,' said Daisy.

'If I die sad and hopeless,' explained the Ickabog, 'my babies won't survive. I've watched my fellow Ickabogs die in despair, one by one, and their babies survived them only by seconds. An Ickabog can't live without hope. I'm the last Ickabog left, and my Bornding will be the most important Bornding in history, because if my Bornding goes well, our species will survive, and if not, Ickabogs will be gone forever...

'All our troubles began from a bad Bornding, you know.'

'Is that what your song's about?' asked Daisy. 'The bad Bornding?'

The Ickabog nodded, its eyes fixed on the darkening, snowy marsh. Then it took yet another deep bagpipe breath, and began to sing, and this time it sang in words that the humans could understand.

*'At the dawn of time, when only*
*Ickabogs existed, stony*
*Man was not created, with his*
*Cold, flint-hearted ways,*
*Then the world in its perfection*
*Was like heaven's bright reflection*
*No one hunted us or harmed us*
*In those lost, beloved days.*

*Oh Ickabogs, come Bornding back,*
*Come Bornding back, my Ickabogs.*
*Oh Ickabogs, come Bornding back,*
*Come Bornding back, my own.*

*Then tragedy! One stormy night,*
*Came Bitterness, Bornded of Fright,*
*And Bitterness, so tall and stout,*
*Was different from its fellows.*
*Its voice was rough, its ways were mean,*
*The likes of it had not been seen*
*Before, and so they drove it out*
*With angry blows and bellows.*

*Oh Ickabogs, be Bornded wise,*
*Be Bornded wise, my Ickabogs.*
*Oh Ickabogs, be Bornded wise,*
*Be Bornded wise, my own.*

*A thousand miles from its old home,*
*Its Bornding time arrived, alone*
*In darkness, Bitterness expired*
*And Hatred came to being.*
*A hairless Ickabog, this last,*
*A beast sworn to avenge the past,*
*With bloodlust was the creature fired,*
*Its evil eye far-seeing.*

*Oh Ickabogs, be Bornded kind,*
*Be Bornded kind, my Ickabogs.*

*Oh Ickabogs, be Bornded kind,*
*Be Bornded kind, my own.*

*Then Hatred spawned the race of man,*
*'Twas from ourselves that man began,*
*From Bitterness and Hate they swelled*
*To armies, raised to smite us.*
*In hundreds, Ickabogs were slain,*
*Our blood poured on the land like rain,*
*Our ancestors like trees were felled*
*And still men came to fight us.*

*Oh Ickabogs, be Bornded brave,*
*Be Bornded brave, my Ickabogs.*
*Oh Ickabogs, be Bornded brave,*
*Be Bornded brave, my own.*

*Men forced us from our sunlit home,*
*Away from grass to mud and stone,*
*Into the endless fog and rain*
*And here we stayed and dwindled,*
*'Til of our race there's only one*
*Survivor of the spear and gun*
*Whose children must begin again*
*With hate and fury kindled.*

*Oh Ickabogs, now kill the men,*
*Now kill the men, my Ickabogs.*
*Oh Ickabogs, now kill the men,*
*Now kill the men, my own.'*

Daisy and the Ickabog sat in silence for a while after the Ickabog had finished singing. The stars were coming out now. Daisy fixed her eyes on the moon as she said:

'How many people have you eaten, Ickabog?'

The Ickabog sighed.

'None, so far. Ickabogs like mushrooms.'

'Are you planning on eating us when your Bornding time comes?' Daisy asked. 'So your babies are born believing Ickabogs eat people? You want to turn them into people killers, don't you? To take back your land?'

The Ickabog looked down at her. It didn't seem to want to answer, but at last it nodded its huge, shaggy head. Behind Daisy and the Ickabog, Bert, Martha, and Roderick exchanged terrified glances by the light of the dying fire.

'I know what it's like to lose the people you love the most,' said Daisy quietly. 'My mother died, and my father disappeared. For a long time, after my father went away, I made myself believe that he was still alive, because I had to, or I think I'd have died as well.'

Daisy got to her feet to look up into the Ickabog's sad eyes.

'I think people need hope nearly as much as Ickabogs do. But,' she said, placing her hand over her heart, 'my mother and father are both still in here, and they always will be. So when you eat me, Ickabog, eat my heart last. I'd like to keep my parents alive as long as I can.'

She walked back into the cave, and the four humans settled down on their piles of wool again, beside the fire.

A little later, sleepy though she was, Daisy thought she heard the Ickabog sniff.

*In darkness, Bitterness expired*
*And Hatred came to being.*

*By Ewan, age 11 years, United Kingdom*

# CHAPTER 55

# Spittleworth Offends the King

After the disaster of the runaway mail coach, Lord Spittleworth took steps to make sure such a thing would never happen again. A new proclamation was issued, without the king's knowledge, which allowed the Chief Advisor to open letters to check them for signs of treason. The proclamation notices helpfully listed all the things that were now considered treason in Cornucopia. It was still treason to say that the Ickabog wasn't real, and that Fred wasn't a good king. It was treason to criticise Lord Spittleworth and Lord Flapoon, treason to say the Ickabog tax was too high, and, for the first time, treason to say that Cornucopia wasn't as happy and well fed as it had always been.

Now that everybody was too frightened to tell the truth in their letters, mail and even travel to the capital dwindled to almost nothing, which was exactly what Spittleworth had wanted, and he started on phase two of his plan. This was to send a lot of fan mail to Fred. As these letters couldn't all have the same handwriting, Spittleworth had shut up a few soldiers in a room with a stack of paper and lots of quills, and told them what to write.

'Praise the king, of course,' said Spittleworth, as he swept up and down in front of the men in his Chief Advisor's robes. 'Tell him he's the best ruler the country's ever had. Praise me, too. Say that you don't know what would become of Cornucopia without Lord Spittleworth. And say you know the Ickabog would have killed many more people, if not for the Ickabog Defence Brigade, and that Cornucopia's richer than ever.'

So Fred began to receive letters telling him how marvellous he was, and that the country had never been happier, and that the war against the Ickabog was going very well indeed.

'Well, it appears everything's going splendidly!' beamed King Fred, waving one of these letters over lunch with the two lords. He'd been much more cheerful since the forgeries had started to arrive. The bitter winter had frozen the ground so that it was dangerous to go hunting, but Fred, who was wearing a gorgeous new costume of burnt-orange silk, with topaz buttons, felt particularly handsome today, which added to his cheerfulness. It was quite delightful, watching the snow tumble down outside the window, when he had a blazing fire and his table was piled high, as usual, with expensive foodstuffs.

'I had no idea so many Ickabogs had been killed, Spittleworth! In fact – come to think of it – I didn't even know there was more than one Ickabog!'

'Er, yes, sire,' said Spittleworth, with a furious glance at Flapoon, who was stuffing himself with a particularly delicious cream cheese. Spittleworth had so much to do, he'd given Flapoon the job of checking all the forged letters before they were sent to the king. 'We didn't wish to alarm you, but we realised some time ago that the monster had, ah—'

He coughed delicately.

'—reproduced.'

'I see,' said Fred. 'Well, it's jolly good news you're finishing them off at such a rate. We should have one stuffed, you know, and hold an exhibition for the people!'

'Er… yes, sire, what an excellent idea,' said Spittleworth, through gritted teeth.

'One thing I don't understand, though,' said Fred, frowning over the letter again. 'Didn't Professor Fraudysham say that every time an

Ickabog dies, two grow in its place? By killing them like this, aren't you in fact doubling their numbers?'

'Ah... no, sire, not really,' said Spittleworth, his cunning mind working furiously fast. 'We've actually found a way of stopping that happening, by – er – by—'

'Banging them over the head first,' suggested Flapoon.

'Banging them over the head first,' repeated Spittleworth, nodding. 'That's it. If you can get near enough to knock them out before killing them, sire, the, er, the doubling process seems to... seems to stop.'

'But why didn't you tell me of this amazing discovery, Spittleworth?' cried Fred. 'This changes everything – we might soon have wiped Ickabogs from Cornucopia forever!'

'Yes, sire, it *is* good news, isn't it?' said Spittleworth, wishing he could smack the smile off Flapoon's face. 'However, there are still quite a few Ickabogs left...'

'All the same, the end seems to be in sight at last!' said Fred joyfully, setting the letter aside and picking up his knife and fork again. 'How very sad that poor Major Roach was killed by an Ickabog just before we began to turn the tables on the monsters!'

'Very sad, sire, yes,' agreed Spittleworth, who, of course, had explained away Major Roach's sudden disappearance by telling the king he'd laid down his life in the Marshlands, trying to prevent the Ickabog coming south.

'Well, this all makes sense of something I've been wondering about,' said Fred. 'The servants are constantly singing the national anthem, have you heard them? Jolly uplifting and all that, but it does become a bit *samey*. But this is why – they're celebrating our triumph over the Ickabogs, aren't they?'

'That must be it, sire,' said Spittleworth.

In fact, the singing was coming from the prisoners in the dungeons, not the servants, but Fred was unaware that he had fifty or so people trapped in the dungeons beneath him.

'We should hold a ball in celebration!' said Fred. 'We haven't had a ball for a very long time. It seems an age since I danced with Lady Eslanda.'

'Nuns don't dance,' said Spittleworth crossly. He stood up abruptly. 'Flapoon, a word.'

The two lords were halfway towards the door when the king commanded:

'Wait.'

Both turned. King Fred looked suddenly displeased.

'Neither of you asked permission to leave the king's table.'

The two lords exchanged glances, then Spittleworth bowed and Flapoon copied him.

'I crave Your Majesty's pardon,' said Spittleworth. 'It's simply that if we are to act on your excellent suggestion of having a dead Ickabog stuffed, sire, we must act quickly. It might, ah, rot, otherwise.'

'All the same,' said Fred, fingering the golden medal he wore around his neck, which was embossed with the picture of the king fighting a dragonish monster, 'I remain the king, Spittleworth. *Your* king.'

'Of course, sire,' said Spittleworth, bowing low again. 'I live only to serve you.'

'Hmm,' said Fred. 'Well, see that you remember it, and be quick about stuffing that Ickabog. I wish to display it to the people. Then we shall discuss the celebration ball.'

*It was quite delightful, watching the snow tumble down outside the window,*
*when he had a blazing fire.*

*By Shannon, age 11 years, United Kingdom*

# CHAPTER 56

# The Dungeon Plot

As soon as Spittleworth and Flapoon were out of earshot of the king, Spittleworth rounded on Flapoon.

'You were supposed to check all those letters before giving them to the king! Where am I supposed to find a dead Ickabog to stuff?'

'Sew something,' suggested Flapoon with a shrug.

'Sew something? *Sew* something?'

'Well, what else can you do?' said Flapoon, taking a large bite of the Dukes' Delight he'd sneaked from the king's table.

'What can *I* do?' repeated Spittleworth, incensed. 'You think this is all *my* problem?'

'You were the one who invented the Ickabog,' said Flapoon thickly, as he chewed. He was getting very bored of Spittleworth shouting at him and bossing him about.

'And you're the one who killed Beamish!' snarled Spittleworth. 'Where would you be now, if I hadn't blamed the monster?'

Without waiting for Flapoon's response, Spittleworth turned and headed down to the dungeons. At the very least, he could stop the prisoners singing the national anthem so loudly, so the king might think the war against the Ickabogs had taken a turn for the worse again.

'Quiet – QUIET!' bellowed Spittleworth, as he entered the dungeon, because the place was ringing with noise. There was singing and laughter, and Cankerby the footman was running between the cells fetching and carrying kitchen equipment for all the different prisoners, and the smell of Maidens' Dreams, fresh from Mrs Beamish's oven, filled the warm air. The prisoners all looked far better fed than the last time Spittleworth had been down here. He didn't like this, didn't like it at all. He especially didn't like to see Captain Goodfellow looking as fit and strong as ever he had. Spittleworth liked his enemies weak and hopeless. Even Mr Dovetail looked as though he'd trimmed his long white beard.

'You are keeping track, aren't you,' he asked the panting Cankerby, 'of all these pots, and knives and whatnots you're handing out?'

'Of – of course, my lord,' gasped the footman, not liking to admit that he was so confused by all the orders Mrs Beamish was giving him, that he had no idea which prisoner had what. Spoons, whisks, ladles, saucepans, and baking trays had to be passed between the bars, to keep up with the demand for Mrs Beamish's pastries, and once or twice Cankerby had accidentally passed one of Mr Dovetail's chisels to another prisoner. He *thought* he collected everything in at the end of each night, but how on earth was he to be sure? And sometimes Cankerby worried that the warder of the dungeons, who was fond of wine, might not hear the prisoners whispering to each other, if they took it into their heads to plot anything after the candles were snuffed out at night. However, Cankerby could tell that Spittleworth was in no mood to have problems brought to him, so the footman held his tongue.

'There will be no more singing!' shouted Spittleworth, his voice echoing through the dungeons. 'The king has a headache!'

In fact, it was Spittleworth whose head was beginning to throb. He forgot the prisoners as soon as he turned his back on them, and fell back to pondering how on earth he was going to make a convincing stuffed Ickabog. Perhaps Flapoon was onto something? Might they take the skeleton of a bull, and kidnap a seamstress to stitch a dragonish covering over the bones, and pad it out with sawdust?

Lies upon lies upon lies. Once you started lying, you had to continue, and then it was like being captain of a leaky ship, always plugging holes in the side to stop yourself sinking. Lost in thoughts of skeletons and sawdust, Spittleworth had no idea that he'd just turned his back on what promised to be his biggest problem yet: a dungeon full of plotting prisoners, each of whom had knives and chisels hidden beneath their blankets, and behind loose bricks in their walls.

# CHAPTER 57

# Daisy's Plan

Up in the Marshlands, where the snow still lay thick upon the ground, the Ickabog was no longer pushing the boulder in front of the cave mouth when it went out with its baskets. Instead, Daisy, Bert, Martha, and Roderick were helping it collect the little marsh mushrooms it liked to eat, and during these outings they also prised more frozen food from the abandoned wagon, which they took back to the cave for themselves.

All four humans were growing stronger and healthier by the day. The Ickabog, too, was growing fatter and fatter, but this was because its Bornding time was drawing ever closer. As the Bornding was when the Ickabog said it intended on eating the four humans, Bert, Martha, and Roderick weren't very happy about the Ickabog's growing belly. Bert, in particular, was certain the Ickabog meant to kill them. He now believed he'd been wrong about his father having an accident. The Ickabog was real so, clearly, the Ickabog had killed Major Beamish.

Often, on their mushrooming trips, the Ickabog and Daisy would draw a little ahead of the others, having their own private conversation.

'What d'you think they're talking about?' Martha whispered to the two boys, as they searched the bog for the small white mushrooms the Ickabog particularly liked.

'I think she's trying to make friends with it,' said Bert.

'What, so it'll eat us instead of her?' said Roderick.

'That's a horrible thing to say,' said Martha sharply. 'Daisy looked after everyone at the orphanage. Sometimes she took punishments for other people, too.'

Roderick was taken aback. He'd been taught by his father to expect the worst of everybody he met and that the one way to get on in life was to be the biggest, the strongest, and the meanest in every group. It was hard to lose the habits he'd been taught, but with his father dead, and his mother and brothers doubtless in prison, Roderick didn't want these three new friends to dislike him.

'Sorry,' he muttered, and Martha smiled at him.

Now, as it happened, Bert was quite right. Daisy *was* making friends with the Ickabog, but her plan wasn't only to save herself, or even her three friends. It was to save the whole of Cornucopia.

As she and the monster walked through the bog on this particular morning, drawing ahead of the others, she noticed that a few snowdrops had managed to force their way up through a patch of melting ice. Spring was coming, which meant soldiers would soon be returning to the edge of the marsh. With a funny seasick feeling in her stomach, because she knew how important it was that she got this right, Daisy said:

'Ickabog, you know the song you sing every night?'

The Ickabog, who was lifting a log to see whether there were any mushrooms hiding beneath it, said:

'If I didn't know it, I couldn't sing it, could I?'

It gave a wheezy little chuckle.

'Well, you know how you sing that you want your children to be kind, and wise, and brave?'

'Yes,' agreed the Ickabog, and it picked up a small silvery-grey mushroom and showed it to Daisy. 'That's a good one. You don't get many silver ones on the marsh.'

'Lovely,' said Daisy, as the Ickabog popped the mushroom into its basket. 'And then, in the last chorus of your song, you say you hope that your babies will kill people,' said Daisy.

'Yes,' said the Ickabog again, reaching up to pull a small bit of yellowish fungus off a dead tree, and showing it to Daisy. 'This is poisonous. Never eat this kind.'

'I won't,' said Daisy, and drawing a deep breath she said, 'but d'you really think a kind, wise, brave Ickabog would eat people?'

The Ickabog stopped in the act of bending to pick up another silvery mushroom and peered down at Daisy.

'I don't *want* to eat you,' it said, 'but I have to, or my children will die.'

'You said they need hope,' said Daisy. 'What if, when the Bornding time comes, they saw their mother – or their father – I'm sorry, I don't quite know—'

'I will be their Icker,' said the Ickabog. 'And they'll be my Ickaboggles.'

'Well, then, wouldn't it be wonderful if your – your Ickaboggles saw their Icker surrounded by people who love it, and want it to be happy, and to live with them as friends? Wouldn't that fill them with more hope than anything else could do?'

The Ickabog sat down on a fallen tree trunk, and for a long time it said nothing at all. Bert, Martha, and Roderick stood watching from a distance. They could tell something very important was happening between Daisy and the Ickabog, and although they were extremely curious, they didn't dare approach.

At last the Ickabog said:

'Perhaps… perhaps it would be better if I didn't eat you, Daisy.'

This was the first time the Ickabog had called her by her name. Daisy reached out and placed her hand in the Ickabog's paw, and for a moment the two smiled at each other. Then the Ickabog said:

'When my Bornding comes, you and your friends must surround me, and my Ickaboggles will be Bornded knowing you're their friends too. And after that, you must stay with my Ickaboggles here on the marsh, forever.'

'Well… the problem with that is,' said Daisy cautiously, still holding the Ickabog's paw, 'that the food on the wagon will run out soon. I don't think there are enough mushrooms here to support the four of us and your Ickaboggles too.'

Daisy found it strange to be talking like this about a time when the Ickabog wouldn't be alive, but the Ickabog didn't seem to mind.

'Then what can we do?' it asked her, its big eyes anxious.

'Ickabog,' said Daisy cautiously, 'people are dying all over Cornucopia. They're starving to death, and even being murdered, all because some evil men made everyone believe you wanted to kill people.'

'I *did* want to kill people, until I met you four,' said the Ickabog.

'But now you've changed,' said Daisy. She got to her feet and faced the Ickabog, holding both of its paws. 'Now you understand that people – most people, anyway – aren't cruel or wicked. They're mostly sad, and tired, Ickabog. And if they knew you – how kind you are, how gentle, how all you eat is mushrooms, they'd understand how stupid it is to fear you. I'm sure they'd want you and your Ickaboggles to leave the marsh, and go back to the meadows where your ancestors lived, where there are bigger, better mushrooms, and for your descendants to live with us as our friends.'

'You want me to leave the marsh?' said the Ickabog. 'To go among men, with their guns and their spears?'

'Ickabog, please listen,' begged Daisy. 'If your Ickaboggles are Bornded surrounded by hundreds of people, all wanting to love and protect them, wouldn't that feed them more hope than any Ickaboggle ever had, in history? Whereas, if the four of us stay here on the marsh and starve to death, what hope will remain for your Ickaboggles?'

The monster stared at Daisy, and Bert, Martha, and Roderick

watched, wondering what on earth was happening. At last, a huge tear welled in the Ickabog's eye, like a glass apple.

'I'm afraid to go among the men. I'm afraid they'll kill me and my Ickaboggles.'

'They won't,' said Daisy, letting go of the Ickabog's paws and placing her hands instead on either side of the Ickabog's huge, hairy face, so her fingers were buried in its long marsh-weedy hair. 'I swear to you, Ickabog, we'll protect you. Your Bornding *will* be the most important in history. We're going to bring Ickabogs back… and Cornucopia too.'

# CHAPTER 58

# Hetty Hopkins

When Daisy first told the others her plan, Bert refused to be part of it.

'Protect that monster? I won't,' he said fiercely. 'I took a vow to kill it, Daisy. The Ickabog murdered my father!'

'Bert, it didn't,' Daisy said. 'It's never killed *anyone*. Please listen to what it's got to say!'

So that night in the cave, Bert, Martha, and Roderick drew close to the Ickabog for the first time, always having been too scared before, and it told the four humans the story of the night, years before, when it had come face-to-face with a man in the fog.

'... with yellow face hair,' said the Ickabog, pointing at its own upper lip.

'Moustaches?' suggested Daisy.

'And a twinkly sword.'

'Jewelled,' said Daisy. 'It *must* have been the king.'

'And who else did you meet?' asked Bert.

'Nobody,' said the Ickabog. 'I ran away and hid behind a boulder. Men killed all my ancestors. I was afraid.'

'Well, then, how did my father die?' demanded Bert.

'Was your Icker the one who was shot by the big gun?' asked the Ickabog.

'Shot?' repeated Bert, turning pale. 'How do you know this, if you'd run away?'

'I was looking out from behind the boulder,' said the Ickabog. 'Ickabogs can see well in fog. I was frightened. I wanted to see what the men were doing on the marsh. One man was shot by another man.'

'Flapoon!' burst out Roderick, at last. He'd been afraid to tell Bert before now, but he couldn't hold it in any longer. 'Bert, I once heard my father tell my mother he owed his promotion to Lord Flapoon and his blunderbuss. I was really young... I didn't realise what he meant, at the time... I'm sorry I never told you, I... I was afraid of what you'd say.'

Bert said nothing at all for several minutes. He was remembering that terrible night in the Blue Parlour, when he'd found his father's cold, dead hand and pulled it from beneath the Cornucopian flag for his mother to kiss. He remembered Spittleworth saying that they couldn't see his father's body, and he remembered Lord Flapoon spraying him and his mother with pie crumbs, as he said how much he'd always liked Major Beamish. Bert put a hand to his chest, where his father's medal lay close against his skin, turned to Daisy, and said in a low voice:

'All right. I'm with you.'

So the four humans and the Ickabog began to put Daisy's plan into operation, acting quickly, because the snow was melting fast, and they feared the return of the soldiers to the Marshlands.

First, they took the enormous, empty wooden platters that had borne the cheese, pies, and pastries they'd already eaten, and Daisy carved words into them. Next, the Ickabog helped the two boys pull the wagon out of the mud, while Martha collected as many mushrooms as she could find, to keep the Ickabog well fed on the journey south.

At dawn on the third day, they set out. They'd planned things very carefully. The Ickabog pulled the wagon, which was loaded up with the last of the frozen food, and with baskets of mushrooms. In front of the Ickabog walked Bert and Roderick, who were each carrying a sign. Bert's read: THE ICKABOG IS HARMLESS. Roderick's said: SPITTLEWORTH HAS LIED TO YOU. Daisy was riding on the Ickabog's shoulders. Her sign read: THE ICKABOG EATS ONLY MUSHROOMS. Martha rode in the wagon along with the food and a large bunch of snowdrops, which were part of Daisy's plan. Martha's sign read: UP WITH THE ICKABOG! DOWN WITH LORD SPITTLEWORTH!

For many miles, they met nobody, but as midday approached, they came across two ragged people leading a single, very thin sheep. This tired and hungry pair were none other than Hetty Hopkins, the maid who'd had to give her children to Ma Grunter, and her husband. They'd been walking the country trying to find work, but nobody had any to give them. Finding the starving sheep in the road, they'd brought it along with them, but its wool was so thin and stringy that it wasn't worth any money.

When Mr Hopkins saw the Ickabog, he fell to his knees in shock, while Hetty simply stood there with her mouth hanging open. When the strange party came close enough, and the husband and wife were able to read all the signs, they thought they must have gone mad.

Daisy, who'd expected people to react like this, called down to them:

'You aren't dreaming! This is the Ickabog, and it's kind and peaceful! It's never killed anyone! In fact, it saved our lives!'

The Ickabog bent down carefully, so that it wouldn't dislodge Daisy, and patted the thin sheep on the head. Instead of running away, it *baaa*-ed, quite unafraid, then returned to eating the thin, dry grass.

'You see?' said Daisy. 'Your sheep knows it's harmless! Come with us – you can ride on our wagon!'

The Hopkinses were so tired and hungry that, even though they were still very scared of the Ickabog, they heaved themselves up beside Martha, bringing their sheep too. Then off trundled the Ickabog, the six humans, and the sheep, heading for Jeroboam.

# CHAPTER 59

# Back to Jeroboam

Dusk was falling as the dark grey outline of Jeroboam came into view. The Ickabog's party made a brief stop on a hill overlooking the city. Martha handed the Ickabog the big bunch of snowdrops. Then everyone made sure they were holding their signs the right way up and the four friends shook hands, because they'd sworn to each other, and to the Ickabog, that they would protect it, and never stand aside, even if people threatened them with guns.

So down the hill towards the winemaking city the Ickabog marched, and the guards at the city gates saw it coming. They raised their guns to fire, but Daisy stood up on the Ickabog's shoulder, waving her arms, and Bert and Roderick held their signs aloft. Rifles shaking, the guards watched fearfully as the monster walked closer and closer.

'The Ickabog has never killed anyone!' shouted Daisy.

'You've been told lies!' shouted Bert.

The guards didn't know what to do, because they didn't want to shoot the four young people. The Ickabog shuffled ever closer, and its size and strangeness were both terrifying. But it had a kindly look in its enormous eyes, and was holding snowdrops in its paw. At last, reaching the guards, the Ickabog came to a halt, bent down, and offered each of them a snowdrop.

The guards took the flowers, because they were afraid not to. Then the Ickabog patted each of them gently on the head, as it had done to the sheep, and walked on into Jeroboam.

There were screams on every side: people fled before the Ickabog, or dived to find weapons, but Bert and Roderick marched resolutely in front of it, holding up their signs, and the Ickabog continued offering snowdrops to passers-by, until at last a young woman bravely took one. The Ickabog was so delighted it thanked her in its booming voice, which made more people scream, but others edged closer to the Ickabog, and soon a little crowd of people was clustered around the monster, taking snowdrops from its paw and laughing. And the Ickabog was starting to smile too. It had never expected to be cheered or thanked by people.

'I told you they'd love you if they knew you!' Daisy whispered in the Ickabog's ear.

'Come with us!' shouted Bert at the crowd. 'We're marching south, to see the king!'

And now the Jeroboamers, who'd suffered so much under Spittleworth's rule, ran back to their houses to fetch torches, pitchforks, and guns, not to harm the Ickabog, but to protect it. Furious at the lies they'd been told, they clustered around the monster, and off they marched through the gathering darkness, with only one short detour.

Daisy insisted on stopping at the orphanage. Though the door was of course firmly locked and bolted, a kick from the Ickabog soon put that right. The Ickabog helped Daisy gently down, and she ran inside to fetch all the children. The little ones scrambled up into the wagon, the Hopkins twins fell into the arms of their parents, and the larger children joined the crowd, while Ma Grunter screamed and stormed and tried to call them back. Then she saw the Ickabog's huge hairy face squinting at her through a window and, I'm happy to tell you, she passed out cold on the floor.

Then the delighted Ickabog continued down the main street of Jeroboam, collecting more and more people as it went, and nobody noticed Basher John watching from a corner as the crowd passed. Basher John, who'd been drinking in a local tavern, hadn't forgotten the bloody nose he'd received from Roderick Roach on the night the two boys stole his keys. He realised at once that if these troublemakers, with their overgrown marsh monster, reached the capital, anybody who'd made pots of gold from the myth of the dangerous Ickabog would be in trouble. So instead of returning to the orphanage, Basher John stole another drinker's horse from outside the tavern.

Unlike the Ickabog, which was moving slowly, Basher John was soon galloping south, to warn Lord Spittleworth of the danger marching on Chouxville.

*Its size and strangeness were both terrifying. But it had a kindly look in its enormous eyes, and was holding snowdrops in its paw.*

*By Evelyn, age 8 years, United Kingdom*

# CHAPTER 60

# Rebellion

Sometimes – I don't know how – people who live many miles apart seem to realise the time has come to act. Perhaps ideas can spread like pollen on the breeze. In any case, down in the palace dungeons, the prisoners who'd hidden knives and chisels, heavy saucepans and rolling pins beneath their mattresses and stones in their cell walls, were ready at last. At dawn on the day the Ickabog approached Kurdsburg, Captain Goodfellow and Mr Dovetail, whose cells were opposite each other, were awake, pale, tense, and sitting on the edges of their beds, because today was the day they'd vowed to escape, or die.

Several floors above the prisoners, Lord Spittleworth, too, woke early. Completely unaware that a prison break-out was brewing beneath his feet, or that a real live Ickabog was at that very moment advancing on Chouxville, surrounded by an ever-growing crowd of Cornucopians, Spittleworth washed, dressed in his Chief Advisor's robes, then headed out to a locked wing of the stables, which had been under guard for a week.

'Stand aside,' Spittleworth told the soldiers on guard, and he unbolted the doors.

A team of exhausted seamstresses and tailors were waiting beside the model of a monster inside the stable. It was the size of a bull, with leathery skin, and was covered in spikes. Its carved feet bore fearsome claws, its mouth was full of fangs, and its angry eyes glowed amber in its face.

The seamstresses and tailors watched fearfully as Spittleworth walked slowly around their creation. Close up, you could see the stitching, tell that the eyes were made of glass, that the spikes were really nails pushed through the leather, and that the claws and fangs were nothing but painted wood. If you prodded the beast, a trickle of sawdust ran from the seams. Nevertheless, by the dim light of the stables, it was a convincing piece of work and the seamstresses and tailors were thankful to see Spittleworth smile.

'It will do, by candlelight, at least,' he said. 'I'll simply have to make the dear king stand well back as he looks at it. We can say the spikes and fangs are still poisonous.'

The workers exchanged relieved looks. They'd been working all day and all night for a week. Now at last they'd be able to go home to their families.

'Soldiers,' said Spittleworth, turning to the guards waiting in the courtyard, 'take these people away. If you scream,' he added lazily, as the youngest seamstress opened her mouth to do so, 'you'll be shot.'

While the team that had made the stuffed Ickabog was dragged away by the soldiers, Spittleworth went upstairs, whistling, to the king's apartments, where he found Fred wearing silk pyjamas and a hairnet over his moustaches, and Flapoon tucking a napkin beneath his many chins.

'Good morning, Your Majesty!' said Spittleworth with a bow. 'I trust you slept well? I have a surprise for Your Majesty today. We have succeeded in having one of the Ickabogs stuffed. I know Your Majesty was eager to see it.'

'Wonderful, Spittleworth!' said the king. 'And after that, we might send it around the kingdom, what? To show the people what we're up against?'

'I would advise against that, sire,' said Spittleworth, who feared that if anybody saw the stuffed Ickabog by daylight, they'd be sure to spot it as a fake. 'We wouldn't want the common folk to panic. Your Majesty is so brave that you can cope with the sight—'

At that moment, the doors to the king's private apartments flew open and in ran a wild-eyed, sweaty Basher John, who'd been delayed on the road by not one, but two sets of highwaymen. After getting lost in some woods and falling off his horse while jumping a ditch, then being unable to catch it again, Basher John hadn't managed to reach the palace much ahead of the Ickabog. Panicking, he'd forced entry to the palace through a scullery window, and two guards had pursued him through the palace, both of them prepared to run him through with their swords.

Fred let out a scream and hid behind Flapoon. Spittleworth pulled out his dagger and jumped to his feet.

'There's – an – Ickabog,' panted Basher John, falling to his knees. 'A real – live – Ickabog. It's coming here – with thousands of people – the Ickabog – is real.'

Naturally, Spittleworth didn't believe this story for a second.

'Take him to the dungeons!' he snarled at the guards, who dragged the struggling Basher John from the room and closed the doors again. 'I do apologise, sire,' said Spittleworth, who was still holding his dagger. 'The man will be horsewhipped, and so will the guards who let him break into the pal—'

But before Spittleworth could finish his sentence, two more men came bursting into the king's private apartments. These were Spittleworth's Chouxville spies who'd had word from the north about the Ickabog's approach, but as the king had never laid eyes on them before, he let out another terrified squeal.

'My – lord,' panted the first spy, bowing to Spittleworth, 'there's – an – Ickabog, coming – this – way!'

'And it's got – a crowd – with it,' panted the second. 'It's *real!*'

'Well, of course the Ickabog's real!' said Spittleworth, who could hardly say anything else with the king present. 'Notify the Ickabog Defence Brigade – I shall join them shortly in the courtyard, and we'll kill the beast!'

Spittleworth ushered the spies to the door and thrust them back into the passageway, trying to drown out their whispers of, 'My lord, it's real, and the people like it!', and, 'It's on its way south, my lord, our contacts seen it with their two eyes!'

'We shall kill this monster as we've killed all the others!' said Spittleworth loudly, for the king's benefit, and then under his breath he added, '*Go away!*'

Spittleworth closed the door firmly on the spies and returned to the table, disturbed, but trying not to show it. Flapoon was still tucking into some Baronstown ham. He had a vague idea that Spittleworth must be behind all these people rushing in and talking about live Ickabogs, so he wasn't frightened in the slightest. Fred, on the other hand, was quivering from head to foot.

'Imagine the monster showing itself in daylight, Spittleworth!' he whimpered. 'I thought it only ever came out at night!'

'Yes, it's getting far too bold, isn't it, Your Majesty?' said Spittleworth. He had no idea what this so-called real Ickabog could be. The only thing he could imagine was that some common folk had rigged up some kind of fake monster, possibly to steal food, or force gold out of their neighbours – but it would still have to be stopped, of course. There was only one true Ickabog, and that was the one Spittleworth had invented. 'Come, Flapoon – we must prevent this beast from entering Chouxville!'

'You're so brave, Spittleworth,' said King Fred in a broken voice.

'Tish, pish, Your Majesty,' said Spittleworth. 'I would lay down my life for Cornucopia. You should know that by now!'

Spittleworth's hand was on the door handle when yet more running footsteps, this time accompanied by shouting and clanging, shattered the peace. Startled, Spittleworth opened the door to see what was going on.

A group of ragged prisoners was running towards him. At the head of them was the white-haired Mr Dovetail, who held an axe, and burly Captain Goodfellow, who carried a gun clearly wrestled from the hands of a palace guard. Right behind them came Mrs Beamish, her hair flying behind her as she brandished an enormous saucepan, and hot on her heels came Millicent, Lady Eslanda's maid, who held a rolling pin.

Just in time, Spittleworth slammed and bolted the door. Within seconds, Mr Dovetail's axe had smashed through the wood.

'Flapoon, come!' shouted Spittleworth, and the two lords ran across the room to another door, which led to a staircase down to the courtyard.

Fred, who had no idea what was going on, who'd never even realised that there were fifty people trapped in the dungeons of his palace, was slow to react. Seeing the faces of the furious prisoners appear at the hole Mr Dovetail had hacked in the door, he jumped up to follow the two lords, but they, interested only in their own skins, had bolted the door they had escaped through from the other side. King Fred was left standing in his pyjamas with his back to the wall, watching the escaped prisoners hack their way into his room.

*Right behind them came Mrs Beamish, her hair flying behind her as she brandished an enormous saucepan.*

*By Béibhinn, age 8 years, Republic of Ireland*

# CHAPTER 61

# Flapoon Fires Again

The two lords dashed out into the palace courtyard to find the Ickabog Defence Brigade already mounted and armed, as Spittleworth had ordered. However, Major Prodd (the man who'd kidnapped Daisy years before, who'd been promoted after Spittleworth shot Major Roach) was looking nervous.

'My lord,' he said to Spittleworth, who was hastily mounting his horse, 'there's something happening inside the palace – we heard an uproar—'

'Never mind that now!' snapped Spittleworth.

A sound of shattering glass made all the soldiers look up.

'There are people in the king's bedroom!' cried Prodd. 'Shouldn't we help him?'

'Forget the king!' shouted Spittleworth.

Captain Goodfellow now appeared at the king's bedroom window. Looking down, he bellowed:

'You won't escape, Spittleworth!'

'Oh, won't I?' snarled the lord, and kicking his thin yellow horse, he forced it into a gallop and disappeared out of the palace gates. Major Prodd was too scared of Spittleworth not to follow, so he and the rest of the Ickabog Defence Brigade charged after His Lordship, along with Flapoon, who'd barely managed to get onto his horse before Spittleworth set off, bouncing along at the rear, holding onto his horse's

mane for dear life and trying to find his stirrups.

Some men might have considered themselves beaten, what with escaped prisoners taking over the palace and a fake Ickabog marching through the country and attracting crowds, but not Lord Spittleworth. He still had a squad of well-trained, well-armed soldiers riding behind him, heaps of gold hidden at his mansion in the country, and his crafty brain was already devising a plan. Firstly, he'd shoot the men who'd faked this Ickabog, and terrify the people back into obedience. Then he'd send Major Prodd and his soldiers back to the palace to kill all the escaped prisoners. Of course, the prisoners might have killed the king by that time, but in truth, it might be easier to govern the country without Fred. As he galloped along, Spittleworth thought bitterly that if only he hadn't had to put so much effort into lying to the king, he might not have made certain mistakes, like letting that wretched pastry chef have knives and saucepans. He also regretted not hiring more spies, because then he might have found out that someone was making a fake Ickabog – a fake, by the sound of it, that was far more convincing than the one he'd seen that morning in the stables.

So the Ickabog Defence Brigade charged through the surprisingly empty cobbled streets of Chouxville and out onto the open road that led to Kurdsburg. To Spittleworth's fury, he now saw why the Chouxville streets had been empty. Having heard the rumour that an actual Ickabog was walking towards the capital with a large crowd, the citizens of Chouxville had hurried out to catch a glimpse of it with their own eyes.

'Out of our way! OUT OF OUR WAY!' screamed Spittleworth, scattering the common people before him, furious to see them looking excited rather than scared. He spurred his horse onwards until its sides were bleeding, and Lord Flapoon followed, now green in the face, because he hadn't had time to digest his breakfast.

At last, Spittleworth and the soldiers spotted the huge crowd advancing in the distance, and Spittleworth hauled at his poor horse's reins, so that it skidded to a halt in the road. There, in the midst of the thousands of laughing and singing Cornucopians, was a giant creature as tall as two horses, with eyes glowing like lamps, covered in long greenish-brown hair like marsh weed. On its shoulder rode a young woman, and in front of it marched two young men holding up wooden signs. Every now and then, the monster stooped down and – yes – it seemed to be handing out flowers.

'It's a trick,' muttered Spittleworth, so shocked and scared he hardly knew what he was saying. 'It must be a trick!' he said more loudly, craning his scrawny neck to try and see how it was done. 'There are obviously people standing on each other's shoulders inside a suit of marsh weed – guns at the ready, men!'

But the soldiers were slow to obey. In all the time they'd been supposedly protecting the country from the Ickabog, the soldiers had never seen one, nor had they really expected to, yet they weren't at all convinced they were watching a trick. On the contrary, the creature looked very real to them. It was patting dogs on the head, and handing out flowers to children, and letting that girl sit on its shoulder: it didn't seem fierce at all. The soldiers were also scared of the crowd of thousands marching along with the Ickabog, who all seemed to like it. What would they do if the Ickabog was attacked?

Then one of the youngest soldiers lost his head completely.

'That's not a trick. I'm off.'

Before anybody could stop him, he'd galloped away.

Flapoon, who had at last found his stirrups, now rode up front to take his place beside Spittleworth.

'What do we do?' asked Flapoon, watching the Ickabog and the joyful, singing crowd drawing nearer and nearer.

'I'm thinking,' snarled Spittleworth, 'I'm thinking!'

But the cogs of Spittleworth's busy brain seemed to have jammed at last. It was the joyful faces that upset him most. He'd come to think of laughter as a luxury, like Chouxville pastries and silk sheets, and seeing these ragged people having fun frightened him more than if they'd all been carrying guns.

'I'll shoot it,' said Flapoon, raising his gun and taking aim at the Ickabog.

'No,' said Spittleworth, 'look, man, can't you see we're outnumbered?'

But at that precise moment, the Ickabog let out a deafening, blood-curdling scream. The crowd that had pressed around it backed away, their faces suddenly scared. Many dropped their flowers. Some broke into a run.

With another terrible screech the Ickabog fell to its knees, almost shaking Daisy loose, though she clung on tightly.

And then a huge dark split appeared down the Ickabog's enormous, swollen belly.

'You were right, Spittleworth!' bellowed Flapoon, raising his blunderbuss. 'There are men hiding inside it!'

And as people in the crowd began to scream and flee, Lord Flapoon took aim at the Ickabog's belly, and fired.

# CHAPTER 62

# The Bornding

And now several things happened at almost the same time, so nobody watching could possibly keep up, but luckily, I can tell you about all of them.

Lord Flapoon's bullet went flying towards the Ickabog's opening belly. Both Bert and Roderick, who'd sworn to protect the Ickabog no matter what, flung themselves into the path of that bullet, which hit Bert squarely in the chest, and as he fell to the ground, his wooden sign, bearing the message **THE ICKABOG IS HARMLESS**, shattered into splinters.

Then a baby Ickabog, which was already taller than a horse, came struggling out of its Icker's belly. Its Bornding had been a dreadful one, because it had come into the world full of its parent's fear of the gun, and the first thing it had ever seen was an attempt to kill it, so it sprinted straight at Flapoon, who was trying to reload.

The soldiers who might have helped Flapoon were so terrified of the new monster bearing down upon them that they galloped out of its path without even trying to fire. Spittleworth was one of those who rode away fastest, and he was soon lost to sight. The baby Ickabog let out a terrible roar that still haunts the nightmares of those who witnessed the scene, before launching itself at Flapoon. Within seconds, Flapoon lay dead upon the ground.

All of this had happened very fast; people were screaming and

crying, and Daisy was still holding onto the dying Ickabog, which lay in the road beside Bert. Roderick and Martha were bending over Bert, who, to their amazement, had opened his eyes.

'I – I think I'm all right,' he whispered, and feeling beneath his shirt, he pulled out his father's huge silver medal. Flapoon's bullet was buried in it. The medal had saved Bert's life.

Seeing that Bert was alive, Daisy now buried her hands in the hair on either side of the Ickabog's face again.

'I didn't see my Ickaboggle,' whispered the dying Ickabog, in whose eyes there were again tears like glass apples.

'It's beautiful,' said Daisy, who was also starting to cry. 'Look… here…'

A second Ickaboggle was wriggling out of the Ickabog's tummy. This one had a friendly face and wore a timid smile, because its Bornding had happened as its parent was looking into Daisy's face, and had seen her tears, and understood that a human could love an Ickabog as though it was one of their own family. Ignoring the noise and clamour all around it, the second Ickaboggle knelt beside Daisy in the road and stroked the big Ickabog's face. Icker and Ickaboggle looked at each other and smiled, and then the big Ickabog's eyes gently closed, and Daisy knew that it was dead. She buried her face in its shaggy hair and sobbed.

'You mustn't be sad,' said a familiar booming voice, as something stroked her hair. 'Don't cry, Daisy. This is the Bornding. It is a glorious thing.'

Blinking, Daisy looked up at the baby, which was speaking with exactly the voice of its Icker.

'You know my name,' she said.

'Well, of course I do,' said the Ickaboggle kindly. 'I was Bornded knowing all about you. And now we must find my Ickabob,' which, Daisy understood, was what Ickabogs called their siblings.

Daisy stood up and saw Flapoon lying dead in the road, and the first-born Ickaboggle surrounded by people holding pitchforks and guns.

'Climb up here with me,' said Daisy urgently to the second baby, and hand-in-hand the two of them mounted the wagon. Daisy shouted at the crowd to listen. As she was the girl who'd ridden through the country on the shoulder of the Ickabog, the nearest people guessed that she might know things worth hearing, so they shushed everyone else, and at last Daisy was able to speak.

'You mustn't hurt the Ickabogs!' were the first words out of her mouth, when at last the crowd was silent. 'If you're cruel to them, they'll have babies who are born even crueller!'

'Bornded cruel,' corrected the Ickaboggle beside her.

'Bornded cruel, yes,' said Daisy. 'But if they're Bornded in kindness, they will be kind! They eat only mushrooms and they want to be our friends!'

The crowd muttered, uncertain, until Daisy explained about Major Beamish's death on the marsh, how he'd been shot by Lord Flapoon, not killed by an Ickabog, and that Spittleworth had used the death to invent a story of a murderous monster on the marsh.

Then the crowd decided that they wanted to go and talk to King Fred, so the bodies of the dead Ickabog and Lord Flapoon were loaded onto the wagon, and twenty strong men pulled it along. Then the whole procession set off for the palace, with Daisy, Martha, and the kind Ickaboggle arm-in-arm at the front, and thirty citizens with guns surrounding the fierce, first-born Ickaboggle, which otherwise would have killed more humans, because it had been Bornded fearing and hating them.

But after a quick discussion, Bert and Roderick vanished, and where they went, you'll find out soon.

*Then a baby Ickabog, which was already taller than a horse,*
*came struggling out of its Icker's belly.*

By Grace, age 8 years, Australia

## CHAPTER 63

# Lord Spittleworth's Last Plan

When Daisy entered the palace courtyard, at the head of the people's procession, she was amazed to see how little it had altered. Fountains still played and peacocks still strutted, and the only change to the front of the palace was a single broken window, up on the second floor.

Then the great golden doors were flung open, and the crowd saw two ragged people walking out to meet them: a white-haired man holding an axe and a woman clutching an enormous saucepan.

And Daisy, staring at the white-haired man, felt her knees buckle, and the kind Ickaboggle caught her and held her up. Mr Dovetail tottered forward, and I don't think he even noticed that an actual live Ickabog was standing beside his long-lost daughter. As the two of them hugged and sobbed, Daisy spotted Mrs Beamish over her father's shoulder.

'Bert's alive!' she called to the pastry chef, who was looking frantically for her son, 'but he had something to do… He'll be back soon!'

More prisoners now came hurrying out of the palace, and there were screams of joy as loved ones found loved ones, and many of the orphanage children found the parents they'd thought were dead.

Then a lot of other things happened, like the thirty strong men who surrounded the fierce Ickaboggle, dragging it away before it could kill anyone else, and Daisy asking Mr Dovetail if Martha could come and live with them, and Captain Goodfellow appearing on a balcony with a weeping King Fred, who was still wearing his pyjamas, and the crowd cheering when Captain Goodfellow said he thought it was time to try life without a king.

However, we must now leave this happy scene, and track down the man who was most to blame for the terrible things that had happened to Cornucopia.

Lord Spittleworth was miles away, galloping down a deserted country road, when his horse suddenly went lame. When Spittleworth tried to force it onwards, the poor horse, which had had quite enough of being mistreated, reared and deposited Spittleworth onto the ground. When Spittleworth tried to whip it, the horse kicked him, then trotted away into a forest where, I am pleased to tell you, it was later found by a kind farmer, who nursed it back to health.

Lord Spittleworth was therefore left to jog alone down the country lanes towards his country estate, holding up his Chief Advisor's robes lest he trip over them, and looking over his shoulder every few yards for fear that he was being followed. He knew perfectly well that his life in Cornucopia was over, but he still had that mountain of gold hidden in his wine cellar, and he intended to load up his carriage with as many ducats as would fit, then sneak over the border into Pluritania.

Night had fallen by the time Spittleworth reached his mansion, and his feet were terribly sore. Hobbling inside, he bellowed for his butler, Scrumble, who so long ago had pretended to be Nobby Buttons's mother and Professor Fraudysham.

'Down here, my lord!' called a voice from the cellar.

'Why haven't you lit the lamps, Scrumble?' bellowed Spittleworth, feeling his way downstairs.

'Thought it best not to look like anyone was home, sir!' called Scrumble.

'Ah,' said Spittleworth, wincing as he limped downstairs. 'So you've heard, have you?'

'Yes, sir,' said the echoing voice. 'I imagined you'd be wanting to clear out, my lord?'

'Yes, Scrumble,' said Lord Spittleworth, limping towards the distant light of a single candle, 'I most certainly do.'

He pushed open the door to the cellar where he'd been storing his gold all these years. The butler, whom Spittleworth could only make out dimly in the candlelight, was once again wearing Professor Fraudysham's costume: the white wig and the thick glasses that shrank his eyes to almost nothing.

'Thought it might be best if we travel in disguise, sir,' said Scrumble, holding up old Widow Buttons's black dress and ginger wig.

'Good idea,' said Spittleworth, hastily pulling off his robes and pulling on the costume. 'Do you have a cold, Scrumble? Your voice sounds strange.'

'It's just the dust down here, sir,' said the butler, moving further from the candlelight. 'And what will Your Lordship be wanting to do with Lady Eslanda? She's still locked in the library.'

'Leave her,' said Spittleworth, after a moment's consideration. 'And serve her right for not marrying me when she had the chance.'

'Very good, my lord. I've loaded up the carriage and a couple of horses with most of the gold. Perhaps Your Lordship could help carry this last trunk?'

'I hope you weren't thinking of leaving without me, Scrumble,' said Spittleworth suspiciously, wondering whether, if he'd arrived ten minutes later, he might have found Scrumble gone.

'Oh no, my lord,' Scrumble assured him. 'I wouldn't dream of leaving without Your Lordship. Withers the groom will be driving us, sir. He's ready and waiting in the courtyard.'

'Excellent,' said Spittleworth, and together they heaved the last trunk of gold upstairs, through the deserted house and out into the courtyard behind, where Spittleworth's carriage stood waiting in the darkness. Even the horses had sacks of gold slung over their backs. More gold had been strapped onto the top of the carriage, in cases.

As he and Scrumble heaved the last trunk onto the roof, Spittleworth said:

'What is that peculiar noise?'

'I hear nothing, my lord,' said Scrumble.

'It is an odd sort of grunting,' said Spittleworth.

A memory came back to Spittleworth as he stood here in the dark: that of standing in the icy-white fog on the marsh all those years before, and the whimpers of the dog struggling against the brambles in which it was tangled. This was a similar noise, as though some creature were trapped and unable to free itself, and it made Lord Spittleworth quite as nervous as it had last time when, of course, it had been followed by Flapoon firing his blunderbuss and starting both of them onto the path to riches, and the country down the road to ruin.

'Scrumble, I don't like that noise.'

'I don't expect you do, my lord.'

The moon slid out from behind a cloud and Lord Spittleworth, turning quickly towards his butler, whose voice sounded very different all of a sudden, found himself staring down the barrel of one of his own guns. Scrumble had removed Professor Fraudysham's wig and glasses, to reveal that he wasn't the butler at all, but Bert Beamish. And for just a moment, seen by moonlight, the boy looked so like his father that Spittleworth had the crazy notion that Major Beamish had risen from the dead to punish him.

Then he looked wildly around him and saw, through the open door of the carriage, the real Scrumble, gagged and tied up on the floor, which was where the odd whimpering was coming from – and Lady Eslanda sitting there, smiling and holding a second gun. Opening his mouth to ask Withers the groom why he didn't do something, Spittleworth realised that this wasn't Withers, but Roderick Roach. (When he'd spotted the two boys galloping up the drive, the real groom had quite rightly sensed trouble, and stealing his favourite of Lord Spittleworth's horses, had ridden off into the night.)

'How did you get here so fast?' was all Spittleworth could think to say.

'We borrowed some horses from a farmer,' said Bert.

In fact, Bert and Roderick were much better riders than Spittleworth, so their horses hadn't gone lame. They'd managed to overtake him and had arrived in plenty of time to free Lady Eslanda, find out where the gold was, tie up Scrumble the butler, and force him to tell them the full story of how Spittleworth had fooled the country, including his own impersonation of Professor Fraudysham and Widow Buttons.

'Boys, let's not be hasty,' said Spittleworth faintly. 'There's a lot of gold here. I'll share it with you!'

'It isn't yours to share,' said Bert. 'You're coming back to Chouxville and we're going to have a proper trial.'

*And Lady Eslanda… holding a second gun.*

*By Martha, age 12 years, United Kingdom*

# CHAPTER 64

# Cornucopia Again

Once upon a time, there was a tiny country called Cornucopia, which was ruled by a team of newly appointed advisors and a Prime Minister, who at the time of which I write was called Gordon Goodfellow. Prime Minister Goodfellow had been elected by the people of Cornucopia because he was a very honest man, and Cornucopia was a country that had learnt the value of truth. There was a country-wide celebration when Prime Minister Goodfellow announced that he was going to marry Lady Eslanda, the kind and brave woman who'd given important evidence against Lord Spittleworth.

The king who'd allowed his happy little kingdom to be driven to ruin and despair stood trial, along with the Chief Advisor and a number of other people who'd benefited from Spittleworth's lies, including Ma Grunter, Basher John, Cankerby the footman, and Otto Scrumble.

The king simply wept all through his questioning, but Lord Spittleworth answered in a cold, proud voice, and told so many lies, and tried to blame so many other people for his own wickedness, that he made matters far worse for himself than if he'd simply sobbed, like Fred. Both men were imprisoned in the dungeons beneath the palace, with all the other criminals.

I quite understand, by the way, if you wish Bert and Roderick had shot Spittleworth. After all, he'd caused hundreds of other people's deaths. However, it should comfort you to know that Spittleworth really would have preferred to be dead than to sit in the dungeon all day and night, where he ate plain food and slept between rough sheets, and had to listen for hours on end to Fred crying.

The gold that Spittleworth and Flapoon had stolen was recovered, so that all those people who'd lost their cheese shops and their bakeries, their dairies and their pig farms, their butcher's shops and their vineyards, could start them back up again, and begin producing the famous Cornucopian food and wine once more.

However, during the long period of Cornucopia's poverty, many had lost the opportunity to learn how to make cheese, sausages, wine, and pastries. Some of them became librarians, because Lady Eslanda had the excellent idea of turning all the now useless orphanages into libraries, which she helped stock. However, that still left a lot of people without jobs.

And that is how the fifth great city of Cornucopia came into being. Its name was Ickaby, and it lay between Kurdsburg and Jeroboam, on the banks of the River Fluma.

When the second-born Ickaboggle heard of the problem of people who'd never learnt a trade, it suggested timidly that it might teach them how to farm mushrooms, which was something it understood very well. So successful did the mushroom growers become that a prosperous town sprang up around them.

You might think you don't like mushrooms, but I promise, if you tasted the creamy mushroom soups of Ickaby, you'd love them for the rest of your life. Kurdsburg and Baronstown developed new recipes that included Ickaby mushrooms. In fact, shortly before Prime Minister Goodfellow married Lady Eslanda, the King of Pluritania offered Goodfellow the choice of any of his daughters' hands for a year's supply of Cornucopian pork and mushroom sausages. Prime Minister Goodfellow sent the sausages as a gift, along with an invitation to the Goodfellows' wedding, and Lady Eslanda added a note suggesting that King Porfirio might want to stop offering people his daughters in exchange for food, and let them choose their own husbands.

Ickaby was an unusual city, though, because unlike Chouxville, Kurdsburg, Baronstown, and Jeroboam, it was famous for three products instead of one.

Firstly, there were the mushrooms, every single one of them as beautiful as a pearl.

Secondly, there were the glorious silver salmon and trout which fishermen caught in the River Fluma – and you might like to know that a statue of the old lady who studied the fish of the Fluma stood proudly in one of Ickaby's squares.

Thirdly, Ickaby produced wool.

You see, it was decided by Prime Minister Goodfellow that the few Marshlanders who'd survived the long period of hunger deserved better pastures for their sheep than could be found in the north. Well, when the Marshlanders were given a few lush fields on the bank of the Fluma, they showed what they could really do. The wool of Cornucopia was the softest, silkiest wool in the world, and the sweaters and socks and scarves it produced were more beautiful and comfortable than could be found anywhere else. The sheep farm of Hetty Hopkins and her family produced excellent wool, but I'd have to say that the finest garments of all were spun from the wool of Roderick and Martha Roach, who had a thriving farm just outside Ickaby. Yes, Roderick and Martha got married, and I'm pleased to say they were very happy, had five children, and that Roderick began to speak with a slight Marshlander accent.

Two other people got married, as well. I'm delighted to tell you that on leaving the dungeon, and though no longer forced to live next to each other, those old friends Mrs Beamish and Mr Dovetail found that they couldn't do without each other. So with Bert as best man, and Daisy as chief bridesmaid, the carpenter and the pastry chef were married, and Bert and Daisy, who'd felt like brother and sister for so long, now truly were. Mrs Beamish opened her own splendid pastry shop in the heart of Chouxville where, in addition to Fairies' Cradles, Maidens' Dreams, Dukes' Delights, Folderol Fancies, and Hopes-of-Heaven, she produced Ickapuffs, which were the lightest, fluffiest pastries you could possibly imagine, all covered with a delicate dusting of peppermint chocolate shavings, which gave them the appearance of being covered in marsh weed.

Bert followed in his father's footsteps and joined the Cornucopian army. A just and brave man, I wouldn't be at all surprised if he ends up at the head of it.

Daisy became the world's foremost authority on Ickabogs. She wrote many books about their fascinating behaviour, and it is due to Daisy that Ickabogs became protected and beloved by the people of Cornucopia. In her free time, she ran a successful carpentry business with her father, and one of their most popular products were toy Ickabogs. The second-born Ickaboggle lived in what was once the king's deer park, close to Daisy's workshop, and the two remained very good friends.

There was a museum built, in the heart of Chouxville, which attracted many visitors each year. This museum was set up by Prime Minister Goodfellow and his advisors, with help from Daisy, Bert, Martha, and Roderick, because nobody wanted the people of Cornucopia to forget the years when the country believed all Spittleworth's lies. Visitors to the museum could view Major Beamish's silver medal, with Flapoon's bullet still buried in it, and the statue of Nobby Buttons, which had been replaced, in Chouxville's biggest square, with a statue of that brave Ickabog who walked out of the Marshlands carrying a bunch of snowdrops, and in doing so saved both its species and the country. Visitors could also see the model Ickabog that Spittleworth had made out of a bull's skeleton and some nails, and the huge portrait of King Fred fighting a dragonish Ickabog that never existed outside the artist's imagination.

But there's one creature I haven't yet mentioned: the first-born Ickaboggle, the savage creature who killed Lord Flapoon, and who was last seen being dragged away by many strong men.

Well, in truth, this creature was something of a problem. Daisy had explained to everyone that the savage Ickaboggle must not be attacked or mistreated, or it would hate people more than it already did. This would mean that at its Bornding, it would bring forth Ickaboggles even more savage than itself, and Cornucopia could end up with the problem Spittleworth had pretended it had. At first, this Ickaboggle needed to be kept in a reinforced cage to stop it killing people, and volunteers to take it mushrooms were hard to find, because it was so dangerous. The only people this Ickaboggle even slightly liked were Bert and Roderick, because at the moment of its Bornding they'd been trying to protect its Icker. The trouble was, of course, that Bert was away in the army and Roderick was running a sheep farm, and neither of them had time to sit all day with a savage Ickaboggle to keep it calm.

A solution to the problem arrived at last, from a very unexpected place.

All this time, Fred had been crying his eyes out down in the dungeons. Selfish, vain, and cowardly though he'd definitely been, Fred hadn't meant to hurt anyone – though of course he had, and very badly too. For a whole year after he lost the throne, Fred was sunk into darkest despair, and while part of the reason was undoubtedly that he now lived in a dungeon rather than in a palace, he was also deeply ashamed.

He could see what a terrible king he'd been, and how badly he'd behaved, and he wished more than anything to be a better man. So one day, to the astonishment of Spittleworth, who was sitting brooding in the cell opposite, Fred told the prison guard that he'd like to volunteer to be the one to look after the savage Ickabog.

And that's what he did. Though deathly white and trembly-kneed on the first morning, and for many mornings afterwards, the ex-king went into the savage Ickabog's cage and talked to it about Cornucopia, and about the terrible mistakes he'd made, and how you could learn to be a better, kinder person, if you really wanted to become one. Even though Fred had to return to his own cell every evening, he requested that the Ickabog be put into a nice field instead of a cage and, to everyone's surprise, this worked well, and the Ickabog even thanked Fred in a gruff voice the following morning.

Slowly, over the months and years that followed, Fred became braver and the Ickabog gentler, and at last, when Fred was quite an old man, the Ickabog's Bornding came, and the Ickaboggles that stepped out of it were kind and gentle. Fred, who'd mourned their Icker as though it had been his brother, died very shortly afterwards. While there were no statues raised to their last king in any Cornucopian city, occasionally people laid flowers on his grave, and he would have been glad to know it.

Whether people were really Bornded from Ickabogs, I cannot tell you. Perhaps we go through a kind of Bornding when we change, for better or for worse. All I know is that countries, like Ickabogs, can be made gentle by kindness, which is why the kingdom of Cornucopia lived happily ever after.

*And that is how the fifth great city of Cornucopia came into being. Its name was Ickaby, and it lay between Kurdsburg and Jeroboam.*

*By Florence, age 11 years, United Kingdom*

*With thanks to the following
for their wonderful illustrations:*

J.K. Rowling is the author of the seven *Harry Potter* books, first published between 1997 and 2007. The adventures of Harry, Ron and Hermione at Hogwarts School of Witchcraft and Wizardry have sold over 500 million copies, been translated into over 80 languages, and been made into eight blockbuster films. Alongside the book series, she has written three short companion volumes for charity, including *Fantastic Beasts and Where to Find Them*, which later became the inspiration for a new series of films, also written by J.K. Rowling. She then continued Harry's story as a grown-up in a stage play, *Harry Potter and the Cursed Child*, which she wrote with playwright Jack Thorne and director John Tiffany, and which has been playing to great acclaim in theatres in Europe, North America and Australia.

J.K. Rowling has received many awards and honours for her writing. She also supports a number of causes through her charitable trust, Volant, and is the founder of the children's charity Lumos, which fights for a world without orphanages and institutions, and reunites families.

For as long as she can remember, J.K. Rowling has wanted to be a writer, and is at her happiest in a room, making things up. She lives in Scotland with her family.

*The Ickabog* is J.K. Rowling's first book for children since *Harry Potter*, and was initially published online for families to enjoy and engage with creatively whilst in lockdown in 2020. It is beautifully brought to life throughout with full-colour illustrations by the young winners of *The Ickabog* Illustration Competition.